S0-BDM-827

MY FAVORITE SCAR

ALSO BY THE AUTHOR

Cruz

MY FAVORITE SCAR

NICOLÁS FERRARO

TRANSLATED FROM THE SPANISH BY
MALLORY CRAIG-KUHN

SOHO CRIME

First published in Spanish under the title *Ámbar*
in Argentina by Editorial Revólver, 2021.

First published in English in 2024 by
Soho Press, Inc.
227 W 17th Street
New York, NY 10011

Library of Congress Cataloging-in-Publication Data
Names: Ferraro, Nicolás, author. | Craig-Kuhn, Mallory, translator.
Title: My favorite scar / Nicolás Ferraro ; translated from the Spanish by
Mallory Craig-Kuhn. | Other titles: Ámbar. English
Description: New York : Soho Crime, 2024. | Identifiers: LCCN 2023014656

ISBN 978-1-64129-515-4
eISBN 978-1-64129-516-1

Subjects: LCGFT: Thrillers (Fiction) | Novels.
Classification: LCC PQ7798.416.E873 A8313 2024
DDC 863/.7—dc23/eng/20230331
LC record available at https://lccn.loc.gov/2023014656

Interior illustrations by Diego Jiménez
Interior design by Janine Agro

Printed in the United States of America

10 9 8 7 6 5 4 3 2 1

To Damián Vives and Ariel Mazzeo

MY FAVORITE SCAR

I

FROM NOWHERE

1.

"You're my favorite scar."

That's what my dad says, patting his forearm where he has my name tattooed:

Á M B A R.

And two red hibiscus flowers, one on each side.

He says those were my favorite flowers when I was little. I don't remember having a favorite flower. I don't remember him being around much when I was little, either. And I definitely don't remember being little.

He wears my name near his elbow, right where he rolls his sleeves up to, so it's almost always hidden. *They can use your tattoos to identify you*, he'll say, and then he'll tell me a story about Furia Roldán, who got caught because of an eight ball on the back of his neck.

But what covers my name now is the blood dripping from a bullet hole in his chest, next to his shoulder. I hand him a towel. He wipes the tattoo off first and smiles at me. I give him a look that says *get on with it* and he finally starts cleaning the wound. The towel turns red, little by little.

"It went straight through," he says and flops down on the couch, crushing the book I was reading when I saw the VW 1500's high beams and then him, with no shirt, leaning on the doorframe just long enough to catch his breath and leave a puddle of blood.

I do everything from memory; he doesn't have to ask. I pull aside the curtain of the window that looks out over the road to see if anyone's coming. I can't see the car, but he left the headlights on, and they're crashing against the side of the house. As evening falls, they become more visible. I get out the tackle box we use as a first aid kit, give him a couple of pills and a glass of water, and set a bottle down next to him. Blood loss makes you thirsty. The muscles in his arms are shaking in a strange way.

"What were you wearing?"

"My shirt."

Dad taught me how to remove bullets and sew up cuts when I was twelve. He taught me how to shoot at thirteen, and how to hotwire a car a few months later.

If the bullet went straight through, infection is the problem. Cloth or bits of the bullet that might be stuck inside. I pour hydrogen peroxide over it until there's an eruption of pink foam. He swears, but I don't care. I take a close look. The entry wound is round, the exit wound looks like a pothole. A medium caliber, 9mm for sure. A .45 would have taken out a chunk, a .22 wouldn't have made it through. At one point I was surprised—or scared—that I knew all this. Now I know it the same way I can identify a bird by its feathers, tell a bill is fake just by touching it, or know the difference between a garden snake and a viper by the scales on its head.

Blood flows out like it doesn't want to be inside him. I pour more peroxide on it so I can see the wound. Dad grits his teeth and holds his breath. All I find is torn flesh.

"It doesn't look so bad."

"Thanks, Freckles."

I'm glad he calls me that, something other than his favorite scar.

Coming from almost any other man, that wouldn't mean much. All most of them have is a little scar on their eyebrow from when they fell as a kid, or the reminder of when they had their appendix out, or a cut from some fight where the only thing hanging in the balance was their pride.

Dad carries his scars like medals. His whole body tells his story better than he could himself. Víctor Mondragón is a man who can be read in Braille better than he can be heard, but he can't be truly understood in any language.

He might carry my name on his skin, but he never held me in his arms. He chose my name, but he was never around until he didn't have any other choice. He became my father the way other people become survivors. It's something that happens after an accident. For my parents, love was an accident they both managed to drag themselves away from, covered in scars. So I guess it does make sense that he says I'm his favorite scar.

I go to look for more gauze in the bathroom. When I come back, I can see through the open door that the car's windshield is full of holes and shattered into a spiderweb, covered in blood. There's a dead person in the front seat on the passenger side, but I can't see who it is. I don't care. There's no one it would hurt for me to lose.

I soak a piece of gauze in disinfectant and press it against the wound.

"Hold that," I tell him, and he does as I say.

I put another piece of gauze on the exit wound while I tear off a piece of tape with my teeth. I press down and watch my fingernails turn red.

"What are you laughing at?" he asks.

He hates when I paint my nails, but he doesn't seem to mind painting them himself with his blood.

"Nothing."

I continue wrapping up his chest and shoulder. I go around once, twice, three and a half times, and then the tape runs out. He touches the bandage and moves his shoulder.

"Leave it alone, will you?" I say, and he laughs.

Then his smile fades and finally disappears. He hangs his head, looking at the flowers in his tattoo, and scratches at the streaks of blood next to them. It looks like the petals fell off, like the hibiscus flowers have dried out, but no one's decided to throw them out—yet.

"Get your stuff," he says. Before I can reply, he adds, "Yeah, I know I promised."

He heads to his room and comes out wearing an under-shirt, doing up his button-down. He puts the guns from all the different rooms into a bag. *You never know where they might find you.* He goes from the bathroom to my bedroom, sees me standing still in the middle of the living room, and says, *get moving*, tells me again to get my things. He says not to forget the shotgun the way other fathers tell their daughters not to forget their jacket. But I just stand there, rubbing the blood off my fingernails, because everything's already packed away in my bag, like always. Because Dad might make promises, but even if he doesn't know it, his promises always have an expiration date.

I go into my room and pick up my bag. Back in the living room, I throw in my Walkman and book.

"Grab something warm, it's getting cold out," he says and stops in the doorway, his boot in the puddle of blood that used to be his and now belongs to no one. He looks at me, and I already know what he's going to say. "Someday you'll understand."

I still don't understand him, and I hope I never will.

I stand next to the window. Dad turns off the VW 1500's headlights. He pulls the dead man around to the trunk using just his good arm. It's a clumsy job because of his wound, but I'm not going to help him.

Not this time.

The evening lengthens his shadow until it stretches across the grass and climbs up the walls of the house. When I was a little girl, I liked to watch my shadow at this time of day. I would say to my dad that I was nine, but my shadow was already fifteen, and that's how big my body was going to be when I grew up.

Far off, on the cusp of the land, the sun is a match that the wind finally blows out, and the shadows of everything, the car, the house, Dad, me, become one and sink into the grass. Now that I really am fifteen, I don't have a shadow, just darkness.

2.

I always thought driving during a storm was hardest. That was up until tonight, when I had to drive at night with a shattered and blood-stained windshield.

Dad insisted I take the wheel. He said he needed to rest his wound, but I think he did it so I wouldn't have to sit on top of the mess the dead man left in the seat. Before we got in, he cleaned up as best he could with newspaper. He got the solids out, bone and brain, but the blood stuck to the windshield and pooled on the floor and on top of the glove compartment.

On my side, the cracks are the problem. The highway looks like it's been censored. I try to see out a big hole that's right in front of me. The seat back has been destroyed by bullets. I wonder where he was for them not to have hit him. The wind blowing in makes my eyes water. Every once in a while, a mosquito bounces off, and I'm afraid one will get in my eye. I wish I had glasses. After all this is over, I'm going to ask him to buy me some.

"Well?"

"It's not far now."

He moves in his seat. There's the sticky sound his blood-soaked shirt makes, sucking against the leather upholstery. He's holding the .38 between his legs the way an old lady would hold a rosary in church.

I'm waiting—hoping—for an explanation. I want him to tell me how someone goes to work as a trucker and comes home with Death in the passenger seat. But Dad is a solutions guy, not an explanations guy. It doesn't matter how much I wish that was different. He has a sharp gaze. He's always squinting, as if he were constantly aiming at something or doubting what's in front of him.

Every so often, he switches between the rearview and sideview mirrors, the little he can see in the dark. The moonlight helps uncover some of the highway and landscape. There are no gas stations around here. No body shops. Nothing like that. There's also nowhere to eat, which he says makes it less likely there'll be cops around. *Nowhere to sit their fat asses down and eat choripán, nowhere to take bribes.*

The highway is full of potholes, like it used to have horrible acne. I feel bad that the first thing that pops into my head is Yanina Gorostiza, my classmate. "Moonface" to everybody else. That's the name Melina "I have bigger boobs than you" Loria and Hanna "I pretend I'm German but my last name is Garmendia" gave her. Yanina leaves huge zits mixed in with the pock marks because she's afraid she'll get more scars. Sometimes I want to pop them, wipe them all off her face. Or wipe the smirks off Melina and Hanna's faces. If I was Yanina's friend, I would have done something.

I look at my skin in the rearview. I don't get zits very often. I'm closer to having a scar than a pockmark.

My hands are cramping up from gripping the wheel so hard. We can't listen to music in the VW. The radio never worked. And a while ago, Dad's Barboza cassette got stuck in the tape deck. I was glad at the time, but right now I'd be thrilled to hum along with that accordion line I know by heart so I could forget that there's a body in the trunk, that Dad's hurt and that there's someone trying to track him down and kill him.

The only good part is we're going to get rid of the VW 1500.

Finally.

When we moved here, to the town where he grew up, there were three moments that meant that, this time, we were really going to stay, that here we were going to be Ámbar and Víctor Mondragón:

The VW 1500.

Enrolling me in school.

Me dyeing my hair pink.

The VW 1500 was the only car he bought in his whole life, his way of saying that from then on, we were going to be legal. An asthmatic motor, military green paint, and torn upholstery. It was the worst car we'd ever had. And we'd had a few. We changed them as often as we did our clothes. Half of the time, we used whatever Dad's crowbar provided. If the car was worth keeping for a while, we painted it and changed the license plates, and that was enough. It took a few days to get the paint off our hands, and we had to say we worked painting houses. *So young and already working*, people said, always up in our business.

The other times, we get by with what Mendéz provides us. We used to see him occasionally, especially when we had to lie low after something went wrong—read: Dad fucked up (again)—and we would use his garage as a hideout. Mendéz is around fifty and always smiling, like a tic, probably a souvenir from his time as a junkie. It's nice to be around him; he likes to talk a lot, not like the other men Dad surrounds himself with. Mendéz speaks firing one word after another, like his mouth has to compensate for the speed his body lost. He drags his right leg as if it were attached to a ball and chain. I never knew how it happened, and never dared to ask. Sometimes he touched his ankle and looked at Dad with a mix of admiration and fear. And I wondered if Dad avenged him or was the one who reduced his ankle to bone dust. Mystery #231 about my father. The last time we saw him, we stayed for a couple of days, until the blood dried, and we left in an old car that Mendéz insisted on calling a classic. *You are leaving in a gem, darling*. But the hard reality was that the car was closer to junkyard than museum. *Just like people, Ámbar, it's what's under the hood that counts,* he said. That old bastard couldn't prepare a decent meal to save his life, but give him a screwdriver and some oil and he could turn a beaten piece of crap into the getaway car we needed. It has to be said: all the cars were boring as hell. They had to be grey, brown, or maroon. Never red or blue. The key was not to drive anything flashy. A 504, a Ford Escort, or a Senda. Never a 206 or a Ford Fiesta. Definitely not an Alfa Romeo.

In one way or another, everything was disposable.

Our clothes.

Our identities.

Every time we got to a new town or city, we'd use a different name. We took turns picking them. So, we were María and Miguel Navarro, Beatriz and Bautista Alcazar, Estefanía and Emilio Molina—that was when we went through what he called our *Spanish phase*. Then there was the *Independiente phase*, when Dad went through all the players' last names: we were the Villaverdes, the Clausens, the Outes. That time I picked our first names. I called myself Arami, Anyelén, and Abigail. Dad liked being called Raul, after Barboza, and he hated being José, especially if people called him Pepe, *you wanted to be just an average Joe, huh?*, but the worst of all for him was Antonio, the name of the man who'd stolen his first girlfriend. That was my way of getting back at him. He'd used my only dress as a tourniquet. I didn't have many options in the way of revenge, but I never let an opportunity pass me by.

In most of the highway motels we stayed at, the only thing that had to be real was our money. They almost never asked for ID. Dad let me fill out the forms so I could practice printing. We always ate out or ordered something to the room. Coke, fries, and *milanesas*. Hamburgers were my favorite, but he saved those for when he'd really screwed up and had to make it up to me. I got to eat hamburgers pretty often.

The good thing about motels as opposed to houses out in the middle of nowhere—hideouts—was that there was cable. I could watch all the movies I wanted, as long as I turned the volume down and kept an eye on the door, locked and barred with a chair shoved under the doorhandle. I'd watch a horror movie, or something with DiCaprio or Johnny Depp. I didn't like Brad Pitt. He was too into himself and couldn't act.

When Dad bought me the Sega, I played Sonic for hours, or Earthworm Jim or Mortal Kombat II. I always played as Scorpion. I hated Sonya. I'd wait there, listening to the sounds from the other rooms, the TVs turned up loud to drown out the shouting, crying, moaning, while Dad went out and did his stuff. To get out from under some problem.

Or to get tangled up in a new one.

After Mom left, I lived with Nuria, my grandma on her side. Every so often an envelope of money would arrive from Dad, sent from somewhere around the tri-border area. He'd turn up every six months, if I was lucky. Always with a new look and a new scar.

When other dads travel, they come back with souvenirs. Dad didn't believe in that. *Bringing back chocolates is overrated. They suck. There's ten to a box and only one of them is any good.* He'd bring me back words that showed where he'd been. At first, I thought it was because he was cheap, but I got used to it. He'd replace "Freckles" with *sardenta* if he came back from Brazil or call me *cuñataí* when he was coming from Paraguay. After every trip, he gave me a new word. *Saudades de você.* I missed you. *Melancia.* Watermelon. *Chato.* Boring. And if he'd been somewhere they spoke Guarani: *Mbaracaja.* Cat. *Tatácho.* Drunk. When I nagged him about something, instead of saying I was being a pain, he'd say I was a *juky vosa.* He worked with a Basque guy for a while, and he said hi to everyone with *kaixo* and goodbye with *agur.* He knew how to blend in, gain people's trust. Some might say he had people skills. I wouldn't go that far.

Three years went by like that, until Grandma Nuria had a heart attack. One day she was there and the next, she was ashes. Dad came and didn't know what to do with me.

He still doesn't.

A car comes up behind us, fast, its high beams lighting us up. He clicks off the safety on the .38. The car flies past us. My hair flutters, the pink streaks twisting like they're caught in a tornado. This is the first time I've been able to choose the cut and color of my hair. I didn't have to wear it plain to go unnoticed anymore. I could be myself: Ámbar.

I could be remembered.

"Who is it?" I ask, tossing my head toward the trunk.

"Something we've got to get rid of. Be careful at the roundabout."

I can't see anything, but I slow down, and the roundabout suddenly appears. Next to it are green signs with the names of towns and distances eaten away by rust. But he could tell you the names of all of them, plus the best bar and body shop in each one. And other places he wouldn't tell his daughter about.

"Slow down." He peers into the darkness until he sees a break in the underbrush. "Turn here."

The road is so narrow that no one who didn't know it was there could have found it. We bump along because no tires have flattened the ground. I switch off the high beams and keep driving with the low beams. The pointy trees in the distance blend into a black mass. Some pieces of the windshield fall off with all the shaking. We go by a couple of low houses with no doors or windows. A cracked silo looks like it was struck by lightning. A little farther on, I see the burned-out shell of a car. The grass never grew back around it. I bite back my question before it can leave my mouth.

"Pull in behind the silo."

I park and leave the lights on. He has trouble getting out. He does everything with his good arm. He hands me my bag, grabs his, and takes the keys out of the ignition. I stand aside. His back is covered in blood. The car's headlights make the rest of the night seem deeper, and I can't see the top of the silo. If there are stars, I can't see them, either.

He opens the trunk. He screws the cap off a gas can with his teeth and splashes the contents over the dead man and the car. I both want and don't want to see who it is. I let my eyes follow the mosquitos in the beams of the headlights. They must be chewing up my legs, but I can't feel them. Tomorrow morning I'll be covered in bug bites. It feels like tomorrow morning is five days away.

"Shit," he says.

"What's wrong?"

He shows me his lighter. It just throws off sparks. Half of the body is hidden inside the trunk.

"He must have one."

I try to think which of the people he hangs out with smokes. The guy with the thick beard and horrible breath. What was his name? Ludueña. And Baigorria, too. No. I think Baigorria's in jail. What an idiot. I'd forgotten the most obvious person: Giovanni. The closest thing my dad has to a brother.

"God damn it. This asshole decided to quit smoking. Didn't do you much good, huh?" he says to the dead body. The head is sticking out of the trunk. "Got any matches?"

"They ran out."

"Check in the first aid kit."

"I'm telling you, they ran out."

"Why didn't you get more?"

I scratch my forehead.

"I forgot. I didn't know it was Set-a-Car-on-Fire Sunday."

I walk into the darkness so he won't see that I'm shaking. I press my lips together, as if I could rewind my words. I can't see his eyes. He must be giving me a look even worse than the one he uses when he's decided a conversation is over. I still haven't come up with a name for that one.

He gets into the VW 1500, starts it up, sits with his legs hanging out, and murmurs a song by Cartola, a loose, off-key version. I can't remember what it's called. When I'm about to ask him what the hell he's doing, he touches something. He uses his teeth to tear off a piece of his shirt so he won't hurt his arm. I hear a *shink*. He slides out with the car lighter in his hand. He holds it against the fabric until it catches, and then he drops that into the trunk. The flames leap up, and suddenly we turn orange. It's as if dawn came early just for the two of us.

We move away from the car. He doesn't take his eyes off the trunk.

"Giovanni always wanted to be cremated."

His best friend, eaten by the flames, and he doesn't even shed a tear. The car explodes when the fire reaches the tank.

"Let's go."

He groans when he slings the bag across his chest. I follow him, always one step behind. After a while, the fire doesn't light our way anymore. It takes us a while to get back to the highway, surrounded by his groans and the sound of the stones I kick off onto the shoulder. One hits his heel, he stops short, and before I can catch up to him, he says:

"I'm sorry."

He says it very quietly.

"Did you say something?" I ask.

He snorts.

"I said there's a motel a few kilometers away. If we hurry, we'll get there before the sun comes up."

He starts walking again, hunched over. Blood drips from the tips of his fingers. Like sweat. I move up next to him, pull the sleeve of my sweater over my palm, and wipe off his hand. I never liked this sweater anyway.

"I'm sorry," he says.

Then we get a move on, before dawn comes for everyone else.

3.

"That doesn't count as an animal."

"Why not?" he says.

"No. A dog is pretty much a person. Cats, too. It has to be one you couldn't keep in the house."

Dad thinks, or pretends to think. The shoulder is so narrow it's almost like walking on the road.

"A cow."

"Seriously? That's the most boring animal in the world."

"But it's the tastiest."

He stops and moves the bag to his other shoulder.

"So, what's your favorite animal?"

"Are you asking me for real?"

"When you were little, it was a unicorn. I guess you don't believe in that stuff anymore."

I can't remember having been so silly—so girly—that I believed in unicorns.

"A jaguar," I say.

"You've never even seen one."

"So what? They're beautiful. Have you seen their fur? No two jaguars have the same spots. They're like fingerprints. The only bad part is they're going extinct."

"If they weren't so pretty, they wouldn't be going extinct."

I pick up a little stone and throw it at his back.

"Have some respect, I'm wounded."

The first thing we see is a light on the motel roof. It lights up an aluminum sign with a name painted on it that removes all doubt as to what kind of motel it is:

Cupid.

The logo is surrounded by rusted and peeling hearts.

"Are you kidding?"

"It's this or nothing."

The motel has rooms upstairs and space for cars on the ground level. Each parking spot is protected by strips of plastic hung from the ceiling. The door is painted a furious red. It's my favorite color. I think it's called vermilion. The concrete floor is spotted with paint, and there's a ladder lying next to the floor along with some buckets. I want to look and see what the exact name of the color is to know what hair dye to look for. If it's vermilion or scarlet red or whatever. Some people would say it's blood red. But those people haven't seen blood. They don't know that it's different colors when it comes out, when it pools, when it dries.

Above the door, a light with three families of dead flies behind the glass lets me see that Dad is sweating. I don't know if it's because of the walk or because he has an infection.

I'm not sure whether to leave my hood up or pull it down. I have no idea how to look older. Maybe I should show the pink in my hair, or maybe it's better to pretend I don't want people to recognize me, like I'm here for a one-night stand.

The lobby is small, with blue and red lights. Behind a window is a man who looks about thirty. He's watching a television that faces away from us. The show is talking about aliens that live on a mountain in Chile.

"Wait there," Dad says, pointing at a couch.

When I sit down, I realize how tired I am. The adrenaline fades away, and I'm out like a light. For the moment, we don't have to run and we aren't doing anything illegal, except for the fact that minors aren't allowed in this sort of motel.

I pull my bag off my shoulder and set it in my lap. I run my fingers over the pins. The one that says Soundgarden. The Pearl Jam stick figure. There's one that says Incubus, and I don't like them at all, but it was a present from a guy two towns ago, when I was Anabela. Those were the calmest five weeks I've had. I keep the pin there as a possibility that maybe things will get better. And because I liked the guy. Rogelio. His name was the only thing about him that wasn't perfect. He was three years older than me and had a gap between his front teeth. The way he looked at me made me feel special and scared at the same time.

Dad talks to the man, but the volume is so high on the TV that all I can hear is that there's a UFO landing strip in Cajón del Maipo. The guy stretches his neck and sees me on the couch. I've been told a few times that I look older than fifteen. Usually by older men. *I thought you were eighteen.* Guys who have been men longer than I've been alive. It was easy to be disgusted. But I also heard it from boys and girls my age. *I don't know. There's something about your face. Your eyes*, they'd say when I asked them why. I never knew how to feel about that.

Who knows what the guy at the reception desk thinks. Whether he's considering calling the cops because a forty-something guy showed up to have sex with an underage girl. People say a lot of things about Dad—so many that some of them must be true—but I wouldn't like it if they said that. The guy leans over the desk and looks at me a little more closely. I unzip my hoodie so my boobs show. That's where my body first stopped being a little girl's. The guy looks at me for a few more seconds and then settles back behind the desk. I relax my back and shoulders and let out my breath.

So, this is the famous Cupid. The boys joke about it, boasting about experience they don't have, saying they want to bring you here, but I'm sure that if a girl told them, *okay, let's go*, they wouldn't know what to do. Hanna and Melina talk about the Cupid sometimes. That little wannabe German brought an ashtray with the motel's logo to school with her. She pretended it fell out of her backpack and left it lying between the benches at school. She only "rushed" to put it away when she was sure everyone had seen it. For two weeks, it was the only thing anyone talked about. *Hanna has a sister who's five years older than she is, she stole it from her*, I told Yanina. *I don't know. People are saying she's going out with an older guy. A doctor who gives them notes so they can skip school whenever they want.*

Yanina was the only one who would always talk to me. The rest didn't trust me because I was new, because of my porteño accent and my pink streaks. *I'm sure she does drugs*, I heard one of the teachers say. People love to talk. Especially about stuff they don't know the first thing about.

Nobody ever invited Yanina to the Cupid. Me, neither. People hardly invited me to parties. Especially after Esteban, the guy Melina was leading on, started to like me. He was actually pretty cute, tall with curly hair. I remember Melina's face when he stopped paying attention to her and started talking to me, and even unbuttoning an extra button on her shirt wasn't enough to get his attention back. We went off together. There was some kissing. It was clumsy. His hands went searching, but I stopped them before they found anything. He thought I'd be easy just because I was new. He pushed it. I kneed him in the balls. He was still lying there on the ground when I left. Later he told everyone he'd deflowered me. At the time, I was comforted to know that Dad would probably screw up again and I'd be able to start over somewhere new.

I wasn't wrong.

Next to me is a table with game schedules from the World Cup, still sitting there half a year later. I remember we watched the game against Sweden in a motel that only had a TV in the lobby. Dad yelled at Verón throughout the whole game. If any of the boys at school had come to the Cupid, they would have taken a game schedule to show off. Next to that is a fish tank lit up from the inside that covers a whole wall. I can't tell if the glass is dirty or if it's the water. Or both. I can barely see the stairway on the other side. I don't see any fish, but I do see my reflection with my hoodie unzipped. *What am I doing?* I say to myself and zip it back up. I look at my face and think, no, the first part of my body that stopped being a little girl's was my mouth. It was my smile.

Bubbles climb toward the surface in one corner. Lying on the little stones at the bottom, there's a cigarette butt, bottle caps, coins. A wedding band, too. I imagine the person coming down from the room and throwing the ring in there. And saying *that's it*. I think it must have been a woman.

Dad shifts his weight from one leg to the other and stretches out one arm, pointing outside. Then he shrugs his shoulders and opens his hands. How hard is it to get a room? He takes his bag off his shoulder and puts it on the floor. As he pulls it across his back, his shirt rides up and leaves the butt of the .38 showing. I look at all four corners of the ceiling. I don't see any security cameras. There must be one. I find it above the reception desk. I hope Dad doesn't turn around. He pulls out his wallet, the brown leather one where he keeps the fake IDs. He slides a bill through the slot in the window. The guy behind the desk looks at the TV and says something to him.

"I don't know," Dad replies, scratching the side of his head. "If I came from outer space and landed in Chile, I'd tell my species not to bother coming."

There's a noise upstairs. Laughter. Footsteps. The man talks loudly, and the woman gives a long *shh*. I don't know if I should stand up and pull his shirt back over the .38. I don't want to give the guy in reception a good look at me. If I try to get his attention, Dad might turn around and immortalize his back on the security tape. If it's even recording. The couple comes down the first few stairs. My dad turns his head a little and then looks forward again. I always thought that guns are a kind of second skin, that he can feel the metal like it was another part of his skeleton. And it seems that way because as soon as their footsteps come closer, Dad moves his shirt back in place to hide the .38, like he knew the whole time that it was showing.

The girl must be twenty and is wearing a faded black shirt and jeans, the typical kind of neutral clothes you wear under a work apron. I think she works at the Iris bakery. He's wearing a suit and is at least a decade older. Two worlds that can only meet in a motel.

"They said there aren't many aliens on Earth because space travel is really expensive," says the guy behind the desk. "The ones who stayed here must be having a rough time. It must be hard not to be able to go home."

My dad grabs the key, turns around, and nods to me. *God damn nutjob*, he says under his breath. We go upstairs. The hallway is long and dimly lit. The room is the third one on the right.

"After you," he says, opening the door.

There's a double bed with a blanket with satin trim, just like the ones Grandma Nuria had. They're about the ugliest thing there is. The headboard is made of wood. There's a sticker on it listing the porn channels. Dad sets his bag and the .38 on a table below the TV. He goes into the bathroom. He closes the door and turns on the water. He lets out grunts of pain. There's a couch next to the window. I run into my reflection in a mirror that covers one wall. I pull my bag off my shoulder and sit down on the bed. The edges of the sticker with the porn channels are peeling and dirty. Someone got bored and tried to rip it off. The ashtray is different from the one Hanna brought to school. This one is glass and glued to the bedside table. Stupid German wannabe. It was obvious she stole it from her sister. But what am I going to say? *Hey, I went to the Cupid.* Nobody would believe me. I'm never going to see them again, anyway.

There are some switches on the wall. I try them out. A red light turns on, then a green one. I leave just the red one on. I'd like someone to take a picture of me like that, lying on the bed. It looks like a music video.

Dad comes out of the bathroom without his shirt on and I rush to change the lights, but I end up turning all of them on. He uses his *you're too old for this stuff* look. The one he's been using since I turned ten.

I click the switches until the light goes back to normal.

"How are you feeling?"

The wound doesn't look inflamed, and it's yellowish from the disinfectant.

"It hurts. That's always a good sign."

He takes out a piece of gauze, and the movement is an order. I'm too tired to get up, but I do it anyway. There are noises in the next room. Someone flushes the toilet, and I can hear the water running through the pipes in the wall.

I rip off a piece of tape and put the bandage on tight. Dad gets out another shirt and puts the old one in a bag along with the used gauze. They'll go in the first garbage can we come across.

I flop down on the bed with my arms wide.

"Do you want something to eat?"

I don't look at him. I'm more tired than mad, but I want him to think I'm mad. When he knows he's screwed up, he's nicer to me. Now that we're safe—or something like it—I can afford to be angry. I can see in his reflection in the TV that he's holding some kind of menu. He's looking at me, waiting, but I'm comfortable. I like things to move at my pace. He picks up the phone. There's no dial tone. He clicks his tongue. He buttons up his shirt and goes out.

My eyes wander across the ceiling, and I wonder what women think while they're lying here, during or after, when everything's finished, or at least when the guys have finished. They probably look at the ceiling, at the peeling paint, and say, *what am I doing here?* And then they walk out and throw their wedding band in the fish tank, and all that force dissipates when it hits the water. It falls slowly, twirling, muffled. Sinking is slower than falling.

How does someone decide to leave everything behind?

Sometimes I'd like to find Mom just so I could ask her that.

Sometimes I wish she'd explain it to me.

Or that I could tell her to go fuck herself.

Dad comes back with a bottle of water for him and a Coke for me. He hands it to me with a plastic champagne glass. He doesn't let me drink Coke at night. He sits down on the edge of the bed and pulls a salami and cheese sandwich out of a bag. I'm hungry as soon as I look at it, even though I don't like salami. I should have told him I wanted something. He wipes the crumbs off his shirt and then hands me the paper bag.

"In case you get hungry."

There are two ham and cheese sandwiches in it. How long can I keep pretending to be mad? There's a short, loud moan from the next room. Then there are more. The man is louder. Dad and I avoid each other's eyes. He grabs the remote and points it at the TV, but his finger just sits on the power button. He can't sleep without the TV on. He always has it on in the background, the news or a channel where the shows are over for the night. He needs the white noise. I read that that's what it's called. It's a way to isolate yourself. He decides to leave the remote aside. He must be afraid that a porn channel will come on. I think it's funny. I can see a bullet wound, but not two people having sex.

"You stay in the bed, I'll take the couch."

Now she's the one moaning. And asking for it. Dad paces back and forth like he's in a cage. I like to see him uncomfortable like this. And I like listening to them. I grab a sandwich and dig in my bag until I find my Walkman. I press play and give us a ceasefire. Pearl Jam. The end of Vitalogy. Eddie sings about trying to find comfort. I don't speak much English, but for the sorrow in his voice I feel that he is far from finding any peace at all. "Sleep well," I see Dad's lips say.

He drags the couch over to a corner so it isn't in front of the door and settles in with the .38. I put my hands on the wall and feel the bumps of the headboard on the other side.

I'll never forget this, I think. I could pry off the ashtray and take it with me, talk about the fish tank and the discarded wedding band, but I don't have anyone to tell it to. I turn out the light.

4.

There isn't much to do when you're waiting.

My Walkman ran out of batteries after a half hour. Vedder's voice got lower than ever. It stretched out, distorted. Even rolling the batteries didn't help.

The book is on my stomach with my finger marking the place. I've been lying like this for half an hour. I tried to read, but my eyes slid across the lines, and I turned the pages without knowing what was happening.

In the novel.

And outside.

My stomach wants breakfast. I look at the menu. Dad always leaves money on the bedside table. Not this time. That tells me he's got something else on his mind.

I could buy myself something with the money I'm saving up to get a tattoo, but maybe he'll come back right then and ask me where the money came from. I don't want him to know I have it. Three years hanging on to coins and changing them for bills. From two to five. To twenty. To a hundred. Two hundred pesos I hid in a shotgun shell. I took out the buckshot, put the money in, and put it back together. Dad might take my Walkman, the Sega, or a ring to scrape together some money, but he'd never touch the guns or ammo.

Sometimes I think I'd like to get a tattoo of a book surrounded by flowers, like I saw on a waitress at a truck stop. Or part of a song, but I'm afraid I'll hate the band later, or that they'll spell something wrong.

I have time. What I don't have yet is his permission.

I press on the mattress with my hand. I always thought they'd be more comfortable here, or be water beds or something. I test it out, bouncing up and down. It's firm, really firm. I feel cheated. I set the book aside. I never got into it. I understand why someone left it at the house. A lot of the time there's nothing to entertain yourself with but the stuff other people have left behind. That's the fun part. Trying to imagine them based on those leftovers. Books about medicinal plants, pull-back toy cars missing a wheel, old VHS tapes of kids' movies or with labels that say "Civil Ceremony" or "María's Fifteenth." Novels with sentences underlined. Cookbooks with notes written in pen. Those are the most interesting ones. The ones that feel lived in.

Mom was always watching cooking shows, but she never turned on the stove except to light a cigarette. The fridge was covered in magnets that came with the food we got delivered, hiding the drawings I did of the two of us and the piece of paper with the diet plan she never started.

One time, we wrote down a recipe for chocolate cake. I don't remember what it was called, but it had, like, four kinds of chocolate in it. *I'll buy the stuff and make it. If you behave.* She hung the piece of paper on the fridge. It got yellow over time, just like the walls, wilting from the cigarette smoke.

You didn't behave, she said.

What did she know about how I behaved? She'd have to have been home for that.

Mom always thought I was younger than I was; Dad thinks I'm older.

I realize I'm breathing through my mouth. Waiting is something that, no matter how much you do it, never gets any easier.

I didn't hear Dad go out. And he must have made noise. The bag of stuff to throw away is gone, and his backpack looks emptier. He must have taken the other gun.

I remember seeing him sitting at the desk, writing, but I don't know if I dreamed it or if it was in another motel room. Sometimes I'm not sure what's a memory and what I made up. And even when I'm with him, I'm not sure what he's doing.

Dad has a scar on his chest where his heart must be. It's long and looks like a worm. I know three people who claim to be responsible for it, just in this city alone. Velázquez says he gave it to him because he owed him money. Karina said she was just drunk and didn't like Dad. Simionato swears up and down that he cut him with a Quilmes bottle outside a bar because he'd stolen his girlfriend. There are no witnesses to any of those stories. That's not the only scar people fight over.

Sometimes I wish Dad would make me a part of what's happening.

Most of the time, I don't.

My hair smells like smoke, and my skin is sticky and damp. The shower is disgusting. There was no wrapper on the bar of soap. It doesn't look like anyone has used it, but I don't want to take the risk. I scrub my hands with water to clean the blood out from under my nails. The sink is clogged, and I can see the blood coming off my hands and my nails and dissipating when it hits the water. When it drains, there are red streaks on the ceramic. I cup my hands together and splash it clean.

Make it look like you were never there, another one of Dad's rules.

I settle for changing my clothes. When I put my hand in the bag, the first thing I touch is the shotgun. Dad gave it to me on my thirteenth birthday. *Take care of it*, he said, as if he were giving me a pet. He sawed off the barrel so I could carry it more easily and so it wouldn't be so heavy. He explained how I should stand, how to make it another part of my body. It's the only thing that's always with me. I take it out. It doesn't look so big anymore. I point it at the mirror, and it's like I'm aiming at myself. I imagine firing, the image falling to pieces. I wonder what would be left after I pulled the trigger. A few shards of mirror, hanging on, stuck to the wall, and there, where I used to see my whole body, I'd only find the reflection of one eye, of a pink lock of hair, of the corner of a lip, reflections hanging on by a thread before falling to the floor with everything else.

I put it away. I grab a T-shirt and smell it. It's wrinkled and smells musty. Like all the other ones. I used to be sure to leave my favorite clothes folded and ironed in the bag so I wouldn't risk losing them if we had to leave in a hurry, but that meant I never wore them. For a while now, I've left it up to chance, wearing the first thing I grab. It's also been a while since I had favorite clothes. It's easier that way.

I put on the T-shirt and a pair of jeans. I feel just as dirty as before, maybe worse. Except for the hoodie, I put the rest of the dirty clothes in a bag along with the book. This is going to end up in the trash, too.

Someone is vacuuming in the hallway. When the vacuum cleaner is turned off, I can hear the voices of two women. They're talking about the mess someone left in room 7. *We should just burn everything. I'll bet it was González. He shouldn't be allowed in.*

I think about turning on the TV. But with the noise of the vacuum cleaner, I might not hear him coming, and he'll get mad. He wouldn't believe me if I said I wasn't watching porn. There isn't even a closet or drawers. I used to play with those in hotel rooms. Open them up, look through everything. A few times, I found letters that people had gotten or hadn't sent or that were stuck in the middle of a Bible or caught in the edge of a drawer, letters left unfinished or smeared by tears, sentences crossed out, letters that started out with neat handwriting and were rushed chicken scratches by the fourth line. *I hope you understand* is the classic sentence for something that usually doesn't make sense and that the other person won't be able to understand. A letter is the closest thing I know to cowardice. And the most honest thing, too.

I remember my dad—and I'm sure of this, that one of all the times I saw it must have been real—writing in the dark, with just the glow of the TV, so he wouldn't bother me or so I wouldn't wake up and see him. He always wrote with a Parker. Every word took time. He had really neat handwriting, like a woman's. I thought he was writing to Mom, or that's what I wanted to believe. He never mentions her, not even to say bad things about her. I would lie awake watching him. Most of the time I'd fall back to sleep before he finished, or I'd see him rip the letter in half, then in half again, and again, until it was confetti. Once I went to the bathroom, and he didn't see me coming. He was startled and hid the letter under the TV and went back to bed. The next day, when he went out, I looked for it. He'd forgotten it there. It said Á M B A R. The tail of the R was stretched out and looked so pretty. And then there were just a bunch of little weird dots scattered in the margin. It was like the nub of the Parker had been bouncing up and down on the page while he tried to find the best way to tell me what he couldn't say out loud. To abandon me. Like Mom.

I'm terrified he won't come back. That something will happen to him. I want to cry. But he doesn't like to see me cry. Time passes slowly. It circles around and seems to stay in the same place, like a bird with a broken wing.

Giovanni had a wife. Beatriz. I met her two or three times. I'd stay with her while they went out to do their business. I can't say they left me with Beatriz so she could take care of me. We waited together. She was tall and wore big earrings and blouses. She cooked a lot. She'd make potato gnocchi and sauce from scratch, serve everything up, and then barely touch her food. She had a tired gaze, like her surroundings had nothing to do with her.

Dad comes in. I don't know if he knocked or not. I feel something that should be relief but isn't very much like it.

He's wearing a red jacket that's too big for him, even though he's 6'3". He sets a brown paper bag down on the desk and takes out a coffee with a plastic top and stirrer and hands it to me.

"Did you get any sugar?"

He checks the bag. He empties his jacket pockets out on the desk. There are a couple of receipts, slips of paper, a few bullets. Car keys. The keychain has a wallet-sized picture of a kid in a school uniform, covered in hard plastic. It's worn. The kid must be in high school now. He looks familiar. Dad paws through everything.

"Here." He hands me two packets of sugar. "There are pastries, too."

The coffee is still hot. There's nothing left of the pastries but crumbs on the floor within two minutes. They're still vacuuming outside. Dad tries to open the window, but it's stuck. He hates artificial light. I read that that happens to people who were in jail. He grabs another cup of coffee for himself and sits on the edge of the bed, next to me. He checks to see the remote is still where he left it.

"So, what do we do now?" I ask.

He digs around in the pile of stuff he took out of his pockets until he finds a canister for a roll of film. He opens it and shakes two red and white pills out onto his palm. He washes them down with coffee.

"Take it easy with those."

"A doctor prescribed them."

"A doctor?"

"He used to be a doctor."

We drink our coffee. The vacuum cleaner turns on and off. I look at us in the mirror in front of us and think this must be the weirdest image that's been reflected there, and the competition must be pretty stiff. Dad scratches at his eyebrow. His knuckles are split. From yesterday, I think, but the broken skin is still soft, and the blood hasn't scabbed over yet. Our eyes meet in the mirror.

"Where'd you get the car from? Who's that kid?"

I can see a little steam rising from his cup.

"I need to know what's going on."

"It wouldn't do you any good."

Now I'm the one who gets up the nerve, through the mirror, to use my *I'm not a little girl anymore* look.

"What happened?"

Dad looks tired. If he got any sleep, his body didn't get the memo. He pulls a flap of skin off his knuckle and throws it in his cup. He stretches and grabs a folded-up piece of paper and hands it to me. I unfold it. It's a list of names. There are a few snakes drawn at the top, like he was trying to get the shape right.

Sinaglia.

Mitelman. (X)

Zucchini.

Mendieta.

Macizo Padilla.

Camerlingo.

I recognize some of them. They're friends of his. Acquaintances.

"Are you making a list of people to invite to your birthday party?"

He laughs.

"It's a list of people I made angry in the last two years."

"Are you sure you didn't forget anybody?"

"Turn it over."

On the other side, there are seven or eight more. All the names are written elegantly, like he was planning to dedicate a love letter to them and not a bullet. His memory reaches farther back on this side. It's less exact. There are first and last names but also things like:

The pistoleiro de aluguel *from Porto Alegre.*

The añamembú *who worked with Alvarenga.*

I wonder what he did to them. There are no women.

"I think you're right, Freckles. I did forget someone."

He takes the paper back from me, pulls out his Parker, and writes. He blows on the ink and gives it back to me. At the end of the list:

ÁMBAR.

I shake my head.

"What's with the snake?"

He waves away the question.

"I at least deserve to know what's going on."

Dad leans back against the headboard.

"What did I tell you about tattoos?"

"That I could get one."

"Don't be smart."

"That that's how people get caught."

He nods.

"Yesterday we stopped at the Shell station at the roundabout. Giovanni had to take a leak, and I made a phone call. That's when I heard the shots." With one finger, he rubs the line of a wrinkle in his forehead. "The guy was wearing a ski mask. But on his shooting arm he had a tattoo of a snake, something like that." He points at the paper. "I don't know if one of these guys decided to get inked or if it was someone they hired."

"He came out of nowhere?"

"I think he must have been following us."

"And you don't know why?"

"Everyone's got their own 'why.'"

"And what are you going to do?"

"Find him."

"I'll come with you."

"You're staying here."

He stands up and organizes the stuff on the desk. He sets the bullets off to one side and puts the rest into a shopping bag along with the jacket. He has to push everything down to fit it in. He opens the .38 and takes out three empty shells. The smell of gunpowder spreads through the room like a battlefield-scented air freshener.

"What if they find me?"

"They're not going to find you."

He reloads the .38 and sticks it in his waistband.

"They found you."

His back is to me, but I can see his grimace in the mirror.

"I can see your face. You know I'm right."

He grunts and turns around. He rubs his split knuckle and pulls off another piece of skin. He shrugs.

"Don't forget any of your stuff."

He puts on his light military shirt, his trademark, and puts the rest of the bullets in one pocket, *so they're handy, Freckles*, and in the other, the film canister with his pills.

"Who's next?" he asks, pointing at the list.

"We have to go see somebody first."

"Who?"

"She needs to know what happened."

Dad closes his eyes, sighs, and nods.

HE'S BEEN INSIDE FOR ten minutes. But it feels like more. The house is squat and flat, like the rest of them on this block, all with a backyard. This is the only one with the shutters closed. The outside light is on, as if inside, they think it's still nighttime—like they're still living through last night. I know some nights last forever.

I didn't want to go in. Dad didn't insist. He reached into the backseat, pulled some bills out of an envelope, and got out. The Renault 19 I'm waiting in reeks of cat piss. I roll down the window. A neighbor walks by carrying groceries. I can see cans through the bag. Big ones. Peaches. He finishes a cigarette and pops a stick of gum in his mouth.

I can't stop moving my feet. Or my hands. Behind the house, I can see a line with clothes hanging on it, swaying in the wind. A striped polo shirt. A red one. Dad always wears polos, and I never saw Giovanni in anything else, either. There's also a flowered dress to one side. A pair of panties and some old boxer shorts. Farther back, against the dividing wall, a plastic table and iron chairs. The wind picks apart the clouds in the sky. Soon it'll be hot and sticky.

The door opens, and Dad comes out eating a chocolate chip cookie.

"Happy?" he says when he gets in the car.

At least she won't have to wait anymore, I think, but I don't say anything. I try to imagine how pain and relief can live inside one body at the same time. I envy her a little. I feel something in my stomach, an irritation I can't quite name but that makes it hard to breathe because even though I have Dad here, even though I can touch him, I still have the same feeling every time he goes away. Maybe what I'm waiting for isn't for him to come back. What I'm waiting for is for him to abandon me so that, once and for all, I can stop waiting.

I hear a sound out back of the house, a gate and a screen door slamming. Beatriz goes out onto the patio. She doesn't see us. I don't think she would see us even if we were standing right next to her. She's wearing slippers. She holds her sweatshirt closed with her arms crossed over her chest.

"Did you tell her the truth?"

"I gave her money. That'll do her more good than the truth."

Beatriz walks over to the clothesline. She removes one clothespin first, then another, and takes down the striped polo shirt. She folds it and sets it on the plastic table. Then the dress and the panties. She stands in front of the red polo shirt. The shadow of her face falls on the other side of the fabric. It gets bigger as she moves closer. She snatches it down and presses it against her face, like she wants to smother herself or smell her husband. The lines of her nose and her sharp chin press into the cloth, but there's only the smell of clean clothes. There'll never be the smell of Giovanni again.

Dad starts the car.

"Don't you feel better?" I ask.

"No. Just poorer."

I don't feel any better, either, I would say, but he doesn't ask me.

5.

"I think that's just junkie stuff."

"You're crazy, Dad."

"Come on. The guy's snorting that stuff, cuts a line, tap, tap, tap, then he sniffs up a whole bag and gets all aggressive and goes out looking for them."

"Did you get dropped on the head as a kid?"

"As a grown-up, too."

The Renault 19 moves through town. The plaza slips away behind us with its statues of lions at the corners, and so does the vacant lot where we used to watch the guys play soccer, those guys who were dying to impress us, and the night club I never went into. All of that's behind us now, and I doubt I'll ever see it again.

"I think we're talking about different things."

"I have a friend with that nickname. And he was always snorting something. You'd get there and you could hear him from outside, tap, tap, tap, making lines with what? With a Sacoa card. Coincidence? I don't think so."

"Just because your friend was a cokehead doesn't mean Pac-Man is drug advocacy."

"Advocacy . . . Where'd you read that word?"

"In a book. I look up the words I don't know in a dictionary."

"Bookworm. Are you going to go to law school? It wouldn't be so bad to have a lawyer in the family."

Every so often he moves his arm, pulls his shirt aside to look at the wound.

"Have you got any other crazy theories? I don't know. Tetris?"

"That's a metaphor for life. The stuff you do well disappears and just the bad stuff hangs around."

"Donkey Kong?"

"That one's obvious. A working guy goes up against the gorillas who won't let him get ahead. That's the most Peronist game in history."

To the left, the houses get bigger and more expensive. To the right is open land.

"Going to the arcade with you is boring as hell."

"You should listen to me. All that stuff is full of subliminal messages. Just like the music you listen to."

The plan for me to wait for him in the car changes as soon as he parks and we see them sitting on the curb. Three guys next to a Ford Escort that's just been washed. They're sharing a liter bottle of Quilmes. Dad doesn't let go of the key when he turns the motor off. He thinks about starting it back up and taking off, but the problem is that they see us, too. The one on the end lifts his sunglasses up over his forehead. Judging by his face, you'd think his favorite song just came on the radio.

Dad sighs. He takes the key out of the ignition.

"Come on, but don't listen to them."

"You either."

I've seen two of them around. One of them is named Mike. He's always wearing a rugby sweater with the Los Cardos logo, the club where he used to play until they suspended him for biting an opposing player. The one with the sunglasses is Rafael Mendieta and for the first time I connect his name with the one on the list. I wonder how they know each other. They call him Tank. He's in his twenties and must weigh 220, a good 175 of it from the waist up. His legs have never seen a gym. He goes out with Lucila Mendoza, or at least he picks her up outside school in the Escort. He honks twice so she'll see him, but mostly because he wants people to see she's leaving with him. She walks slowly, too, her school uniform pulled up so it shows off her ass, which all the boys want and all the girls, even though we don't say so, are jealous of. Sometimes Lucila's out of school for whole weeks at a time. Some of the girls say she's out partying with him. Some of the boys say she's staying inside until the bruises fade.

The third guy has long hair tied back in a ponytail and is wearing a Hang Loose T-shirt. Terrible acne is splashed across his face and makes him look younger than the other two.

"Stay close," Dad says and places me on the other side of the guys.

It's a two-story house with white walls. There's a little patio out front with plants I don't know the names of. A line of bushes divides their yard from the neighbor's. It doesn't look anything like the kind of house Dad's friends would live in.

Tank leans on the hood of the Escort and crosses his arms. He's got a few tattoos, none of a snake. Dad jerks his chin at him in greeting and heads toward the house. Tank snaps his fingers.

"Where do we think we're going? Stay right there, nobody invited you in."

Dad stops. He turns to face him.

"Rafael, right?"

"It's Tank to you."

"Right. I was told you work with Charly. But I see you've set up a car wash. Regular entrepreneur."

"Let's just say I'm in the security business now." He thumps the hood of the Escort twice. "And this baby's mine."

Across the street, two guys are cutting the grass with weed whackers. When they turn them off, I hear the music coming from inside the house. It's muffled by doors, windows, curtains. Even so, I can identify it. Cartola. I can recognize his voice like I can recognize Dad's. Whenever Dad was quiet, Cartola was singing in the background. Through the windows, I see someone pass by, then a door shuts, and the Brazilian's voice disappears again.

"You're really getting ahead," Dad says. "The last time I

saw you, you were about old enough to start shaving. And you were riding a bike with training wheels on it. I told Charly to take them off, but he said he didn't want you to fall and bump your head. Overprotective uncle, huh?"

Tank doesn't even look at me. He's blinded by Dad. He stands up too fast, and his sunglasses fall off. He manages to catch them and hangs them from the neck of his sleeveless shirt. The neckline pulls down enough to show the tip of another tattoo. Dad scans his arms. All tribals. There's also one of a yellow and red cassette tape that I like. The tape forms a word I can't read from here. I'd get that one. I'm not sure with what word.

"I don't really remember you, Mondragón. I guess because you spent so much time hiding. What I do remember is that one day my uncle suddenly stopped taking me to the plaza. We had to go visit him in the hospital. They thought he wasn't ever going to walk again. My mom and aunt would whisper that, scared. And they'd whisper your name, too, like you were some kind of disease. The doctors would joke that there was a wing of the hospital named after you where they put everybody you sent in. You gave them a lot of work."

"Small-town gossip."

"No, it wasn't gossip. I was there. I spent three months watching guys roll in beat to shit while my uncle learned to walk again."

Mike looks me up and down and stares at my face. He winks at me. Badly. He's one of those guys that has to move his whole face to wink, like a tic. He must really kill with the ladies.

"What the hell did he do to you for you to come at him like that?"

"He never told you? He must have had a reason."

Tank asks for the beer, takes a drink, and gives it back to the guy with acne.

"I remember when they let him out, he came to live with us. Mom used to mash up all of Lolo's food and his, too. It took about a year for him to be able to eat something you had to cut with a knife."

"Considering what a horrible cook your mom was, that doesn't seem like much of a sacrifice. Is your uncle home?"

"For you, definitely not."

Dad scratches his eyebrow with the knuckle of his thumb.

"My uncle's thirty, and he's got dentures and a cane. You know what it's like to see the guy who raised you in that kind of shape?"

"Charly always had style and personality. I bet he carried it off just fine."

"Suck my fucking dick, Mondragón."

He spits at Dad's feet. Dad looks at the loogie next to his boots.

"Look, kid. Two things. I don't get into anybody's sex life. If you want a guy to suck your dick, good for you. And don't swear, I didn't come alone."

Tank looks over his shoulder at his friends.

"I bet that girl knows more swear words than both of us put together."

Dad puts his hand up around his back, and for a moment I'm—even more—scared. But he just scratches his skin next to the revolver. The .38 must feel itchy because he wants to take it out so badly.

"I don't know if she knows any swear words or not, but she's smart. She's always telling me stuff that makes me think. The other day she told me that, in a while, after pulling our wisdom teeth for so long, we're just going to stop having them right from the get-go. If the Mendietas don't stop screwing around, they're going to start being born without any teeth."

Mike reaches for the bottle, and the guy with acne hands it to him. He turns it over to grab it by the neck like a bat and spills beer on his jacket. He swears. The guy with acne laughs at him. His face is red, his eyes even redder. He's high.

"My uncle told me you were back. He just said it offhand, but you can tell when someone's saying something important. I promised him that if I could do something someday to make him feel better, I would. I had to wait for a long time. But here you are."

"Can you just call him, kid?"

"An ambulance is what I'm going to call. So you can end up in your own little fucking room and go through what we went through."

Dad moves his shoulders. I don't want him to reopen his wound because I'm the one who's going to have to sew it up. I step into his shadow. That's the closest thing to being protected.

"Okay, you've put on your little number, you've shown you're a tough guy. You've got your friends here to back you up, and you can spice up the story however you want. I don't care. If you want, I'll even tell it to Charly, and maybe he'll give you a raise, but I'm just here to talk."

Tank jerks his head from side to side, but his neck doesn't crack. He moves like someone who learned everything he knows about violence from TV. He takes a few steps and stops a foot and a half from Dad. He's taller than I thought. Dad reaches his arm out and taps me twice on the tummy. We didn't work that signal out, but it's not hard to realize he wants me to back off.

"What the hell do you want to talk to my uncle for? If you're here to say you're sorry, you're too late. There are some things you can never be forgiven for, even if you get on your knees and beg. But . . . if *she* gets on her knees, that would be an interesting way to say you're sorry. And maybe I'll let you both go. I don't know about my uncle, but I'd think about forgiving you. But it'd have to be the best blowjob of my life. And she's got some competition."

Tank laughs at his own joke, and Mike follows suit. He points the bottle at my dad. Or at me. I can smell the beer and my own sweat. I realize my mouth is dry.

Tank's still laughing when the kick from my dad knocks him off his feet. He lands on his shoulder and then hits his head. There's a hollow sound, like the pavement is coughing. Dad's boot lands on his stomach. Tank doubles up, shoving his face closer to me. That's where the second kick lands. I stop counting them. There are a lot. Mike looks ready to shit himself and throws down the bottle, which breaks at his feet. When Dad stops kicking him, Tank rolls away, driving shards of glass into his skin. He yells. As well as he can. It's like he's gargling his own blood. The hood of the Escort is splattered with red whiplashes. Dad gives him another kick, softer this time, to roll him over.

"Don't be a moron, you're going to choke. Lay on your side and spit."

The blood pours out of his mouth with bits of teeth surfing the wave. Mike is stock still. There's a stain on his sweatshirt and another on his pants, most likely piss. The guy with acne steps over Tank with his hands raised like a white flag and starts picking up the teeth he finds on the pavement.

"What are you doing? What are you, the Tooth Fairy?"

"It's so they can put them back."

Dad shakes his head. He opens the back door of the Escort so they can get in. They slip in the blood. Tank is making noises, his face peppered with broken glass.

"Go to the hospital. No detours. If you go to the police, you'll end up sharing a room."

The guy with the acne says okay. Mike gets behind the wheel. He doesn't look at Dad. Not even in the rearview. Dad picks up the bucket they were using to wash the car, still full, and splashes it across the street. The water runs along the curb, making a little river that carries away the bits of teeth and glass. They look like little paper boats that disappear down the storm drain. He opens the gate in front of the house and motions for me to come in.

"Wipe your feet," he says.

On the welcome mat, he scuffs off his boots as if the blood were just dirt.

6.

Shit, Charly says when he sees us, and drops his cane. He says shit again when he turns off Cartola and hears Dad out, leaning against the marble countertop, and he says shit one last time and looks at my dad's boots, stained red.

"That jackass . . ."

Charly must be fifty. His beard is grey. The first thing I do is look at his teeth: perfect. He's wearing a gold Rolex like one Dad used to have. I'm sure his isn't from Ciudad del Este.

"Look at it as a glass half full," Dad says. "You can't get loyal people these days."

"What good is a jackass's loyalty?" Charly replies. "Is he going to make it?"

Dad nods and shrugs one shoulder, as if to say he only gave him a scratch. He leans over, picks up the cane in both hands, and looks at it. There's a gold bird on the top. It looks like a cardinal.

"Nice."

He leans it against the counter next to its owner, settles onto one of the benches, and puts the .38 on the wooden bar.

"Hey, stop," Charly says. "What are you doing?"

"It's uncomfortable when I sit down." He points at the stove. "Something's burning."

Charly turns around and checks a huge frying pan. He takes off the lid, and a puff of steam and smoke billows out. He gives it a stir. He has to scrape hard with the spoon to unstick the onion and meat from the bottom. Without the lid, the bubbles in the brown sauce burst, spattering the stove and the floor. Judging by the smell, it must have mustard and cream in it. He turns off the burner. As he wipes his hands on a towel, he looks at me closely for the first time, points at Dad, then at me, then at Dad again, then at me, like he can't do the math.

"Listen, Víctor . . ."

"She's my daughter, sicko."

Charly lets out a deep breath. It's weird to hear someone call Dad by his name.

"I'm Carlos, nice to meet you." He reaches his hand out to me, and I shake it. It's sticky.

"Ámbar."

It's a big kitchen, but everything is set close together so he can lean against things and move around without his cane. There's a sliding glass door that looks out over a small patio. The fridge doesn't have any magnets from takeout places or trips, or any pictures. It's just a fridge. And it's full. Cheese. Cold cuts. Expensive chocolate in the door compartments. He offers me something to drink or eat, but I tell him no, thanks.

"Are we expecting someone?" Dad asks, nodding at the pots and pans.

"Marita, but she'll be here in . . ." He looks at the Rolex. "Half an hour."

He sees a sauce stain on his sweater and rubs at it with a dish rag.

"Give me that," Dad says.

He grabs it and wipes the blood off his boots. Even though he wiped them off thoroughly on the mat, he left bloody footprints on the tile floors of the living room and kitchen. He pulls a piece of tooth from between the laces like someone cleaning dirt from under their nails. He tosses it at a trash can next to the sink and misses. It falls off to the side. Charly picks it up and tosses it in the trash without looking at it, like it grosses him out. Or brings back memories.

"Sometimes a good ass kicking is the best thing that can happen to somebody. Look at me," he says. "I hated my first prosthetic. Dentures, such a crappy set you could see from a mile off they were fake. I always had to keep my mouth shut. It's amazing the shit you don't get into when you keep quiet."

A brown pitbull puppy scratches at the edge of the sliding door.

"Easy, Ginger. A real guard dog, this one. I didn't even hear him bark."

"You can tell he doesn't like Tank."

"I don't like him, either, but Paola asked me to get him a job. I put him on the tank truck to make deliveries, and it was like he was wearing a big sign that said, 'we're moving drugs.' What am I going to tell my sister?"

"Say he had a work-related accident. You weren't paying much attention, either. It's dangerous to turn the music up that loud. And not for your ears."

"If I can listen to it that loud, it's because my conscience is clear. I worked my ass off to buy 100-watt speakers without screwing anybody over."

"Nobody?"

"Almost nobody."

Dad reaches over and picks up the Cartola CD case. The insert's sitting on top of it. I've never seen a picture of him before. It's black and white. He sure looks like he could have been a friend of Dad's.

"You ended up liking him," he says.

"I didn't have much choice. You were always playing this Brazilian bastard in the background. Sometimes it felt like we were living in Rio."

"You're exaggerating."

He isn't. There are times Dad listens to nothing but Cartola. The Brazilian had a raspy voice, like his throat was made of sandpaper. I tried to follow the lyrics, the words I knew standing out from the rest like they were neon signs, and I'd ask about the ones I didn't understand.

Windmill, he'd tell me.

And what's it about, Dad?

About screwing up your own life.

When he came home from his trips, he didn't just bring back words. He brought music, too. Recorded TDK cassettes with the name of the album or the songs written on the label. Sometimes in his handwriting with his long-legged R's. The other ones made me wonder how someone could have dedicated songs like *As Rosas Não Falam* or *Devolva-me* by Adriana Calcanhotto to Dad.

I think, *no one has ever made me a mixtape*. I'd like that. For someone to pick out songs, thinking of me.

"Why did you come here, Víctor? I didn't do anything this time." He rubs his hands together. Dad lets him talk. "Not to you, at least. We're even."

"I don't know if you noticed, but I didn't come here with Giovanni." He gets up, opens the fridge, and grabs a bottle of water. "And you're never going to see me with Giovanni again."

"So, you're the guy in the newspaper." It's half question, half statement of fact.

He looks in a basket and tosses El Noticiario on the counter. *Shooting at gas station.* A black and white picture, glass on the ground, the front of the station with bullet holes. Dad doesn't look at it. He takes a drink of water from the bottle and sets it on the table. Charly's jaw drops when he finally gets it.

"You can't possibly think I had something to do with it. Have you seen my gunmen? They couldn't pass for cowboys in a school play."

"These guys didn't have very good aim, either, because here I am."

"Oh, since when are you so humble?" He tries to walk but just pivots on his good leg. "What makes you think it could have been me?"

Dad gestures at the cane.

"That was ten years ago," Charly says.

"So?"

Charly scratches his chest and shakes his sweater as if it's suddenly ten degrees hotter.

"What do you want me to say? There was a time I would have liked to put a few bullets in you. Sorry, girl, but that's the truth."

The dog jumps up on the frame of the sliding door again. It stands there and gives a high-pitched bark. It must be five or six months old. It looks too nice to be a pitbull.

"He must be out of food."

Dad stands up and walks toward the door.

"What are you doing?" Charly says.

"It's so stupid it could break the glass, and I don't want to see it get hurt."

He opens the door, and the dog runs in, bringing a gust of air that smells like freshly cut grass. It sniffs Dad and licks at the soles of his boots.

"Don't be stupid, you're going to poison yourself."

"Close the living room door," Charly says to me.

But Ginger hears *go to the living room* and heads straight there.

"Why don't you go make sure he doesn't break anything?" Dad says.

It's not a question.

"Don't let him up on the couch," yells Charly.

Ginger sniffs at the boot prints Dad left and licks them. I can see mine next to his, like an echo that gets smaller and smaller until it disappears.

"No, Ginger. No. Be good."

He doesn't listen. It's like nobody lives here. Everything is so organized. The sofa in front of the coffee table with a neat pile of magazines, the bookcase against one wall. A huge TV. There are no ashtrays. No pictures. No art.

"That's enough, Ginger." I give him a slap on his back leg.

The dog stops and licks my face. I laugh, then I see the bloodstains on his snout and shiver. I touch my face and leave my hand there. I don't want to look and see if it's stained red. I find a bathroom with a huge mirror and hang my head so I won't see myself. I wash my face with my eyes closed until I'm sure that if there really was any blood there, it's gone now. I grab a roll of toilet paper, wet it a little, and clean up our prints from the tile before Marita gets here. *Leave everything just like you found it.* I have to use so much toilet paper that I almost plug the toilet. I'll know for next time. Flush every so often.

They're still talking in the kitchen. Naming names. People from the list. Charly says that one of them is a real son of a bitch. He says it loudly. *What were you thinking, Víctor?* Dad tells him to lower his voice, and I can imagine him saying it between clenched teeth. I'm too tired to even listen. As if knowing would make a difference now. Dad says what we do and how we do it.

Ginger walks around the living room. He wags his tail,

and there's nothing for him to knock over or break. I wet my T-shirt and wipe the blood off his jowls. Now there's a vague brick-colored stain on it. The next T-shirt I buy is going to be one I really like. It's going to be just for me.

I sit down on the sofa and lean back. Ginger looks over the armrest. Like he's asking permission. He sniffs at the coffee table, a Persian rug, the CD tower. Everything is interesting to him. They must never let him in here.

"Me, neither."

I pat the cushion next to me, and Ginger jumps up. He rests his head on my leg and looks at me out of the corner of his eye. On one of the pillows, I see a bloody pawprint. It gets a breathy laugh out of me.

"I tried."

I pet him, and for a moment everything is calm.

7.

The empty swing next to the ones we're in moves just a little, as if the wind that drags clouds along up there only has the strength of a sigh down here. Someone wrote in Liquid Paper on the wooden seat that they *love Polo* or maybe *Pola*.

Except for the gas station, the rest is just horizon.

I don't know what Dad's looking at: the man using the pay phone, the kids running around the Renault 19, or the woman who's barely visible on the other side of the glass, cleaning the truck stop tables.

I imagine he's looking at everything, for different reasons.

The man is about thirty. He rode in behind us on a bike, and every two minutes he pulls out more coins and puts them in. It doesn't look like he's giving someone information about us. The kids are maybe twelve at the most. They're throwing little clumps of dried mud at each other and using our car as cover. I'd say they're harmless, even though in Dad's world you stop being harmless as soon as you're old enough to drive. The woman's almost forty. Brown hair and a headband. She's thin and tall. When we were ordering our burgers, I saw she was wearing coral pink lipstick. It makes her look like a French actress from an old movie.

Somewhere in all that are Dad's eyes. I'm not sure about his head.

He wolfed his hamburger down in three bites. I barely nibbled at mine. They toasted the bread so you couldn't tell how old it was. I'm picking it apart, but there aren't even any birds to come and eat the crumbs.

He pulls out the list. There's a name written next to the first one. Mendieta, crossed out. There are some phone numbers, too. He flicks the list with his finger a few times and frowns, like he's waiting for whatever's escaping him to show itself. He stands up and the swing moves, creaks.

"When you were little, you were scared of swings."

Dad likes to talk about things that can't be proven. He always remembers stuff about when I was four or five years old, or younger. He said I liked hibiscus flowers better than roses because they didn't have any thorns and that I liked to pet them like a dog. He tells me about the trip we took to the coast—I don't remember which city—and I saw the beach for the first time, about how I wanted to take home a cat that lived at the hostel we stayed in, *but, Dad, they have lots of them, and I don't have any.* I always wondered why we went to the coast because Dad doesn't take vacations.

I don't know how much of it he makes up.

"What you really loved was the merry-go-round."

He's told me all this before. He's going to talk about lifting me up so I could grab the ring again and again, about Mom giving him hell for bringing me home late, but I'm not sure that's the way it went, that he lifted me up, or that Mom was worried because we didn't come home. Maybe things were different once. Maybe Dad touched people without leaving scars, maybe Mom waited for me with dinner on the table, excited for me to get home.

It's possible, but it's hard to believe.

"Isn't it any good?" he asks. "I know it's not like the AmPm burgers, but it's the best you can get around here."

He talks like he chose this place for the food and not because it's far away from everything. I'm sick of him treating me like an idiot. I bite the inside of my cheek. I tear up some more bread. The blood left dark stains on his jeans. The boot he used to kick Tank is dirtier than the other one. I push myself back and forth on the swing with my toes.

Back.

And forth.

"Did you really have to do all that?" I say.

"What are you talking about?"

"What you did to Tank."

Dad sits back down. The swings are so low that he has to stretch his legs out in front of him.

"What happened to that guy, he did to himself."

He notices that he spilled ketchup on his shirt sleeve and swears. He wipes it off on the edge of the swing.

"What was I supposed to do? Just let him say that stuff about us?"

"They're just words."

"No. It wasn't going to end there. There are failures like him whose only purpose in life is to stir up trouble, and they don't stop till somebody's bleeding. He deserved it."

He digs around in his shirt pocket until he finds the pills. He takes one with water and holds the bottle out to me. I shake my head, and he screws the cap back on.

"Giving is better than receiving," he says. "It took me a lot of scars to figure that one out. At first, I thought that if I just stayed in my lane, the problem would end there. But it doesn't. Those guys just keep going. Hitting back is okay. But hitting first is a whole lot better."

He opens his hands and looks at his fingers from both sides, as if they were someone else's.

"And there were three of them. If you hit first and hit hard, it's two against one instead of three against one. If you really mess him up, the other guys see the consequences, what's waiting for them, and they're not too worried about their honor anymore."

An old car pulls up to the pumps. A man gets out and hands the keys to the attendant. A woman gets out to stretch her legs. She leans against the back window. In the rear windshield I can see a girl younger than ten, playing with dolls I can't quite see. She's blond, and it must have taken her mother half an hour to do up her two little pigtails. Mom never combed my hair. She didn't even comb her own hair. The few times she did, she pulled out big clumps of hair, like she was shearing herself. They'd stay there in the teeth of the comb until I decided to throw them in the trash.

"You could have killed him."

"Trust me. I'm not proud of it, but I've kicked enough guys to know when to stop."

I roll my eyes.

"What are you making that face for?"

"You know when to stop? When we came here, you promised me it was over."

"And it is."

"It sure doesn't seem that way," I say and finally look at him. "What are we doing? Can't we . . . I don't know, go to another town and start over? There must be someplace you haven't . . ." I falter, look for words, but finally use his: ". . . made anybody mad."

"That whole starting over thing doesn't exist."

The sun peeks out and then hides, and our shadows, sitting on the swings, appear and disappear on the grass and the patches of dirt where people have dragged their feet. I can see them appear slowly, take shape, the chains, my hair, our feet, but just as soon as they sharpen up, the sky clouds over and it's like we aren't there anymore.

"So, what? All of this is revenge for Giovanni?"

The man from the car comes back from the bathroom, pays, and they leave. The girl in the rear windshield waves to me.

"It's not just that. You can't do anything for the dead. I'm doing this so we can go home, without having to pray all the time there won't be somebody waiting for us. I'm doing it for us. If people think they have a right to hurt you, they'll do whatever they want to you. I'm not going to give anybody permission to hurt us."

"I didn't ask you to do this."

"Sometimes, stuff happens."

"Yeah . . ."

I feel the sun on the back of my neck again. The man on the bike left at some point. The kids, too. The truck stop lady is at the table at the window with a crumpled napkin in her hands. She stretches her neck back. She waits. She can't leave.

"Aren't you going to eat that?"

I hand him the burger. Dad takes it out of its paper. He bites into it.

"It's cold," he says, but he finishes it anyway.

I push myself far back in the swing, until I'm standing on my tippy toes.

"Dad."

"What?" he says, looking over his shoulder.

"That guy did deserve it. But I don't deserve this."

"I already know that, Freckles."

I shake my head.

"Now you know it."

I take one last step back, grab the chains tight, and let myself fall. I go back and forth, bend my knees, stretch out my legs, a little farther every time, a little higher, my hair gets in my mouth, the chains squeak like they're about to break.

There's no way anyone was ever afraid of this.

8.

The man isn't on the list, but I recognize where we're parking. If he even has a real name, I've never heard it. Dad always calls him Walrus. In his world, the people he's close to have nicknames. A last name if they're lucky.

For a while, no matter where we were, we'd make time to come visit. Dad would leave an envelope for Carolina, and we'd spend the night, him on the living room sofa and me in the girls' room. They were afraid of the dark, so we'd sleep with the night light on. They were awful. I couldn't even play with them. Luckily, we always left early the next morning. That was when Walrus was in jail.

They set him up, Carolina said. She seemed like a sweet, innocent lady. Or naive. *You know him, Mondragón, he's too much of a coward to have done that*. Dad stirred his coffee. He didn't say anything. *The girls are what worry me. Growing up without a father. People talk.*

"You chose him," Dad said, and that put an end to it.

Before we settled in here, we stayed with them for a few weeks. They'd let Walrus out by then. They had a backyard with an in-ground pool. The girls would go in with arm floaties and inflatable life rings like they were swimming in the ocean. I popped one once. They fought over the good one. They peed in the water a lot.

I don't know if I'm supposed to stay with them while he goes to take care of business, like before. But it worries me that he has to leave me here, when he didn't mind kicking a guy's head in in front of me.

He rings the bell. Inside, someone turns down the TV, and I can't hear the news anymore. Dad looks at the plaster Virgin Mary in a recess in the wall, behind a plate of glass. The melted wax from several red candles around her forms a puddle. It looks like Mary is sinking into a swamp of her own blood.

Walrus opens the door and is surprised to see us.

"Look what the rain blew in."

"You mean the storm."

Dad doesn't hug people, he doesn't give people a kiss on the cheek hello, and he doesn't shake hands or anything like that. He nods his head, that's it. It doesn't matter who it is. There's always an awkward moment. Walrus opens the door and invites us in.

A yellowish light hangs from the living room ceiling. The place looks like it's lit by a drop of honey. There's a tea kettle and torta negra buns. Where the old wood-panel Grundig used to be, there's a TV that's way too big. If it fell on someone, it could kill them.

"Want some mate?"

"Don't you have any coffee?"

"Just instant. Yeah, I know. I can make you some tea. I've got . . ."

"I'm fine."

"What about you, Ámbar? I think I've got some Coke." He winks at me. When he opens it, there's no hiss from the carbonation. "Some friends brought it over a few days ago, and we don't drink Coke." Dad laughs. "The girls go crazy."

He pours some into a plastic cup for me.

"Where's the old lady?"

"At work. She's on the afternoon shift this week."

"Are you still at the hardware store?" Walrus nods. "You're going to have to get me a job there, I can see you're not doing too bad." Dad gestures at the TV.

"You know how it is. When you stop making the family bigger, you make the TV bigger. That was our vacation, too," Walrus says, making air quotes with his fingers. "The last time we went to Mar del Plata, and the girls were peeling for days. The sun's bad for them. They've got sensitive skin."

"Looks like lying around in the shade is hereditary."

The Coke must be at least two weeks old. There's a folding door that separates the living room from the rest of the house. I can't hear the girls. They must be at dance class or swimming class. At least they aren't asking me to babysit. Yet.

Dad takes a drawing down from the fridge door. The woman is wearing white, with yellow flowers in her hair.

The man is dressed in black, and both of them have long legs and scarecrow smiles.

"What's this?"

"We got married." He says it without looking up and rubs his wedding band.

Dad raises his eyebrows.

"I didn't get an invitation."

"It was a really small ceremony. For family. We didn't have any money. And . . . You know my in-laws have a different idea about what my friends do."

"But not about what you do?"

"Did. What I did."

"Past tense for me, too. I'm a family man, now. It's crazy, they're so religious, and they were okay with her having daughters without getting married." Then he laughs and Walrus laughs, too. His shoulders relax. "I'll take a mate."

Walrus fills the kettle with water and puts it on the stove. He hands me the remote.

"The cartoons are on channel 22 and up."

What do I care about cartoons? I look for MTV. No. MuchMusic. U2. I hate Bono. The other channel is Latin music. The videos are like soap operas, but with even worse acting.

I hope Caro gets here soon. I don't like being alone with him. He's too affectionate. He always says *I hope my daughters turn out to be as pretty as you.*

I'd rather go with Dad. Whatever it is he has to do.

"What brings you around here?"

The table is to my right. Dad sits down. This time, he

doesn't take the gun out of his waistband. Walrus is leaning against the counter next to the stove.

"You know I've been away for a long time. I don't know most guys' faces these days."

"Well, as you can imagine, I don't, either. The only people who come into the hardware store need the little thingy that goes in the other little thingy in their toilet."

Steam starts to come out of the kettle, and the top rattles.

"I'm looking for a guy by the name of Sinaglia."

Walrus goes over to the trash and empties out his mate.

"Sinaglia? Never heard of him."

"I heard he hangs out at the Gladys."

"I don't go in there anymore, man."

The steam is about the knock the top off the kettle.

"The water's boiling," I say.

"Thanks, sweetie."

He takes the kettle off the stove and sets it on the table on a cork mat.

"Are you sure you've never heard of him? Your paths have crossed more than once." Dad touches his nose.

"If it was back when I was taking my vitamins that way, then maybe. That part of my life's like an old movie. There are a lot of extras I don't have names for. That's what they were. Extras. The guy with the nose. The guy with the curls. The guy who sold blow cut with baby powder."

Walrus drinks the first mate and, judging by his face, burns his tongue. He pours the second one and gives it to Dad.

"I'm one of those jerks who watches the credits after

the movie," Dad says. "Not to know the main characters' names. I'm interested in the background guys. The ones who don't have names. I like seeing what they call them. Boxer. Irate customer. Blond bombshell. They all probably dreamed of being actors and maybe the most they ever managed was 'man in bar' or 'curvy brunette.' Now I've got a guy with a big role in my life, but with an extra's name. Man with snake tattoo," he says, patting his shoulder a few times. "I'm looking for him because I want to know his name, so his role is small. I think you catch my drift."

Walrus notices I'm looking at him, and I turn my eyes back to the TV. Linkin Park, I think. Those bands where one of them raps and the other screams. Backstreet Boys for people who like rock.

"A snake, huh? A prison tat?"

"No, no. A good one. You could put it in a museum."

"Then definitely not. On the inside, everybody gets a dagger and a snake. Die cops die."

"This one wanted me and Giovanni to die. He got half of what he wanted."

Walrus blinks. Dad nods.

"Yesterday."

Walrus gets up, walks over to the sink. He leans against it. He fills a glass with water but doesn't drink it. It's so full, it splashes onto his jeans and shoes when he moves it.

"I can't believe it."

"If you want, I'll show you the bullet wound. That snake had some bite."

Walrus sets the glass down, picks up a kitchen towel, and dries off his jeans.

"Think back."

Dad drinks the mate and hands it back to him. Walrus pours one for himself but sets it down. He looks like he's thinking.

"A snake." Looking off at nothing, he draws one with his finger from his forearm to his hand. Then he scratches his arm like it itches. He drinks the mate and then hands a fresh one to Dad.

"You make the worst mate in the world. Two rounds and the flavor's already gone."

"I'd start over, but Caro must be almost here, and we have plans to go out for dinner with a couple of friends."

Dad laughs. He takes a deep breath and lets the air out his mouth.

"You know, when Charly told me he saw you at Gladys's, that was a surprise. I didn't want to believe him. I thought you'd respect a woman who hung around when you went to jail."

"What do you mean?"

"Now you're going to tell me you go there because they make a great negroni, just like you tell her. I heard this Sinaglia is around there a lot. And I thought, well, that's a coincidence. But the problem is, you gave yourself away. I told you the tattoo was on his shoulder to see if you'd go for it, but you went and touched your arm, which is where this guy's tattoo really is."

Walrus's Adam's apple moves like it's broken.

"Let's hear it," Dad says.

Just then I hear them running down the stairs. They open the folding door and appear, one right behind the other.

"Dad, Carla won't let me use the computer."

"She's been on all day."

They don't even care we're here. They don't even notice us.

"Daddy's busy, girls. I'll come help when I'm finished."

I get up from the couch and go with them.

"Hey, girls." They look at me as if I've just landed here. "You remember me. Ámbar. We played in the pool."

They shrug. They both have bowl cuts. Carla's wearing a powder blue dress with roses on the hem. Manuela's wearing a green Sailor Moon T-shirt.

"Go play with Ámbar," Walrus says.

I take their hands and walk them out. I close the folding door, and we go into a kind of smaller version of the living room. Just the Grundig and two armchairs. A bathroom to one side. Pictures of the girls at the beach. Red, like their skin all over their bodies is embarrassed.

"I like your pink hair."

"Do you want to see our Barbie collection?"

"Mom made clothes for them."

"I used to make clothes for mine, too."

Manuela shows me one she takes out of a basket. I recognize the fabric from a dress of Caro's that I loved. I think about their mother using the clothes she doesn't wear anymore—that she isn't allowed to wear—to make dresses for the dolls. I'm—very—angry and—very—touched.

The voices coming from the kitchen are calm. Dad

doesn't raise his voice. Just his fist. I think about the kettle of boiling water. About the TV. About the set of knives Walrus showed off at one of the worst asados I ever ate at.

"You smell dirty," Manuela says.

I sniff loudly a couple of times, moving closer to her.

"You do, too," I tell her.

Carla laughs.

"How about we play hide and seek?"

"That's boring."

"Maybe, but the winner gets a Kinder egg."

"Mom always gives us Kinder eggs," Carla says, shrugging one shoulder.

"Well, what do you want if you win?"

"Ice cream," Carla says, smiling. I can see she's lost one of her teeth.

"Deal. I'll count, but you have to do a good job hiding. I'll count to one hundred."

"That's really high."

"Yeah, but the winner gets a whole kilo of ice cream." Before they can say that their mom always buys them ice cream, I play the pride card: "To eat all by herself."

"Whatever flavor we want?" Carla asks. I nod. "Vanilla!"

Come on, is she serious?

"No. Because I'm going to win, and I'm going to pick French vanilla." Manuela sticks out her tongue.

What's wrong with these girls? It's like there's a rule against fun in this house. They must fight over the computer to play Minesweeper.

"I'm going to stand here to count." I lean against the

bathroom door. "And no cheating. You can't move. So, stay in your hiding place and don't go anywhere."

From the kitchen, I can hear a tinny sound and a yell, like the kettle fell on the floor. I can imagine the steam rising from the floor, or from Walrus's skin.

"Your dad's really clumsy."

Both of them laugh. I clap my hands to get them moving.

"Come on, lazybones."

Lazybones. That's what Mom called me when there used to be stories at night instead of TV, when her breath smelled like Kolynos and not wine, the nights when she tucked me into bed and not the other way around.

I turn around and start counting, but the memory takes off and drags me along with it for a while. Carolina must tuck them in and turn out the light every night. They must fight over who gets to be the hero in the bedtime stories, and their mom must have to make up new ones where instead of one princess, there are two, and two princes, and I think that I would have liked to have been put to bed that way.

From the corner of my eye, I see them go up the stairs on tiptoe, in a way that makes their dance classes obvious. I open the bathroom door and pretend to be looking for them. I find a bottle of perfume. I put a little on. Walrus isn't going to say anything. With a broken nose, he probably won't be able to smell anything. Or maybe he'll tell me it's nicer on me than on his wife.

I go up the stairs and hear them laughing. I need them to know I can find them. There are pictures of the couple every two steps. The higher I climb, the smaller her smile gets. Like the last smile is going to stay on the stairs and not make it to the bedroom.

At some point, and for a while, Mom and Dad must have had a smile with the other one's name on it. Maybe I'm made of the last smile they had together.

"Where could they be?"

I tiptoe down the stairs. I tiptoe better than they do. It doesn't have anything to do with dance; it's about learning to go in or out without anybody realizing.

I hope to see him burned, with pink-hot skin—people say red-hot, but when you burn your skin, it's pink. I find him holding a bag of frozen peas against his face. When he moves it, I can see his lip is split and he's poking around with his tongue, like he's checking to see he's still got all his teeth. His mouth is covered in blood, so it's hard to say. He spits into the sink.

"I think you almost knocked out one of my teeth, you asshole."

"That's the price of refreshing your memory."

"How the hell do you expect me to remember something I don't know?"

Dad bends over and picks the kettle up, leaves it on the table. The buns fell on the floor. His elbow is bloodstained, and his hands are clean.

"I'm telling you I don't know anything. You're so paranoid, it's like you're the cokehead. If I was right about the tattoo, that's just because everybody gets ink there when they're inside."

I don't know if the guy knows anything, but I surprise

myself by hoping Dad beats the shit out of him. Dad goes over to Walrus, who takes a step back.

"You're still the same old idiot. The god damn altar boy. You used to do the same thing when you said thank you for a job. But on your altar, the Virgin Mary looks more like Carrie. Start talking, or you'll look that way, too. Sinaglia or the guy with the tattoo. Either's fine."

I hear sounds. I think it's the girls, but the front door opens.

"I had to leave the car in the street because some idiot parked in the garage." Caroline comes in backwards, dragging along two suitcases with tags hanging from the zippers. "But I got them." Then she turns around and takes in the scene. One of the suitcases falls to the floor when she lets it go.

"Hey, Caro, how are you?" Dad says. "Close the door, I don't want anybody coming in."

She looks at her husband. Then at me, standing next to the folding door.

"Are the girls okay?"

"Yeah," I say. "They're upstairs, playing hide and seek."

She closes her eyes, takes a breath, opens them again.

"What did you do?" She's talking to her husband.

"I didn't do anything, what are you saying?"

Caro picks up the suitcases and sets them aside.

"Those are nice," Dad says. "But you're going to go crazy trying to find them on the conveyor belt. You should tie a red ribbon on them, so they stand out."

He speaks with the confidence of having everything

under control, like rather than just looking at them, he's got them in his sights.

"Where are you going?" he asks Walrus, but he doesn't answer.

"To Cancún," Caro says. "Our honeymoon."

"Walrus here told me you finally made him an honest man. Or tried to, anyway."

"What's going on?"

"I'm trying to jog your husband's memory. So he can give me a name. That's all I want. Maybe you can help me, so you don't have to play nurse for the next, I don't know, six months, depending on how hard it is to get him to talk."

Caro sits down. She isn't wearing any earrings or necklaces or other rings, like everything melted into her wedding ring. She sees the buns on the floor and puts them on the table.

"I told you they don't like tortas negras."

"Those are the only ones they had."

"Those are the only ones you like, that's different."

"All that can wait," Dad says. "Do you know a guy by the name of Sinaglia, Caro?"

"No."

"And a guy with a tattoo of a snake?"

She shakes her head again.

"It's a tough situation." He rubs his neck. "I'd like to avoid this more than anybody, but I got shot yesterday, and Giovanni got killed, and I need to find one of these guys before something happens. Someone has to pay for what they did to him. To us. Caro, you know the things you'd do to keep your kids safe, right?"

Walrus laughs, the sound muffled by the bag of peas that's going soft as they thaw out.

"You're laughing? You ended up in jail for something you had nothing to do with. Some people think you kept your mouth shut out of loyalty, but you're not loyal, you're just chicken shit. You're scared they'll come over and kick your ass, and now you must be thinking: *Mondragón is my friend. He isn't going to mess me up as bad as the other guys would, if I sold them out*. You're wrong about that. Because if you shut your mouth, I'm going to open it up for you, and nobody here wants that."

Dad looks at both of them.

"Last chance for you to still be able to look each other in the eye. No? Well, it's up to you."

Caro pulls a chain out from under her polo shirt. It has two pendants shaped like little girls. She hooks her finger through the chain and moves the pendants back and forth.

"If you know something, spit it out, Caro," I say. All three of them are surprised to hear me.

"A fifteen-year-old girl is smarter than you, Walrus. Listen to her."

Carolina bites her lips. Dad leans against the counter. He rolls up his sleeves, and one of the hibiscus flowers peeks out.

"Where should I start?" He rubs his mouth. "Caro, however hard you try to lie to yourself, you know he doesn't go to Gladys's for the negronis, or to do business or a little coke." She hangs her head. "One time somebody told me, 'Don't underestimate the power of denial.' That stuck with me. You can be in denial and think, no, he doesn't have anybody else, or maybe you've accepted that in the end, he always comes back here."

Caro is still looking at the floor, playing with the pendants. It's like a boiler room in here. It's hard to breathe. I want to open a window. Or turn on the fan. Pull my sticky shirt away from my skin. Take a shower for two hours. I want someone to say something.

"The crazy part is, Walrus, you've always had a big mouth. Even way back when we used to save up change as kids to buy beer from Arreche. You acted all serious, but half a drink in, and you'd start running your mouth. When you started going out with Caro, you wouldn't stop bragging about it. I'll never forget what you told us after you did it the first time." Dad laughs. It's that laugh that tells me I'm sure I don't want to hear what comes next. "Caro, you can say whether it's true or not. He said as soon as he got your clothes off, he saw you had a birthmark right next to your coochie, but after you were done fucking, he was sure it was a burn mark from how hot your pussy was. *You could smell the burnt cum.* Isn't that what you said, Walrus? I still remember, you even did a drawing of it"—Dad traces an outline in the air with his finger—"like a little lightning bolt. And then all those jackasses, whenever they saw you, they'd say, *Do you smell something burning, Caro?* And you didn't know what they were talking about or why they were laughing."

"Did you burn yourself, Mommy?"

I see both of them in the doorway, but I don't know which one of them spoke. Caro grabs them and takes them upstairs.

"You motherfucker," Walrus says, lunging at him. Dad trips him, and he crashes to the floor. Judging by the sound, it was a nasty fall.

Caro comes back in, closes the door. Her eyes are full of tears, trembling, about to fall. *Don't let him see you cry,* I think. *Not this asshole.*

"The man with the tattoo," she says. "He was here."

"Shut up," Walrus says, trying to stand up. "Shut your damn mouth."

Dad lifts his chin, telling her to go on.

"I don't know his name, he came over a couple of times. But they talked about that other guy you mentioned, with the Italian name, and about somebody's granny."

Dad closes his eyes when he hears *granny.*

"Don't say another word," Walrus says.

"I don't know anything else, asshole."

Caro looks at the TV, at the suitcases, at the tortas negras, at me, out the window.

"A name, Walrus. And where I can find him."

"I don't know, that's the truth, I have no idea." He leans against the wall and rubs his shoulder. "I ran into them at Gladys's. The Italian guy was obsessed with one of the girls. He told her he was raking it in, that he was taking a cut from the shipments he was moving for Granny, and he wanted to start working on his own."

"That girl really trusted you, huh? I'm sure it's because she really liked you."

Caro stands up and throws the tortas negras in the trash, along with the bag of peas. Walrus moves his arm a little.

"I think you popped my shoulder out of joint."

"Keep talking."

"They call the guy with the tattoo Mbói Cuatía or some shit like that in Guaraní. We never talked much. The guy would show up, ask me for a tip, and I'd let him know about a job. And I pointed Sinaglia out to him. I don't know what happened in between. I didn't send them after you or Giovanni. I swear, Víctor."

"I know that, you don't have the balls."

Dad shakes his leg like there are ants crawling up it.

"God damn it, wasn't it easier to just tell me all that from the get-go?"

He rubs his beard so hard, his skin turns red.

"If I find out you lay even a finger on her . . ." He nods at Caro, who's hanging her head, her face hidden behind her hair. "On the plus side, you've already got your suitcases ready, because tonight I think you're not even going to be welcome on the couch."

"Don't tell them I told you," says Walrus. "Please."

"Forget about it. Everyone already knows what you are."

Dad nods at me for us to go. I walk by Caro, and I don't know if I should put my hand on her shoulder or tell her I'm sorry, but I keep going and meet my dad at the door. He's checking out the suitcases.

"Don't worry. Cancún's overrated. Just rocks and seaweed. You're not missing much."

9.

Mom never called me Ámbar. Just when I made her mad. She didn't really say it, it just slipped out.

My name coming from Mom's mouth was an insult.

Even when she was on the phone, she found a way not to say it.

I can't right now, I'm with the kid.

The girl.

You know who.

The problem with being named Ámbar is that there's no way to shorten it. It just is. Whenever someone says it, it feels like they're yelling at me, or it's a person who doesn't know me well enough to call me something else. A teacher tried to call me Ambi once to call attendance, but it sounded like a kindergarten name, and she never said it again. Thank god.

I also never understood why, with so many other nice

things she could have called me, Mom chose lazybones. None of the other girls got called that. And in a weird way, that made me feel special.

Calling Caro's daughters lazybones wasn't an accident. Something opened up. Like the memory had been there, waiting.

Let's dance, lazybones.

I was six. It was hot, but I don't know if it was summertime. Mom turned up the radio, eighties music. She pushed the table over against the fridge and put the stools under it. There were a bunch of cigarettes in the ashtray, our centerpiece, but I don't remember the stink of cigarettes. The oven was on, and there was a nice smell coming from it. Meat and sweet potatoes.

Mom took me by the hands and bent over so we were the same height. She even took off her high heels. She turned up the volume until the music was distorted, full of crackling and background noise, and the singer's voice faded into all the sound.

I wanted to know why she was so happy. So it would happen again.

I can't remember her face, and I know that any feature I try to give her is something I made up and not really that moment. Like if I remember her dress, short and Marlboro red, the one I used to put on when I wanted to be like her, the one she'd get mad at me for touching because *that one, kid, is for special occasions.*

I can remember the sweat on her forehead, on her neck. We danced. We were ridiculous, but neither of us was embarrassed. Mom was laughing so hard that I saw she had a filling in one of her molars, and in that moment, I thought it was the prettiest thing in the world because it was something that only existed when she laughed like that, with her mouth wide open and her head thrown back.

Ads came on the radio, and we sat on the floor, the dirt sticking to our sweaty palms. Mom smoothed my hair a little—or did she? Do I just want her to have done that? I know she told me to wash my hands because dinner was ready.

I never saw Mom's filling again.

Sometimes I think I made it up.

All of it.

Because Mom doesn't dance, and she doesn't laugh, and I don't dance, either.

I hope she danced again, I hope she made someone fall in love with her—that was always easy for her—I hope she fell in love, too—that was so hard for her, I don't know if she could do it—and the other person found out who Mom really is, that he saw her C-section scar from when I was born, the one that no cream could make disappear—I hope that man knows that Mom threw something away, and that he leaves, that he leaves her forever, so she'll remember—or find out—how much it hurts to be abandoned. Maybe, in that moment, she'll remember me and say Ámbar like a curse, like a swear word you say when you realize you made a mistake.

"God damn it."

I come back here, to the mirror that's unfogging, like the

image of me is being developed. I wouldn't want anyone to take a picture of me like this. Sitting on the toilet with messy hair and red eyes, wrapped in a hotel towel with raggedy edges.

In the mirror, my dark roots show up under the pink streaks. I push my hair behind my ears. I can't see a single freckle. I lean in. I look for them. Nope. Not a single one. Not even the shadow of a freckle.

I get dressed and go out.

DAD'S LYING ON THE bed, watching TV. The dried blood on his grey sock has gone dark red and reaches all the way to the heel. The mattress is small and makes him look bigger than he is. At least this is a real hotel. A cheap, ratty one, but a hotel.

"I thought you drowned in there."

The lamp on the nightstand between the two beds is turned on. I put my dirty clothes in a bag and shove it into a compartment in my backpack.

"The water was nice."

It smells like cigarettes even though there's a NO SMOKING sign. Out the window, I can see a stretch of highway lit up by the streetlight. Whatever's on the other side of the asphalt is invisible. A car comes into the parking lot with its high beams on. When they turn them off, I can see it's a Renault 12, and a couple is getting out. She has a big white bag with a box of alfajores on top. They look like the kind of people who buy T-shirts from the places they visit and take them home as gifts. *Somebody who loves me brought me this shirt from East Bumfuck.*

Dad changes the channel. The voices don't quite come together. He hates when people flip through the channels. When I do it, he goes crazy and says *can you just pick something*. Or he takes the remote away from me. He must not even be seeing what's on. If he saw something he liked, he wouldn't have realized. Dad recognizes movies from just a few frames. He always prefers to watch something he's already seen instead of something new because that way he's sure he's going to enjoy it. And he watches them with me. But honestly, Dad's movies bore the crap out of me.

He leaves on a local news channel. It's an old habit, seeing if he's on TV or if some cop trying to make a name for himself lets something slip and gives him a lead. There's nothing right now, just a highway accident. A car flipped over on the shoulder.

The list, folded up, sits on the nightstand along with the pen. My name is still the last one. Next to the phone is a tourism pamphlet. Craft fairs. Local products. Rivers. Carnivals. Traditional holidays. We didn't do any of that. Or we did, but in our own way.

Everywhere we were, the regional products were always the same: alfajores, salami, or cheese. The traditional holidays are for some patron saint, always with similar—and improbable—miracles, carnivals on the outskirts of town or in the plaza in front of the church and the town hall.

Every town halfway to nowhere is the same.

"Have you ever been to Cancún?"

"Do you think I could have gone to Cancún?"

He stretches, and his voice is warped by a yawn. He must not have slept at all. That isn't a first. Usually, I can only tell he's tired by the dark circles under his eyes, but now his voice is raspy and his shoulders sag.

"If you want to eat, get a move on, the kitchen's closing soon."

He hands me a menu.

"What are you getting?"

"Order for yourself. I'm not going to eat."

I don't know if it's because we're low on money or there's something that's ruining his appetite. I call and order a sandwich. It's the cheapest thing there is and the easiest to pass off as dinner to keep him from realizing I'm not hungry either.

"Are you worried about that Granny?"

"Not even a little bit."

His mouth twists, a tiny frown at the edges of his lips, and there's a wrinkle at first that spreads to his eyes, his eyebrows, his forehead. People must think he's older than he is, too.

"Why do they call her that?"

"It's a stupid small-town thing." He realizes that's not enough for me, that he's going to have to answer at least one of my questions. "For a long time now, she's been taking care of some business that other people want to take away from her, or they want to compete with her, but she puts them all in their place. And some people, looking in from the outside, started to say the town was like her kid for so long, now it's her grandkid."

"Were you her kid, too?"

"I wasn't even my parents' kid."

All my other questions evaporate with that answer.

Dad never talks about his parents. He doesn't even mention them when he tells a story from when he was little. There are no meals that remind him of his grandma, no lessons that came from his grandpa. I can't imagine him at my age. I can't imagine him any other way than as the guy who wears the trigger of a gun like a wedding ring.

Maybe it wasn't easy for him, either.

He grabs some clothes and a towel and goes into the bathroom.

I flop down on the bed and change the channel. I don't care about the heatwave in Buenos Aires. Or about what Duhalde's saying. I roll over. There are people talking next door. Her: *I mean, if I'm being honest.* Him: *What.* Her: *Nothing.* Him: *Come on, tell me.* I turn off the TV. I can hear the shower. Her: *It's stupid. Forget it.*

There's a knock at the door. I ask who it is. *Room service. What did you order? A sandwich.* Then I open up. A girl with eyebrows plucked down to almost nothing looks at me like I'm crazy and gives me the sandwich wrapped in cling film and a couple packets of mayo. I put both of them on the sandwich and eat it.

Dad comes out in a tank top, with a new bandage. His hair is slicked back. It got so long once that he tied it back in a ponytail. That's the best if you want to change your identity quickly. That and dyeing your hair. When he dyed his hair blond, it was impossible to keep from laughing. He got mad. Since then, he just cuts it or shaves it off.

He sits on the edge of the bed and pulls his socks on. One of them has a hole in the heel. I'm surprised. Clothes don't usually last us that long. It's silly, but the socks give me hope that someday the washing machine will wear the color out of my shirts. I never had a favorite T-shirt that became pajamas.

He fills a bottle he bought at the gas station with tap water. He hates tap water. His wallet must be light as a feather.

I get into bed. The mattress is like a rock. This must be the last room they had because it's horrible. Dad gets in bed, too. There's a cut on his elbow from Walrus's face.

"Couldn't you have just beat him up to make him talk?"

"If I beat people up, that's wrong. If I don't beat them up, that's wrong, too."

Dad turns his head to look at me.

"It's better than breaking up a family."

"I did it to save ours. And you have to understand, that wasn't a family. That was a hostage situation, and I set them free. They should thank me."

He always manages to be right.

"I can't keep having you question everything, Freckles." The pet name is him asking for a truce.

"Don't call me that anymore."

"Why not?"

I get up and put my face close to his.

"Look."

"What?"

"Do you see any freckles?"

He looks, but he can't find any. If it would make him right, I think he'd draw some on with the Parker.

"They'll show up soon. You can see them more in the summer, you just need to get some sun."

"Yeah, to do that I'd need to spend some time outside. We were shut-ins all last summer. And it looks like this one's going to be the same."

I lie back down, one leg hanging off the bed.

"We said we weren't going to talk about Corrientes anymore."

"Yeah," I say, "and before that we said we weren't going to talk about Campana anymore, either, and I'm sure in a few months we're going to say we aren't going to talk about the guy with the snake tattoo."

"I get the picture, Freckles."

"I told you not to call me Freckles." I raise my voice more than I would have liked, so I let the silence settle a little before saying anything else. "I feel like you're talking to someone who doesn't exist anymore."

Dad lets one arm fall off the edge of the bed. When he moves his muscles, the hibiscus flowers look like they're moving in the wind. I don't know if the red faded to pink over time or if it was always like that. In the only picture I ever saw of my parents together, they're sitting next to each other on a sofa, neither of them looking at the camera. Mom's face is just hair, he's resting his hand on her huge tummy, and his other arm is stretched across the back of the sofa, already tattooed. I wonder if he got it as a promise. To say, *I'm here, I'm not going anywhere*. To her. Or maybe to me.

Dad makes his jaw pop. First one side, then the other. I hate when he does that.

"I never thought about it," he says without looking at me, "but what if I call you Ambareté from now on?"

"Why?"

"Mbareté means strong in Guaraní. It sounds good for you."

I love it, but I pretend not to. He puts the list in his jeans pocket. He checks the .38 and sets it next to the lamp, just like someone making sure they've set the alarm to go to work the next day.

He lies down, his shoulders almost hanging off the mattress. He scratches at the cut on his elbow as if it were a bug bite, and in the ease of that movement, there's something sad. I realize Dad isn't scared. He's alone. In two days, his best friend was murdered and Dad burned him, and he found out his other best friend was a piece of shit, a traitor, which I think is even worse. And here I am worried about whether I have freckles or not. I feel like a moody little girl.

"Are you okay?" I ask

He looks at the bandage.

"It barely hurts."

"That's not what I mean. In two days, you lost both your best friends."

He smooths the wrinkles in the bedcover, but as soon as he moves his hand, they reappear.

"That whole best friends thing is for kids."

"Oh my god, Dad. Come on. It's okay to be sad."

"I'm fine."

Dad might never admit I'm right or give me a hug, and I might not know when he's telling the truth and when he's lying to me, but there are things I don't need him to tell me for me to know them or feel them.

I get up and stand by the edge of his bed.

"What?" he says.

I give him a hug.

"Be careful, kiddo. The bullet wound."

"Didn't you just say it doesn't hurt?"

I hug him tighter. The bed is small, so I kneel on the carpet, my head against his chest.

"I like Ambareté," I say.

"You deserve it," he says through a muffled laugh. "Don't hug your old man so hard, he's weak."

"Whatever you say, Dad."

He blows my hair off his face with a puff of air and tucks it behind my ears. He doesn't really know what to do with his arms. He just leaves them there and pats me like a puppy.

And it's okay.

It's okay.

10.

There's a kid younger than me sitting on the gate, looking sleepy or like he's being punished. He takes a long drag of his cigarette and stares at us like he has all the time in the world. Dad starts in with *we're here to*, but the kid doesn't hear him or doesn't care. He leaves the cigarette in his mouth and jumps down. He opens the gate for us and exhales, blowing smoke. In the sideview, I see him close the gate, kick a stone to the other side of the road, and climb back up.

The house is horizontal and long, painted pink, with sliding glass doors and black grates out front. There's a little overhanging roof along the whole width with chairs and hammocks between the pillars. In the back, there are huge eucalyptus trees and a shed. It looks like a picture of a country house in *Billiken* magazine, but cooler.

Behind the house, I can see a pool. Someone does a cannonball. I don't know if it's a girl or a woman. We're too far away. We drive up, and I lose her behind the house. I can still hear the splashing.

As we get closer, more details appear on the porch. Toys lying around, a bunch of Barbies sitting on flowerpots. A blackboard, a boxing bag, soccer balls, and a lot of plants in planters: lilies, roses, and a bunch more I don't know the names of. In the middle of all that is a guy sitting in a lawn chair, with sunglasses on and a long-barreled revolver resting on his leg.

Dad parks next to an F100 pick-up. In the back windshield, where the round speed limit sign should be, it says *As fast as she'll go*.

The guy with the revolver is playing with a doll that's only wearing a bikini top. He moves one leg and then the other, sets it on his shoulder like a parrot. After he takes two steps, it falls, and he tries to grab it, but it slips through his grasp. He's missing two fingers on his right hand.

"That old bitch," Dad says. "It's just mean putting you on frisking duty."

He holds his arms out straight. Using his free hand, the guy checks his armpits, his waist, and then, to avoid bending over, he uses his foot to rub Dad's ankles.

"Come on, Reynosa. I'm not stupid enough to show up strapped."

"I don't know how stupid you are. So I gotta check."

He comes over to me. Luckily, my jeans are tight, and so is my T-shirt, so he doesn't have to pat me down. He checks my tits out more than he does my waist. Then he goes back over to Dad.

"It's nice to see some of us old boys are still alive," Reynosa says, giving him a pat on the shoulder. Well, half a pat.

"Who'd kill the gardener?"

"Fuck you."

"Don't forget to water the lilies."

Dad walks toward one of the sliding glass doors, and I follow him. On the inside, the place looks less like *Billiken* and more like something out of the pages of *Caras* magazine. Wooden ceilings, white curtains. Lots of natural light. There's a table big enough for three families to sit down to and armchairs littered with dolls. The back wall is another set of huge sliding glass doors leading to the pool. A little girl holding on to the ladder is kicking underwater. There are also two little blond boys. They all look like siblings. A guy with no shirt on and a pistol stuck into his plaid trunks is skimming the pool.

The smell of coffee drowns out the scent of the eucalyptus trees. There's a bar separating the living room from the kitchen and a coffee table with a puzzle on it, partially put together. They've only done the border. And there are framed pictures everywhere. On the walls, on end tables, next to the TV. Dad picks one up, but I can't see who's in it.

"It took you long enough."

The voice comes from a hallway. Then she appears, combing her wet, graying hair with bangs that reach her eyebrows. It looks like she just got it cut. She's not wearing any rings or a wedding band, but she does have a lot of bracelets on, and a long necklace over the front of her blouse. She must be about fifty.

"Dragón, it's been a while."

"Not long enough." Dad sets the frame back on the table. "You're still looking good."

"You aren't. But you didn't look very good before, either. I didn't know you'd be coming with a plus one. The famous girl from the rose tattoo, I guess."

"Hibiscus," I say. "I'm Ámbar, nice to meet you."

"Eleonora. But you can call me Eleo."

I feel like Dracula just told me I could call him by his first name.

She gives me a kiss hello. She smells like tanning oil and lotions.

"The pink looks nice on you," she says. "I always wanted to dye my hair, but I could never decide what color, and in the end, time chose for me." She touches her graying hair. Then she looks at Dad. "I won't give you a proper hello because you don't like it. Come on in, sit down. There's fresh coffee."

"Thanks, but we're not here for breakfast."

"I want some," I say.

Ground coffee, not instant coffee or that burnt stuff, or the kind you get on buses, is impossible to turn down. Whatever's going on, it can wait until after coffee.

"With milk?"

"Black is fine."

She picks up a Volturno and pours a cup for me, then hands another one to Dad.

"Just take it, you look like you need it. There's the sugar."

I put in two spoonfuls. I let the steam moisten my face. Eleo pours herself a small cup, puts in some Chuker, and takes a few sips. I could drink this every morning for breakfast. And every afternoon. Dad looks at his, twice, three times, and then gives in. He can't help but make the *damn that's good* face.

"This is what I miss most about working with you."

"I thought it was the money."

"You could have gotten some better security than that idiot Reynosa. Haven't you got Pandora anymore?"

"Pandora's engaged elsewhere. And Reynosa might be an old lump, but he makes a great asado. Anyway, you know my best security is my reputation."

She wets her smile with some coffee, then sets the cup down on the bar. It's porcelain, the kind that in most houses only gets brought out for special occasions.

"Do you want something to eat? I think there are a couple medialunas left."

"I'm fine, thank you."

"She's got good manners. Let's go over to the sofa so I can watch the kids while we talk."

She sits down in an armchair in front of the back patio doors. We sit on either end of the loveseat.

"I didn't know you were running a day camp," Dad says.

"They're Gabriela's kids. I always thought she would have been good for you."

"She wasn't my type. How's she doing?"

"She's on vacation. Spending the next six summers at Ezeiza Federal. It happens. The kids' dad ended up getting a much longer sentence." She points to the floor. "Honestly, I never liked him. He was always telling her they should go off and work on their own. You can see how well that went for them."

She crosses her legs. Her sandal hangs from her big toe. The puzzle pieces are small, there must be about a thousand of them. I have no idea what the picture is of. There's no box for me to look at.

"I didn't know you and Sinaglia were so close." Eleo makes a calculated pause. "He came in after you left. And I never took you for someone who makes friends playing soccer, or meeting people at concerts. You know, Ámbar, your old man is the only guy who goes to a bar and stands a better chance of leaving with an enemy instead of a friend. He has a terrible temper."

"You don't say."

Dad looks at me and I laugh. I don't know if it's nerves or what.

"I don't know how you could like Sinaglia. He's so boring. All he cares about is money. But I guess you two get along. Yesterday Reynosa said you went by the house three times."

"Listen to me."

"No, Dragón. You listen to me. Because I already know everything you're going to say. Don't treat me like an idiot, you can't play a player."

I've never seen anyone cut Dad off like that. Eleo takes another sip of coffee. Above the armchair, there's a picture of her when she was about my age. She's hugging a much older man.

Except for my Grandma Nuria's, I never lived in a house that had pictures on the walls or the nightstand. Mom kept them in albums, along with a book where she wrote down stuff from the first couple years of my life. Who came to my birthday party. What everybody gave me. How much I weighed. She stopped writing in it after a year and a half. There aren't many pictures of me, except on the fake IDs. There are none of her.

A little girl comes down the hallway wearing a ruffled Minnie Mouse bathing suit. She covers her mouth with her hand when she sees us.

"Come on in, sweetie. These are Granny's friends."

The little girl comes over and whispers in Eleo's ear.

"Did you finish tidying up?" The little girl nods. "Then okay, but tell your uncle to help you put on some sunscreen."

The girl smiles, opens the sliding door, and goes outside. Dad looks at me and points.

"Why don't you go out to the pool with the kids?"

"Oh, Dragón. That place is for kids. She should stay here with the grown-ups." Then she says to me: "I'm sure he always tells you you're grown up now. Or is that just when it works for him?"

Dad scratches his beard, next to his mouth. I can feel the sweat in my armpits. The coffee and the cup in my hand make me feel even hotter.

"I'll save you gas and time," she says. "We've been following Sinaglia for a while. A couple of shipments from up north arrived light. I've been doing business with the Di Pietros and Cruz for a long time. And I know if they're going to fuck me, it won't be for twenty kilos. That's the difference between a son of a bitch and a jackass. If a son of a bitch is going to fuck you, he'll really go for it. Jackasses are more dangerous. To fuck one person, they fuck a whole string of people. And we all get dragged down." She shakes her arm to settle the bracelets on her wrist. "When I started this, I thought the dangerous guys were the broke ones. But then I found out the worst are the ones who don't have any self-esteem. I'm sick of dealing with boys, because they're not men. They like money, but they don't like taking orders from a woman. And that's where they screw it all up. Sinaglia's one of those. There are guys who don't realize the best thing that's going to happen to them in their whole lives is having a woman above them."

She picks her cup up from the table and takes a sip.

"But just like we saw you yesterday, we saw that guy with the snake tattoo the days before. Yeah. The one you've been asking about all over town." She gives a thin smile. "We wanted to understand what the deal was, who he was working with, who he was selling to. If there was someone else, or if it was just Sinaglia. He's not too bright. It didn't seem like something he came up with on his own."

As her hair dries, the gray stands out more. I finish my coffee and don't know what to do with the cup. The table with the puzzle on it looks like the kind you always have to use coasters on.

"Whatever it was, he's not coming up with anything at all now. We found him in one of our sheds, full of holes. What we didn't find were the two hundred kilos that should have been in that shed. I guess the snake wasn't happy with what Sinaglia had on him at the time. He wanted more. We know the snake and Sinaglia had set up an exchange with someone else. The question is, with who." She finishes her coffee and sets the cup down next to a picture of some kids playing in a field of marijuana. "Am I doing okay with the story? Since I took the kids in, they ask me to tell them a story every night, and I'm trying to get better at it. I'd ask you for advice, but if there's one thing I always liked about you, it's that you know how to keep your mouth shut."

Dad stretches his arms over the back of the loveseat. Patches of sweat darken his shirt and make it look like camouflage.

"I swear, when I heard you were back, I thought you'd come and ask for your old job. I about fell on my ass when they told me you were driving a truck."

"It's a shit job like any other."

"They must not be paying you too well if you're rolling around in that Renault 19."

Dad jingles the bullets in his shirt pocket. He keeps them on hand like other people carry coins.

"The crazy part is that this is a such a quiet area," she says. "You could raise a family here. Hardly anything ever happens. We're just a little town on the way to somewhere else. But you show up, and suddenly three trucks get hit, and we're in the papers: *Brutal Attacks by Highway Bandits!*" She moves her hands in the air like she's laying the type for the headline.

Dad leans forward and puts his hands on his knees.

"I don't know what the hell you're talking about. I drive an 18-wheeler and haul cows to the slaughterhouse five days a week."

"Now that I think about it, that's the perfect job for you. Look, I'm no cop, Dragón. I don't need proof. Especially if it's not me you're stealing from. I'm trying to have us be honest."

Eleo leans back in her chair and rubs the armrests. She looks at her wrist, trying to read the time on a watch she must have forgotten in the bathroom.

"This guy, the one with the snake tattoo, Robert Alvarado Sorias, or Mbói, started out as a hitman. Not a very good one, I guess, since you're sitting here. I know he branched out, too. When you're not very good, you don't have much choice. He works with a crew along with his brother and a couple other guys. They were from some bumfuck town near Iguazú, too small for two crews. And these guys got driven out. They moved to another town around there, but they're just trying to get by. Making it up as they go along."

Dad holds up his hand.

"I don't need his whole life story. Did you find him?"

"Pandora found him."

"And?"

Dad wipes his hand across his forehead. He's breathing through his mouth.

"The problem is, Mbói found him first. I haven't heard from him since yesterday afternoon. And you know Pandora always gets the job done."

"Where is he?"

"You're going to love this," she says. "Where you got your biggest scar. How long has it been since you've gone there?"

Dad scratches at the hair on the back of his neck, and it sticks up with his sweat.

"Twenty grand," he says.

"Dragón, don't treat me like an idiot."

"I'm not getting your shit back for free."

"I couldn't care less about the dope. What matters is the message. What you always say about people thinking they can hit you and there won't be any consequences."

"The message costs money, too."

He taps his hand against the armrest in a pay up gesture.

"Oh, that's enough, Mondragón. Now you're pissing me off." She leans forward. "Your problem is, you've always surrounded yourself with deadbeats who'd believe anything you said, and I know you like you were my own kid. You didn't get shot at because you're the legendary Mondragón, no matter how often you repeat that to every shit-for-brains you meet. You don't give a good god damn about Giovanni. All you care about is getting back what they stole from you. You got shot to shit for the money for the exchange. I don't know whether you were set up by Sinaglia and Mbói, or what. It doesn't matter. But don't waste my time talking to me like I don't know my ass from a hole in the ground."

Dad relaxes his shoulders and leans back. I'm about to ask if it's true, but only an idiot or someone who didn't know him would ask that. I clench my teeth. I hold myself back from smashing the cup over his head. For a few seconds, all I hear is the water in the pool, the kids getting in and out, and the sound of the bullets in Dad's fingers like the beads of a rosary.

"Are we all on the same page now?"

"So, what do you want?"

"My old man used to say you've always got to lend a hand. A pat on the back for a friend. And a bitch slap for somebody who gets too big for his panties."

"Good thing your dad wasn't a poet."

She raises her arm and waves in the direction of the pool. The guy in the plaid trunks opens the patio door and throws her something. When it lands in the middle of the puzzle, I see it's the keys to a car and an envelope full of money. Dad's money.

"What is this?" Dad asks. "Why the fuck are you touching my stuff?"

"If you'd just been honest, this would have been for free, but since everything's business with you . . ." She checks the envelope. "Still, it's not like I'm ripping you off . . . it looks like there isn't much money in driving trucks, or in robbing them."

Dad looks out the window. The guy in the plaid trunks makes sure we can see the gun in his hand.

"That Renault you have is a piece of shit," says Granny. "Take the Neon that's around the back. You're going to go see Miliki. He's in the same place as always. He's going to take care of what's in the trunk. Here." She doesn't talk again until Dad puts the keys in his pocket. "After that, you can do what you want, go after Mbói, kill him, take a tour of Iguazú Falls with your daughter, do whatever you like and call it whatever you like, revenge, honor. Up to you."

The patio door opens, and one of the little blond boys runs in, the other one chasing on his heels.

"Hey," Eleo yells. "What did I say about coming in here with your feet wet?"

The kids freeze, dripping on the tiles.

"Sorry, Granny. We forgot our towels."

"And you couldn't ask me to go get them?"

Eleo gets up and walks behind me. Dad doesn't look at me. He's leaning his neck against the back of the loveseat with his eyes closed. I want him to say something or do something, but I have no idea what. He should say he's sorry. Again. I think that silence is the most honest thing he can give me. And silence is bullshit.

Eleo stands behind me and rests her hands on either side of my head. Her bracelets pile up on her wrist. She wears them as elegantly as a viper.

"At first, it made me feel good when people called me Granny. All that nonsense about them being my grandkids. But really, they're the only ones I want to call me Granny."

Dad straightens his neck and looks at her. The bones in his jaw pulse like veins.

"Everybody fights over your scars, to see who it was that hurt you. You always loved that. With me, nobody fights to say they did this or that. That's the difference between pissing people off and making them respect you. Don't be stupid, Dragón. There are two ways to treat people like your kids."

"Shut up, Gran, I know you're going to try and charge me for the advice, too." He gets up. "And when you see her, say hi to Gabriela for me. Since your kids are doing so great."

He leaves without waiting for an answer. On his back is one big sweat mark and many little ones.

"It was nice to meet you, Ámbar. I hope next time it's under different circumstances."

I set the cup down on the puzzle table.

"Pink would have looked like shit on you."

I find Dad around back, on the other side from where the pool is, opening the driver's side door of a black Neon. Reynosa is standing nearby, the revolver in his hand.

"Don't worry. I already put all your stuff in the backseat." Then he says to me: "Nice shotgun, but isn't it a few sizes too big for you, princess?"

Dad opens the door for me, and I lean against the edge of the door.

"It's not that it's big, Reynosa, it's just you've got small hands."

When I get in, Dad's smiling with one side of his mouth, but I give him a look that stops his laughter dead in its tracks.

"Drive."

11.

The shoulder is red dirt when we stop for the second time. The gas station is tiny. The guy who pumps gas also works behind the counter.

I roll down the window, but I can't hear what Dad's saying. He clamps the phone between his ear and shoulder and writes something down on a piece of paper. Another list, I think. He takes a step back, but the phone cord is short and tugs on the receiver. A truck drives out and hides him and his words.

It's the first time I've heard Dad's voice in a while. He barely said two words to me to ask if I wanted something to eat when we stopped five hours ago, another gas station, another phone call. I didn't answer him. I got out to go to the bathroom and read what was written on the door. *My period's late. Help. I don't understand you, but I love you. I'd like to run you over just to know you're dead because of me.* And lots of hearts and dicks. I counted them. It was a tie at eight, if you counted the broken hearts. I stayed in there a while, sitting on two layers of toilet paper, with the smell of piss, the sticky floor, the overflowing trash can. I didn't want to get back in the car. If I'd had a marker, I would have written something.

When I got back, there was a bag with a sandwich in it on top of the glove box. I didn't say thank you. It's still there, hot from the sun. I don't even know what kind it is. I'll be too tempted if I open the bag. I prefer going hungry to giving ground. A war of silence is the only thing I can beat him at, no matter how much I have to chew my nails and tear up my cuticles.

Dad fishes around in his pockets looking for another coin until he finds one and puts it in the phone.

I feel like getting out again, but I've already been in enough bathrooms to know that I wouldn't use this one even if I had the runs. I turn on the radio, but all I can get are FM stations that play cumbia or chamamé or that kind of stuff. I grab the bag from the backseat and set it between my feet. I bet that sicko Reynosa touched my underwear. Maybe he even kept some. I want to burn everything. The money, I think. I'm already sure that perv robbed me. I sort through the shotgun shells until I find the lightest one. I have trouble prying it open. If I just had longer nails—or if I had my Victorinox on me—it would be easier, but I manage to open it as if I were pulling the petals off a flower, and see the money is still there.

I'm startled when Dad gets in. I drop the shell and rush to put it in my jacket pocket.

"Don't worry, it's just me."

He starts the engine, checking the mirror to see no one's coming, and we get back on the road.

"Did you lose something?"

Where we're driving, there's no twilight and no streetlights. Just the Neon's headlights. There could be anything at all next to us, we'd never know. My stomach grumbles and I put my hand on it, as if I could hide it. Dad lets out a chuckle through his nose.

"Are you going to keep that up much longer? Do you want me to stop somewhere else and get something? The mayo on that one will make you sick."

My stomach protests again, and I cover it up with my voice.

"Are you going to keep pretending nothing happened?" I say. "How do you say stupid girl in Guaraní? Maybe you can start calling me that."

There's the sound of bugs hitting the windshield. They're starting to tint the glass a brownish green. They keep smacking into it, one after the other.

"What did you want me to do?"

"What you promised. Or at least tell me the truth."

"I told you part of the truth."

He shifts into fifth. We're going so fast that the asphalt looks staticky.

"You know I tried."

"I don't even know what's true with you anymore."

"Don't be dramatic, Ámbar." He slows down, takes a curve. I can see green beyond the shoulder, lots of green, close. It must be beautiful here in the daytime. "I can't be just another guy. At least not just another guy without a cent to his name, like everybody else. I risked my neck a million times, and for what? To end up living like a hobo? No. I really did want to stop, but I always felt less like going home. If you can call that a home. I'd rather be dead."

"Well, you almost got your wish. Didn't you think about what would happen to me?"

The road goes up and down, it's impossible to see very far ahead.

"I understand what you're going through. I've been there. And you have every right to be mad. There are a few things I'd love to change, but I can't."

"Not even for me?"

He doesn't take his eyes off the road. My blood boils in my face, in my hands, I can't describe what's tearing me up from the inside. Maybe it's anger.

"Not until I get back what's mine."

He opens his mouth and makes his jaw pop. I never understood how he still has all his teeth, how they haven't been broken or smashed or pulled out. I'd like for someone to knock a few out. I'd like for someone to smash his face in, step over him, pick up a tooth, and make a necklace out of it. String it on a piece of wire. I'd like for them to always have it on them like other people carry around rosaries, and in every bar they went into, they'd sit down on a stool and tell the story of how they knocked a tooth out of Víctor Mondragón's head.

"Or until you lose the only thing you have left," I say, too late and too quiet.

I buckle up. He takes his hand off the gear shift and plays with the bullets in his pocket. I don't know if it's ritual or what, whether he's asking the bullets what the hell he should do with his life. Maybe it's a tic. Sometimes I think I don't know him at all.

Now I'm mirroring him, playing with the shotgun shell in my hand, touching the edges of the bills inside, thinking about the possibilities. Two hundred pesos isn't much, but it might cover two weeks in a hotel. And then what? A job in a bar, cleaning up vomit or shit. Waitressing, if I'm really lucky. But better that than scrubbing your dad's blood out from under your nails, better that than knowing he'll die in your arms, that this time there's nothing you can do, it's better to have shit under your nails than your own blood, and I want to cry, but Dad taught me not to cry. And I'm his best student.

The road keeps going up and down. There are no houses, no lights, just a bright glow, a fire in the distance. Off to the sides of the road, I can see fleeting little specks, the eyes of animals that watch us go by and could run into the road and get hit, hit us, little eyes that glow and look like stars, as if there were a sky down here, our own sky, made of animals.

Dad isn't wearing his seatbelt. Maybe it wouldn't be so bad if an animal ran out in front of us. It makes me sick that he just sits there in silence, that he still has all his teeth, that he's pretending nothing happened.

"I'm tired of running from place to place," I say, ready to

dig into my own wound to open up one of his. "If we'd just stayed put, Mom could have found me."

"She'd have to have been looking for you."

"I'm sure she did."

Maybe it's not just in silence that I can beat him. Maybe I can do it with words, too, when I sharpen them, throw them, stab them in. I turn sideways to look at him.

"You have no idea what you're talking about, kid."

"I never found out what you did to fuck her up that much. You ruined her. You ruined *us*."

Dad looks at me for a second with an expression I've never seen before. I can't name it, and it sticks with me even though I've turned my eyes back to the road. He slams on the brakes and puts his arm out to hold me back. Even so, and with the seatbelt that locks up, I'm thrown forward and hit the door when the back tires skid out and leave us on the shoulder. Where the lights scratch at the last bit of darkness, an animal runs away, and I can't see what it is. It looks too big to be a dog. He asks me if I'm okay. He grabs my face and looks me over. He gets out and whistles, but we can only see the animal's eyes. It turns and then disappears.

Dad gets back in, leaving the door open. He's shaken up, and the muscles in his neck are straining. He takes a few steps away from the car, punches the hood, and comes back.

"I found her," he says. "She was living an hour away from us."

He opens his mouth to say something else, but then decides against it.

"Say it. If you've got something to say, let's hear it."

"I talked to her. To come and see us. I waited for her at a hotel."

"Of course, you had to get me off your back, huh?"

He runs his tongue across his top teeth first, then the bottom ones.

"You're saying a lot of things that are wrong."

I laugh, I laugh right in his face.

"Fine, since you're so big on the truth. She never showed up, but she left this for you at the desk."

He opens up his wallet, almost empty, just two bills inside and a letter, or something that looks like a letter, the one I always thought he was going to give me, and now I finally have it in my hands. But it's not from him. It's Mom's handwriting. It's written on the back of a pizzeria menu in blue pen that ran out of ink after two lines, then in green pen.

I'm talking to you woman to woman.

"If you want out, here's your chance," Dad says. He pulls the last twenty pesos out of his wallet, unzips the coin purse, and shoves it all into my pocket along with a few bullets. One falls under the seat. "Here. Go find your mom. Or shut up and never mention that bitch again."

Dad gets up and slams the door. The dome light goes out, and I can't read the letter.

I can't think. I feel . . . I don't know how I feel. I see something coming toward us, lighting us up, and I'm so dazed—dazed, that's how I feel—that I think the fire is coming toward us, but when it comes right up behind us, I realize it's a police cruiser. Two cops get out. I turn around to look at them, but the high beams blind me, passing through the Neon. I shade my eyes with my hand. One of them stays behind the trunk, and the other one comes up to Dad's window.

"What's going on, officer?"

"I don't know, you tell me."

"An animal ran out in front of us, and I had to slam on the brakes to keep from getting killed."

I can't see either of their faces. The one at the window isn't fat, but the buttons on his uniform are straining. The one behind the car is just a silhouette, with the light from the cop car making him look like a saint on a prayer card.

"They told me over the radio you were doing ninety."

"Do you think this thing could get up to ninety?"

"Check it out, Lucio. We've got ourselves a real mechanic here," he says to his partner, who turns and comes up to my window. I lay my bag down and push it under the seat with my heels.

"Let's see your papers."

"Look, Officer . . . Cordero," Dad says, straining to read his name tag. "We had an emergency, my wife was in an accident, and a friend lent me the car." He reaches over and opens the glove box. I'm afraid there'll be drugs in there, a gun. But there are old newspapers, a shammy case. He digs farther back. Something falls between my feet, and when the cop at my window shines his flashlight on it, I see that it's a Barbie. Someone drew nipples on it in marker. Her mouth is covered in Liquid Paper. She's missing two fingers on one hand, and the rifle from some Rambo doll is glued onto the other. "I told my brother to put the registration in here. That idiot . . ."

"Registration and step out of the vehicle."

"Officer, with all due respect, we've been driving for eight hours, I just . . ."

The cop opens his hand and motions for him to get out. They go to the shoulder, where the flashing blue lights come and go, rescuing them from the dark.

The other one sits down in Dad's seat with his legs outside the car. He's old. Sweat is pouring down his sideburns. He looks at the Barbie and leans over to pick it up, leaning his head against me while he gropes around for it. I jerk my knee a little, and he straightens up.

"You're a little pervert," he says.

He brushes the dirt off the Barbie, first by blowing on it, then with his fingers.

"It's not mine."

"You're about old enough for other kinds of toys now, huh?" He adjusts the belt buckle that's digging into his stomach. "I see you like older guys."

"He's my dad."

"He didn't want to pay you, and you threatened to jump out, and he had to hit the brakes?" He sniffs every few seconds and checks his nostrils in the mirror. "Or maybe we're your heroes and we saved you. A lot of bodies get dumped out here. You should be grateful we came along."

The pin with his last name—Manzoni—hangs at an angle and is very shiny, unlike the faded blue of his uniform.

I look down. I still have the letter in my hands, wrinkled from holding it so tight.

The cop outside hisses to get his attention. Manzoni gets out and walks over to them.

"If you don't have the papers for the car, I'm sure you can find some other paper that'll do the trick."

Dad shows them his empty wallet. The twenty pesos in my pocket.

"I got the call and ran out with what I had on me. My wife . . ."

"These porteños think we're idiots, Lucio."

I open the letter. With the lights from the cop car cutting through us, I can see what it says.

Now that you're thirteen, a little lady, you'll understand me.

There are a few words spelled wrong. *Mistak. Dreems. Servint.*

On one side, an empanada order is marked down in shorthand, two H&C and one B. I want to tear the letter up, stop reading. Not know it exists.

Dad raises his voice. One of the cops rests his hand on his sidearm.

A woman has to pay attention to her feelings.

That bitch.

That fucking bitch.

I think that whatever's in the trunk will make them happy and get Dad out of my life for a few years. They can drop me off in the next town, I'll pull down a *help wanted* sign in some motel, a hostel, a gas station, put on yellow gloves and scrub floors, count hearts and dicks on the bathroom doors while I scrape shit out of a toilet with no lid or seat, go back to a cockroach-infested room and watch TV, cooking shows with recipes I'm never going to cook, discover the taste of wine and hangovers, make everyone believe I'm eighteen. That I've been a woman for a long time.

One sentence is all it would take: *Officer, the trunk.*

But you shouldn't always trust what you think or feel.

I touch my forearm where I imagined the ink, the tattoo that I haven't decided on yet.

Nothing will grow on my skin yet.

My skin can wait.

My blood can't.

If I'm going to be cleaning up shit, I want it to be my family's.

I pull apart the shell and take out the bills, two fifties and a hundred. I smooth them out as well as I can and put them inside the letter.

"Officer," I say. I get out. "I found the papers."

All three of them look at me. Dad's even more confused than the cops. Manzoni takes the bills. His fingers are sticky, like he's been eating ice cream. He opens the letter.

"Everything seems to be in order."

"You can be on your way, but be careful. There are a lot of accidents around here."

We get back into the car. The cops look at us from the shoulder. Manzoni hands the bills to his partner and keeps the letter, trying to decipher it.

"Goodbye forever, Ámbar," he says, reading the last line

out loud with a laugh. He crumples it up, throws it on the ground, and gets in the cruiser.

Dad asks me if I'm okay, if he did anything to me. I couldn't explain the face I make. The cops make a U-turn. As soon as they're out of sight, Dad throws the Barbie out the window and gets us back on the road. When we pick up speed, the air coming in the window makes me realize I'm drenched in sweat. It takes me a while to understand that the feeling I thought was cold is really something else.

I'm shaking, and I put my hands under my butt so he won't see.

"Where'd that come from?" he asks.

"I was saving up for a tattoo."

Dad starts to say something.

"No," I say. "No more promises."

Cars appear ahead of us. Off in the distance, there are other dots, little lights in front of houses in the middle of nowhere. The red blinking of some antenna above it all. The town comes together, bit by bit, streetlamps lighting up the telephone wires. On the shoulder, there's sign after sign for streams with names in Guaraní. I wonder how many words he brought back for me from here.

"*Tavýcho*," he says, giving me one more.

"What's that?"

"Dumbass in Guaraní."

The houses go from being big lots to just having yards, they get smaller, they pile up on top of each other, they become a neighborhood. He slows down, twisting his neck to see out my window. If it weren't for the lights inside the houses, you'd think they were abandoned. He parks in a makeshift garage with a tin roof. The overgrown grass thumps against the Neon's undercarriage.

"*Aguije*," Dad says after turning off the motor and the headlights, as if he could only say thank you in the dark.

"You're welcome, *tavýcho*."

The house is on an incline. It has a roof and a brick base to lift it in case there's heavy rain or flooding. A covered porch. There's a bathtub full of plants outside. There are wire fences dividing one plot from the next. A dog barks nearby. Dad bends over and sticks his hand into a river boat until he finds a key. He goes in first, like always, to make sure there's no one there. He turns on all the lights in the house as he goes. Then he waves at me to come in. A furious musty smell hits me when I go in. The humidity in the wood, the stink of rot; it's like breathing through a sweaty T-shirt. In the back, next to the window, is a dusty Christmas tree. Dad goes back for the stuff in the car and sets it on a chair. He puts a gun in the fridge, another in the silverware drawer.

Dad's been in this house before. He opens the drawers and cabinets he needs. He knows what he'll find in each one. And I feel like I do, too. A long time ago, when life didn't record memories in cement but in sand. I give it a try: if there's a bathroom to the right with green tile and a skylight, this is it. Yes. There it is. I recognize the bedroom that was mine, too, the crooked bed, the curtains made from a sheet. I set my bag down on a shaky chair. In no time, I find the hiding spot behind a fake baseboard and put my real ID there before he asks me to.

Dad locks the front door. He doesn't unpack. That's good. He plugs in an extension cord in the kitchen and carries it into the bathroom. I hear the clipper buzzing. The blades going back and forth, over Dad's skull. Ten minutes later he comes out with his head shaved and his beard evenly trimmed.

"You look younger," I say.

"As long as I don't look like me. Same goes for you."

I catch the bag and towel he tosses to me. I don't have to check what's inside. Or ask if I really have to.

Don't be remembered.

Don't be identifiable.

The bathroom mirror is tiny, the kind people use to pluck their eyebrows. I angle it so I can see myself. I take the black hair dye out of the package and mix it up, then comb my hair and separate out the pink streaks. I rub Vaseline on my forehead to keep from staining my skin. I look at the ID in the bag. I was twelve in that picture. The girl in the mirror looks nothing like that.

My name is Alejandra. I'm fifteen. My favorite subject is language arts. My best friend's name is Mercedes. I went to a pay-by-the-hour hotel once, but my boyfriend fell asleep. I don't have any scars yet. I like Pearl Jam. Audioslave. I hate Metallica. My mom's working, she works at a tourist resort. A lot of the kids there call her Mom, too.

I grab a brush and the streaks in my hair.

Goodbye, pink.

II

TO NOWHERE

12.

The shirtless guy looks at the Neon parked in the yard at his house. He takes six or seven bricks of cocaine out of the trunk, stacks them against his stomach and chin, and carries them to a little shed where he piles them up together. He weighs them one by one on a food scale until he's sure the needle marks one kilo.

Sitting on two little stools under a beach umbrella, Dad and I watch him walk back and forth.

"You're kidding me," I say.

He shakes his head.

"How come you didn't tell me?"

"I thought you'd seen it. If I hadn't braked, I would have killed it."

"I would have hated you for that."

"You were already busy hating me."

"I would have hated you even more."

"How is it my fault that thing ran out in front of us?"

He moves a little to stay in the shade. His hand that was in the sun looks redder. For having lived around here, Dad's skin is pretty poorly trained. Like he only moved around at night. Or lived behind closed doors.

"If you hadn't been all upset and yelling at me, you would have seen it."

"Let's just drop it."

"Fine by me."

He reaches his hand out toward me, and I shake it. Both our hands are sweaty. I dry mine on my jean shorts. He hates them. He says if you can see the lining of the pockets, they're too short. He can just deal with it. I like my long legs.

"I can't believe it. Was it big?"

"It would have fed you for a month."

I punch him in the shoulder, and he snorts out a laugh. Laughter in Dad's body is a noise, something an animal would make.

"Sure," says the shirtless guy, "you guys laugh it up, I'm the only one doing any work around here. Want me to pour you some tereré while I'm at it?"

His T-shirt is hanging out of his shorts. Every once in a while, he uses it to mop up his sweat.

"Right, Miliki, because that all walked here on its own little legs."

"You've always been one moody fucking *argel*, Mondragón."

"See, I'm not the only one who calls you that," I cut in.

"Even a saint would be *pirevai* in this heat."

"Take your shirt off, then. Or are you shy?"

"I don't want to distract you, you're already working slow enough."

Dad fans himself with a newspaper. He hands me a section so I can, too. It doesn't do any good.

"You should have planted a tree so you'd have a little shade."

"I'll be dead by the time it's big enough for there to be any shade."

"Think of your kids."

"Why do you think I'm doing this? I'd already retired. But the youngest one went and got pregnant. Now they're living in the garage. Having a grandson is great, but sleeping through the night is better."

"Hurry up, then, so you can have a nap."

He loads another couple of bricks. One falls on the ground.

"Don't you have a trolley?"

"Ask your dad what happened to my trolley."

Dad pulls an imaginary zipper across his lips.

"Don't make like you don't love telling stories, go on."

"I don't really remember that one. I do remember Estrella, the Amambay queen."

Miliki stops dead and points his finger at Dad.

"Don't you dare say a word."

"Then keep loading, I've got stuff to do."

"Nobody respects their elders anymore."

"You're not old, Miliki, you're just falling apart."

"I've got three daughters. Three," he says, holding up his

fingers. "Let's see how it goes for you now your pup has grown into a wolf."

Miliki looks down and sees coke stuck to his sweat. He scrapes it up with a finger and rubs it across his gums. He digs into another brick and tries a little more. He gathers up the packets, trying to carry nine this time.

"What did the old lady chat about with you this time?" he asks offhandedly.

"Money, what else is that bitch going to talk about?"

Dad turns on a tap and wets his scalp. I'm not used to seeing him with his head shaved. He has a scar on the back of his neck that looks like branches. I have no idea how he could have gotten it.

"Are you sure it wasn't an ocelot or a margay?"

"Are margays the ones that always look mad?"

"That's you."

"Very funny. No, those are smaller. I told you, this one was big."

I take off my sneakers, set them aside, and put my feet up on the chair. He doesn't let me wear flip-flops. *You can't run in those.* The air feels nice.

"Does yaguareté mean something in Guaraní?" I ask.

Dad tilts his head down and watches the drops of water that run down his face collect on his chin and then fall onto the red ground.

"The beast of beasts. Or something like that."

"That must be why it's my favorite animal."

"If you behave, I'll let you have one."

Sleeping for the first time in almost two days has put him

in a good mood. Like he's in control again. Like being able to put all his hatred in one place keeps it from spreading all over.

I touch my arm. Where the guy has his snake, that's where I'd get a yaguareté.

"I'm going to get a tattoo of one. As soon as I get my money back."

He must be biting his tongue. But he's not going to say anything. There are things he's going to have to accept. I like that. I think about what else I can get out of him. The idea of having some ink in my skin helps me not miss the pink in my hair—at least, not as much. With this heat, I probably should have just cut it. I need a hair tie. Right now.

"You like them because you've never run into one," Miliki says. He talks out of the corner of his mouth, his neck stretching farther and farther as he tries to carry more at a time. It's like those rings on African women, but with bricks of cocaine.

Dad gets up and walks over to the trunk. There's an oniony smell coming from the kitchen.

"This one was ripped," Miliki says, showing it to him before weighing it. "It's about fifty grams short."

"Vacuum out the trunk. What do you want from me? That idiot Reynosa loaded it up."

"Do you know how he lost his fingers?"

Dad nods.

"And you're not planning on telling me?"

"It's because he's a jackass. At this age, if you're in perfect shape, it's because you didn't take enough risks."

"Tell that to Pandora. And he was no spring chicken. We

found him yesterday. One piece. And another one today. I wouldn't be surprised if we find another piece tomorrow."

"He got careless, though. Do you know anything about Mbói?"

Miliki pulls his T-shirt from his waistband and dries off his face.

"He's a two-peso gunman. He kills cheap, but he's sloppy. Those guys don't last long. But they kick up a lot of shit first. And the rest of the crew is about the same, from what I hear. The brother's the only one with half a brain, the cousin's a big guy, but he's useless. And the rest . . . You know when you pick a team at school? Well, these are the guys that get picked last. You know how it is, they're not around very long. The only crew that lasts around here is the police."

"If you hear anything, let me know."

"I'm getting out."

"Me, too."

The guy laughs.

"Lunch'll be ready in five," a woman says through the window.

"You sure you don't want to stay and eat?"

I'm tempted, but Dad doesn't give me time to say anything.

"We're in a hurry. It's a long day."

"It's a long life."

"Only if we're lucky."

We get in the car. The seats are boiling hot. We roll down the windows.

"Is she that bad a cook?" I say.

"Let me put it this way. At Miliki's, you pray after eating."

13.

We're going to go collect payment for his scars.

That's how he puts it. Without a peso to his name, all he can do is call in debts and favors. It's a shorter list, a lot shorter than the other one.

Some of them we can't find, or they're dead or in prison. They aren't friends. They call him Germán or different nicknames—Goat, the Mute, Txakur—so it seems like they're never talking about the same person. They're buddy-buddy nicknames, from some little story they hold onto as a secret.

I heard you were working at an oil well.

Somebody said they'd seen you working in Pedrojuán.

Someone was telling me about a hitman that goes by Cartola, and I thought it was you.

I don't hear much. They don't want to talk in front of me.

After five stops, we find someone who knows Mbói. A woman named Yaharí. She's a bleach blonde with a broken nose. She specializes in tarot readings. She doesn't read the lines on people's palms anymore, *that's old news, babe*; now she reads lines of coke.

She makes Dad choose a card and use it to scrape out three lines. According to her, the first one is the life line, the second one is death, and the third one is the unexpected. Every so often, I have to leave the room to keep from laughing.

"That Mbói, powerful energy," she says. "He's got a spell worked on him."

"Save that spell crap for the idiots who come in here. I want to know where I can find him."

"Let me do my job, babe."

Yaharí keeps going, says that the guy has a spell with snake teeth, that they put them under his skin, that the venom doesn't kill you, it makes you immortal.

She takes the first line.

"You've got powerful energy, too."

"I love you, Yaharí," Dad says. "But I think you took a little too much of your own medicine."

"Coke doesn't lie, Germán."

Dad drops the card on the table. It's a queen of spades. We leave her snorting the lines of destiny and walk out.

"I bet she'd be great for group sessions," I say.

WE KEEP GOING. THE seat of the Neon is like a second skin. I'd give anything for a shower. Or for some deodorant. Sometimes when I go to the bathroom, I wash my armpits.

When we leave the house of a guy named Motoneta, I pull my hair back in a ponytail with a hair tie I stole from his daughter. It's the next best thing to flopping down in front of a fan.

On the plus side, Dad lets me pick the music. He holds out for three songs, which is two more than usual, before starting in on Audioslave.

"I don't see how you can like this. It's noise."

"You just don't understand, Dad."

"You're the one who doesn't understand. Or do you speak English now?"

"I feel it, that's different."

"I think they're depressing."

"Right, because Cartola is a real party."

"That guy had a hard time."

"These guys did, too," I say. "Maybe you didn't notice, but I don't have a life like the girls who listen to Backstreet Boys or Britney Spears."

"I have no idea who they are, but I'm sure you should be thanking me for that."

I take out the tape and throw it on the dash, but it falls on the floor, and I don't bother picking it up. Dad stretches and flexes his fingers on the wheel.

"Do you feel sad?"

"Sometimes."

I look out the window with my head leaning against the glass, like people only do in music videos.

"You lost a friend. I can't imagine what that feels like because I don't even know what it's like to have a friend."

"What do you mean? What about that girl . . . the blond one with the crooked teeth?"

"Marcela?"

"You two were always hanging out."

"Because she helped me with math."

"And the other one, with the acne."

"Yanina. I don't know, maybe, but I think being friends is more than just sitting together in class. A friend is someone you can go eat pizza with or tell a secret to."

Get together and do nothing, call up the boy you like, then hang up and die laughing. Hate the same girl, spread rumors about someone who hurt your friend, skip class and be scared your parents will find out, decide who to invite to your fifteenth birthday party.

"It's sad, but you're the closest thing I've got."

"When you were little, you made me promise we'd always be best friends. So, you can't say I don't keep my promises."

"When I was little, I believed in unicorns."

In a music video, the window would be covered in raindrops that reflect the red and blue neon lights, the city outside. Here, it's just my own reflection, the red dirt, and the countryside that just repeats itself, over and over.

I don't know what it's like to be embarrassed by my dad, to have him pick me up at a dance club, to have him laugh when I say he should park a block away and wait for me, for him to try and be cool in front of my friends.

With Dad, I don't know what it's like to be embarrassed, but I do know what it's like to be scared.

THE LAST PERSON WE see is named Chaves. He's Brazilian, living this side of the border for seven years. *Um pistoleiro de aluguel*, Dad says when we get there, *a hitman, but a good guy*. I have no idea how a hitman can be a good guy.

"God damn, seven years here and your Spanish is still shit. You're worse than Anamá Ferreira."

"Who I am supposed to practice talking with? My shadow also speak only *português*."

"Has all this time alone turned you into a poet? You'd be great. Poet by day, hitman by night."

"Who is the *garota*?"

"My daughter."

Chaves doesn't look like a killer. His smile is too big. His place, a studio apartment at the end of a hallway, is full of packs of cigarettes from Paraguay. There's a Grêmio de Porto Alegre poster on the wall.

"I know this Mbói," he says. "I buy weed for me and for sell. His crew have a hideout house near the river. He work security there. I see him two times, but he get a promotion. The cousin is still there, I see him a couple days ago. They call him Piñata."

He draws a map on the back of a restaurant flyer.

"The house is not too big. And they are no dangerous, but lots of them. Is a job for two."

"That's why I'm here."

"No fuck around. I retired, I already tell you, brother."

"I was retired that night, too."

"What shit you talk? You are not retired even in hell."

"If the *grana* is good . . ."

"But be alone is not good. Alone or dead. Those are the only two exits from our path."

"Brother, I'm not here for enlightenment."

Dad pulls up his T-shirt and shows an uneven scar on his back. Something that could have been made by a knife or wire.

"I heard they were about to send you to the other side, and I didn't hesitate. And Punta Porá's rough. It's not some little cakewalk," he says. "I got more stitches on this one than Grêmio's scored goals in the last ten years. But I got you out."

"Fuck. You don't forget."

"Your head can forget, but your skin can't, *irmão*."

Chaves touches his pockets, the one on his chest and the ones in his jeans. He gets up, opens a carton of cigarettes, and comes back with a pack.

"My skin also don't forget." He lights a cigarette. "You see this?" The scar stretches all the way across his stomach, pouting out against his black skin like a pink worm. You could see it from space. "One year ago, a man and his knife ask about you. They ask very hard. About you and also about Víctor Mondragón and Antonio Outes. You save me in Punta Porá, I owe, and I already pay." He taps the map. "I don't know who you are, what your real name, but I think you are a dead man." He stubs out the cigarette on his scar without so much as blinking. He flicks away the butt, which flies between me and Dad, and lowers his T-shirt. "So, you take care of your little girl before both you are in the land of the dead."

He gets up and stands next to the door. Dad stretches, grabs the map, folds it up, and puts it in his jeans pocket.

"I think you don't have no scar so big that someone owe you help with Mbói and his people."

"I don't know about scars, but I've still got a friend left."

"Knowing you, I think that is hard to believe."

14.

One more call and we're back on the road, heading for Gula's place. It's hard to say he lives on the outskirts of town. Except for a couple of places where the dirt roads are paved, the whole town looks like outskirts. There's not much to see at night except headlights in the distance. With the window down, it's your nose more than your eyes that tell you what's out there. Green and more green.

"Tom Cruise?"

"That midget? Women like tall guys."

"Don't I know it." Dad smiles, takes his hand off the gear shift, and points to himself.

Silence is sacred for him, except when it gets in his way, when that emptiness is filled with a lot of stuff he doesn't want to hear. Then he'll talk about anything to cover it up.

"Let's see . . ." he says. "That blond guy who came to shoot a movie here. Shit, what was his name. The pretty one."

"I don't like pretty guys."

"Oh, come on. Girls your age are all crazy about this guy. You know who I mean. He's in that one where at the end they give him his wife's head in a box and the guy can't even cry right. Damn am I bad with names." He snaps his fingers a few times. "*Seven*. That's the one."

"Great job. You ruined the ending."

"We saw it together. What are you talking about?"

"No. You saw it. I stayed home reading. You said it was too violent for me."

"I was right. It's for sixteen and up."

"You say that like my whole life isn't for sixteen and up."

He laughs.

"And no. It's not Brad Pitt."

"That's the son of a bitch's name. So? You're not going to tell me?"

"Chris Cornell."

He shrugs his shoulders.

"He's a singer."

"I bet he's that junkie with the long hair."

I shake my head in defeat. For the last two minutes, we haven't seen any signs of life.

"What about you? Who's your celebrity crush?"

"Libertad Leblanc," he says immediately.

"Who's that?"

"A gorgeous blonde." He'd define her very differently

if he was describing her to a friend. "She was Coca Sarli's competition."

"I can imagine. I bet she's on those posters like in an auto body shop."

"What do you know about those posters?"

"Are you kidding me? You've taken me to chop shops more times than you've taken me to school. We spent Christmas with Méndez, I don't know, two, three times."

"You're saying like it's a bad thing. That bastard taught you the multiplication tables and the names of all the rivers."

"Sure, he taught me that. He also taught me how to make a tourniquet with my shoelaces, or how to defend myself if someone wants to rape me."

"That shit will take you farther in life than knowing what photosynthesis is."

I shrug. "You're missing my point. What I was trying to tell you is that I've seen more tits there than I really wanted to."

Dad tilts his head to the side, admitting I'm right.

"He has some sort of decoration problem, I'll give you that. But trust me, Freckles, someday you're gonna thank him for all those lessons, and me for taking you there."

"I hope that day never comes."

"You never fucking know."

Dad looks left and right, turns, and heads through an open gate to park the Neon next to a tree with a bunch of bottles hanging from the branches. As soon as we get out, he warns me:

"Gula's kind of a weird guy."

"What a surprise."

Like his inner circle wasn't about ready for a circus or an insane asylum.

The man of the house is waiting for us, sitting at a folding table under a tin roof. Behind him is a lamp surrounded by so many mosquitoes that the light can barely cut through. He shades his eyes to see, and when he recognizes Dad, he opens his hand as if to say, *it's been a long time.*

"*Maitei*, Gula."

"*Mba'éichapa*, Germancito."

He must be the only real friend Dad has left. He knows him so well that he doesn't even bother getting up to welcome him or offer him a beer when we sit down in the cloth chairs. He hands him a bottle of water from a cooler, along with two plastic cups. On the table is a transformer and a bunch of rolls of copper wire.

The place speaks, and it's screaming junkyard. Columns of tires, a few security gates to protect front doors, car parts. A pile of metal, wire baskets, pieces of tin, old radios, and washing machines. I'm glad I got my tetanus shot.

The rotten smell seems to be coming from him. Every time the fan blows on him, I get a whiff of wet dog.

"You brought along the *cuñataí*."

"Alejandra," I say.

Thank God he reaches out his hand instead of giving me a kiss. When I shake it, it's like grabbing a hunk of grease.

"Right," he says. "Ale."

The moment he looks at Dad, I wipe my hand on my shirt.

"Sorry about the mess, but I wasn't expecting any visits from ladies at my age."

I'm sure they've never talked about me. As soon as I'm out of sight, he's going to say, "I didn't know you had a *mitakuña*."

"Have at it," he says, offering us a cutting board with cheese and salami on it.

Dad grabs some and passes it to me. I'm a little unsure, but I'm just too hungry. It's good enough.

"Where have you been, Germancito? Jail, a woman?"

He's sitting in a computer chair with wheels, and the backrest is hanging off it.

"A woman," he says, nodding at me. Then he points at the shotgun leaning against the wall. "I guess I caught you getting ready."

Gula grabs the shotgun, pops out a yellow shell, and hands it to him.

"Rock salt and a few other bits and pieces. The squatter kids from up the way come and try to steal my chickens."

"Does it hurt?" I ask.

"It kicks like a horse. Go have a look at the Luzuriagas' youngest. Doc Loria has been looking after him for about a year, and he says it still hasn't healed."

Dad puts the shell on the table and looks at the butterflies of the night bouncing off a lamp. Gula sets back in on the transformer. He pulls out the copper and rolls it up.

"What brings you back around here?"

The smell is killing me. It would be better if he turned off the fan. If there's one thing I've learned today, it's that Dad doesn't cut straight to the point. He lets them talk, gets their guard down. And I'm five minutes from passing out. I feel like asking to use the bathroom, but my instincts tell me I definitely don't want to go in there. I get up, pretending to see something interesting in the pile of metal.

"Have a look around," he says. "If you see something you like, you can have it."

The house is made mostly of brick, with one added room made of wood. I wonder how long it's been since a woman came here. There's a shed to one side. I turn on the light, and something goes running out, too noisy to be a rat. This place is different from the rest of the property. Everything's neat and organized, a museum of things looking for a second life. Hanging from a few nails in the walls, there are paintings with wooden frames that don't look like they came cheap. A marionette with a pair of women's shoes carved from wood. Horses and cars made from scrap metal, screws, and bolts are arranged on a huge wooden bobbin. If he made them himself, he must be crazy, but he's good. There are so many things that, no matter how well organized they are, I can't really see all of them. I think that when they head out, I could have fun in here.

Or maybe they'll need someone to drive.

The images from Corrientes come flooding back.

I was looking in the rearview, waiting for him to come out, my hands on the wheel, the engine running. The rosary was swinging with the purr of the motor, and it was making me nervous. I grabbed it and threw it out the window. Dad came out with his ski mask on, the bag slung across his chest and his gun in his hand. I was supposed to open the door when I saw him, but I forgot, or I couldn't do it.

There are seconds when so many things are happening that none of them come out right. He opened the door. After that, I mostly remember the noise. An explosion. One time we were living in Tandil, and every once in a while, we'd hear explosions in the quarry, and the sound was like that, or that's how I remember it. I don't know if it was a really long blink or what, but when I opened my eyes, there wasn't a rear windshield anymore. Dad said something to me, I didn't hear him, he was grabbing his arm, his fingers were red, and then there was another explosion and another, and the front windshield disappeared. I felt the impact of the buckshot smacking into my seat, and the heat from outside was pouring in. In the mirror, the man with the shotgun was in the door of the shed, and then his image shattered when the buckshot broke the mirror and his reflection. I peeled out and made him disappear. In the hotel room, I pulled the buckshot out of his shoulder, and the messy flesh mixed in with other, older scars. Later, while I was washing my hands in the bathroom, I saw something glittering in my hair. Pieces of the windshield. I left them there for a minute, twisting my neck to look at them, as if I were at the hair salon, and I thought that Dad bleeding was my fault, that I had to do a better job next time. When I came out, he was sitting on the bed, his arm bandaged up, and he looked at me and said, *It's over, Freckles.*

I didn't know how to feel.

I shake the memory off and when I'm back in the shed, a jaguar is staring me in the face. A wooden mask. Next to it, there's a caiman mask and one of a toucan. I take down the jaguar. It's carved and looks like it was made by some indigenous tribe. I wipe the dust off and look at it more closely. It smells burnt, like the marks were made with fire or something hot. I wonder if it's protection or just decorative.

When I walk back over to them, they're laughing.

"What a son of a bitch," Gula says. "I'd forgotten about Long Dong Silver."

"It's God's honest truth. He just split the oar down the middle and gave half to each girl."

Gula wipes a tear from his eye and shakes with an echo of laughter, like the story is replaying in his head.

"Did you find anything, sweetie?"

"Maybe."

"Mysterious. She gets that from you."

He cuts some cheese and eats it right off the knife.

"So, what can I do for you?"

Dad tosses him a baggie of coke, and Gula catches it.

"You brought dessert. How thoughtful."

What a son of a bitch, I think with a mix of admiration and anger. It was obvious he was the one responsible for the light kilo. He always said the perfect crime wasn't one you got away with but one you could blame on someone else.

"How much?"

"That's a gift."

"Nothing's a gift with you."

Dad tells him about Mbói.

"I've heard about him," Gula says. "People say he's got a hell of a *guyryry* going up there."

Dad keeps talking. He tells him about the weed bunker outside town, Piñata's place.

"You stand there with a shotgun and cover my back, that's it. A picnic compared to the rest of the stuff we've done."

"I'd love to. And my nose would love it even more. But . . ."

"Don't tell me you've gone straight, too."

Gula leans back and slaps his right knee, where the leg of his jeans is rolled up with nothing below it.

"Shit. What happened?"

"A burro race." Dad frowns. "I picked the wrong horse."

Gula talks about a sure thing, a big bet, but Dad's not listening anymore. He rubs his forehead, his eyebrows, his eyes. He zones out. And Gula keeps going, saying sometimes he can still feel his leg. I want to just turn him off like a radio. He stops talking and opens up the baggie with the care of a parent changing their child's diaper. He takes a bump. Dad lifts his head, his gaze lost in the distance, like a castaway who realizes the only land he can reach is the land of the dead.

"I'll go," I say.

He takes his hand away from his face. It's like he's waking up and can't understand if he's here or in a dream.

"I'll go," I say again. "But on one condition."

15.

We land at night.

We land.

Because there are some nights you tumble into, like a deep, dark well.

And this is one of them.

There's a light in the distance, so far away it looks like a star. The lamp marks the wooden shack, with a door in the middle and a DirecTV antenna. If there are windows, I can't see them, or they're boarded up.

I know there are trees. I can smell them, but I can't see them. I can't even see my feet on the ground. The only thing that's real is the shotgun in my hands and Dad, up there ahead of me somewhere, more a noise than something I can see.

The sound of a butterfly's wings could split the night in two. I wonder if I'll ever cast a shadow again. But more than anything else, I wonder why the hell I said, *I'll go.*

I said *I'll go* and after that, everything is foggy.

I put on a huge button-down shirt and sweatpants to hide that I'm a girl, *so they don't think you're weak.* I don't know who handed me the shirt or who said that. It could have been either of them.

Dad gave me the shotgun, my shotgun, the same one as always, the one I shot at cardboard boxes and old cars, but never at a person, and he said again, as if I didn't carry his words with me like a birthmark, *when people see a shotgun, their assholes tighten up, but their tongues loosen*, and I think that Dad's voice is a birthmark that can take any shape. Anything he needs. Just like me.

Dad explains the plan, once, twice, three times, like it's complicated, and in the background Gula's nose keeps snorting coke. *Got it?* And I think I said yes, or I nodded. And then the plan again, and the snorting.

He handed me the yellow shells with salt in them, so I won't have to carry a death on my conscience. I don't know if that's how he said it, I don't think so, but that's how I decide to remember it. *You'll still mess them up pretty good with these.* When he's not looking, I change them out for my own, the regular red ones, because if push comes to shove, I prefer to mess up my conscience but stay alive.

Then there was my condition: I put on the jaguar mask, hoping that something inside it would protect me, make me feel safe.

And now that we're landing, at night, I know it won't.

We go a little farther in, until the light rescues us from the darkness, gives birth to my shadow, and there's something in that I find calming. Then the lamp brings Dad to the surface, glinting first off the double-barrel in his right hand and then the .38 in his left. He turns, and I start giggling when I see him in the caiman mask.

"Shh," Dad hisses.

The shack is about the size of a shipping container. I can hear voices, but I can't make out what they're saying. I have my hood pulled up, and the elastic pinches the back of my neck. My breath, trapped between my skin and the mask, sounds like the wind. The scent of the river. Dad and I always fight about that. To him, it's the stink of the river, not the scent of the river.

As we get closer, the voices dial in, separate from each other. There's a soccer game on TV. *He's got no hustle.* Dad looks at the door. Things must look different in his eyes; the wood must look like cardboard, the people like targets.

What does he see when he looks at me?

A daughter?

An accomplice?

He kicks the door in, and the night splits in two. He goes in first, sweeping the room with his shotgun, and I'm a step behind him. He goes right, I go left. A guy with long hair reaches for the floor, but I aim my sawed-off at him, and he goes still as a statue.

"Anybody who moves is ground beef," Dad says.

I stand next to the TV. There are three guys on my side, all against the opposite wall. There's a girl wearing a bra and soccer pants sitting on a vegetable crate. The other two are on a wooden bench. One's shirtless and has a tupperware container on his knees. The one with long hair still has his hand hovering inches from the floor.

Dad forbade me from talking. *If they realize you're a girl, they'll go for you.* So, I give a hiss, hisses don't have a gender, and I snap my fingers and motion for him to give me the gun.

"Let's go, Rata Blanca," Dad says, "kick it over."

He slides it out with his right foot and toe punts it over. It lands right next to my Converse. It's a revolver with electrical tape on the butt. I give it a kick to get it even farther away. I think, if I wasn't here, that guy would have shot Dad full of holes.

There's a door out the back. The floor is packed dirt. Next to the TV are twenty bricks of weed. On Dad's side are a big man with a rosary spilling across his stomach and a revolver in his waistband, and a kid around my age in a Boca jersey.

"You too, old man."

The guy pulls it out in slow motion and throws it behind Dad.

"Anybody else? If I find a piece on you, I'll make you eat it." The girl shakes her head. "Come on, you two over there." He herds them over to my side.

My face itches with sweat.

"I don't know who you got your tip from," says the old guy, "but this is all we have." He points at the weed with his chin. "With the game today, nobody's working."

"Which one of you is Piñata?"

The guys look at each other. The girl points outside with a long purple fingernail. It must be fake.

"He went out to take a shit."

"Come the fuck on."

"It's true, Wally Gator," says Rata Blanca. "Do you see a bathroom in here?"

"Are you fucking with me? A TV like that and you don't put in a bathroom."

Dad goes over to the back door to look for him, but visibility is only a few yards. It makes me nervous for them all to be looking my way, either at me or the TV, I'm not sure. It's the middle of an ad break, so I think they're keeping an eye on me, waiting for me to get distracted. There are some bags under the bench, but I can't see what's in them. A drop of sweat rolls down my forehead and gets in my eye. I raise my elbow to dry my face, forgetting I have the mask on. I blink a few times to break up the drop of sweat, which is hell-bent on driving me crazy.

"Cat got your tongue, jaguar?"

"He talks with his sawed-off," Dad says. "You want to hear him? And I'm a caiman, kid."

"Well, I'm a Metallica fan, and you're calling me Rata Blanca. You're Carmen's dad, right?"

"This must be Rocío's boyfriend," the girl says. "I told that idiot Piñata she was trouble."

"Shut the fuck up."

The shirtless guy is still eating out of the tupperware. He's using a Sacoa card for a spoon to break up and scoop the rice.

"And you, want to give it a rest with dinner?" Dad says.

"Man, it's my second day on the job, I've got crazy

munchies, and you roll up like Guaraní Sesame Street and tell me not to laugh. Don't be a dick, *che capelú*."

I keep from laughing out loud as best I can, but my shoulders shake. Luckily, Dad doesn't notice, and I don't think anybody else does, either.

"I think you're lying to me."

"It's the second time he's gone out," the old guy says.

"Let me go get him," says the one with long hair. "I want to watch the penalty kicks."

"You'll stay right where you are."

Dad changes position and stands next to the door. He opens it a crack to peek out.

Why are they all fucking staring at me?

My skin is cold, and my heart beats all over my body, as if my chest were too small for it. It beats in my fingers, my ears, the sides of my head. The guy with long hair exchanges a glance with the girl, she looks at the floor, the bags, and nods her head in that direction. I want to talk, to tell them to stop, to scream at them. Rata Blanca slides his hand around behind his back and into a space between the wall and the bench. I could pull the trigger, but I'd kill them all. I hiss, but nobody pays me any attention, not even Dad, who's still looking around outside. They don't care that I've got a shotgun leveled at them. Rata Blanca slides his butt across the chair to lean over better. He closes his eyes with the strain. I push both barrels against his chest, and he's so startled, he bangs his head against the wall. Dad finally looks at us.

"What the hell do you think you're doing?"

He gives him a shove that lands him on top of the girl. He reaches into the bag and pulls out another revolver, then shakes his head.

"Hey, boss, I forgot about that one," Rata Blanca says, with his hands pressed to the side of his head.

"You're not going to forget again."

Dad smashes the butt of his .38 into Rata Blanca's nose and breaks it. Then he hammers it against his teeth, beats his face in. Deformed screams. I aim at the door, and I don't know if it's to protect us or to keep from watching. When he's finished, he opens the cylinder, drops the bullets to the floor, leans over, and sticks the revolver in Rata Blanca's mouth like a pacifier. The guy coughs, chokes, tries to spit it out, but he's so destroyed that it just hangs there, the bloody butt sticking out like a wooden tongue.

"Fucking moron," Dad says.

The caiman mask is spattered with red. It looks like he just devoured some huge animal. They shut up then. All of them. There's just the sound of the TV, the soccer commentary. The girl's gone stiff, her eyes squeezed shut. The old guy has his arm around the kid and gives him a pat on the back. A minute later, there's noise outside, panting and footsteps.

"God damn, it was so big, I almost named it," says Piñata as soon as he walks in.

He sees me, and his face changes. Dad brings his .38 down on the back of his neck and throws him to the floor. He's covered in red dirt.

"Hey there, Piñata."

He pushes the double barrel against his back.

"Get up, we're going for a walk."

"Hang on, what the hell is this?"

"The kind of thing where if you make it hard, I blow your brains out. Get moving."

Dad stands next to me and motions for me to go outside. *And Boca comes out kicking*. I'm sick of Boca. And River. And Rata Blanca, and people thinking they're hot shit, and treating me like a stupid little girl. I pull the trigger and scatter shards of the TV all over the shack, along with silence.

Now everybody really is looking at me.

I roar, and in that roar I'm not a man or a woman or a daughter.

I'm a jaguar.

"WHAT WAS THAT?" DAD asks, back in the car.

The caiman mask is pushed up on his head like a hat. He looks at me with amazement and fear, and if I had to name that look, I'd call it *now you really are grown up*.

Piñata bangs from inside the trunk.

When I'm sure I can wipe the smile off my face, I take off the mask and set it on top of the dash.

"The beast of beasts," I say.

16.

The heat waves rolling up from the cement warp Dad's figure as he walks away, crossing the parking lot. He's got on a cap, sunglasses, and the military shirt he always wears, no matter if it's hot or cold out. If I didn't know him so well, it would be impossible to say he's the same person he was twenty-four hours ago.

He throws the clothes from the robbery into a dumpster stuffed with bags of garbage. I can't imagine how they must smell after baking in the sun all morning.

The Neon doesn't have air conditioning. I lean my head against the headrest and put my feet up on the dash. I press play, but instead of Audioslave, Cartola comes on. He sings something about his heart or his face being deformed. Twisted.

There's blood on the volume dial. I scrape it off with my fingernail until it comes off. I imagine Dad punching Piñata, smashing his face, and then jumping in the car, looking for the TDK, turning it up, and humming along to the words, driving back like that, as calm as if he were coming back from running errands.

I thought I wouldn't be able to sleep, first because of the adrenaline and then because of the *what the hell did I do*, the fear, the thinking about everything that could have happened or could still happen, but my body just shut down. I didn't even hear him come in. I'm surprised to see my feet tapping along to the song. It's been forever since Dad listened to Cartola.

The parking lot is huge, shared by a few businesses on the side of the highway. Tire shops. Restaurants. A crafts stand. A sign on a tarp says the carnival is soon. In the middle of it all is a fountain with an angel. The hand reaching up toward the sky has been broken off. Dad stops next to it. He bends over, cups his hands, and splashes water onto his forehead and the back of his neck. He sits on the edge of the fountain, and at first, I don't understand what he's doing. I finally get it when I see his hand moving from the fountain to his shirt pocket; he's fishing for coins. He holds one in his right hand and flips it, catches it, and checks whether it came up heads or tails. He always picks heads and keeps tossing until he wins. He puts it into the pay phone and dials. He turns and looks at me, then shrugs. I shake my head. He laughs. When they answer, his stance changes.

A truck goes by and casts a shadow on me for a few seconds. I wish it would last forever, a cargo train with a thousand cars. The sky is completely clear, like the ones in the wallpaper pictures at internet cafes. Everything here comes in strips: red dirt, green, and then the blue sky.

I wait.

He hangs up, then makes another call. He hangs up again. Another call. His pocket is dark, wet from the coins. He scratches his shoulder and looks at me. He almost always turns his back to me, stands in front of the phone, picks at the stickers, the ads, peels them off, balls them up, and throws them on the ground at his feet the way other people flick the ash off a cigarette. His nerves take on the form of crumpled paper. He must be thinking about Giovanni. He'll never talk on a pay phone the same way.

Maybe it's me he doesn't see the same way anymore.

He sticks in another coin, pulls out a slip of paper, and dials. The sun prickles on my legs, and I take them off the dash. Cartola stopped playing, and I didn't even realize. I turn the tape over. The label is stained with blood.

Side B starts with a bang to the heart. "Devolva-me" by Adriana Calcanhotto. This song always gets me. I know it's about a couple, but every time I hear it, I think about her, about Mom. I push eject.

Dad gestures for me to get out. The heat hits me like a wall. I have to squint my eyes from the glare. A black T-shirt wasn't the best idea, but it was the only one that didn't look too wrinkled. I don't even like Pantera, but it was a present from Dad. All bands that have guys with long hair are the same to him. *Plus, you like big cats.* I never told him I didn't like the band. The shirt will end up in a trash can soon, anyway. I don't know why all metal band T-shirts are black.

It must be because the people who wear them never leave the house.

Dad leans against the wall next to a store that sells leather stuff.

"Stand there and pretend you're looking at the display window."

I catch sight of my reflection and see that my hair is messy, stuck to the back of my neck.

"Piñata said Mbói isn't staying put. I guess I'm not the only one looking for him. He doesn't know where he is."

"Are you sure he wasn't lying to you?"

"Believe me. I made him live up to his nickname."

He doesn't have any cuts on his hands—at least not new ones. He must have used a stick or something. Or the tire iron that was in the trunk.

"He said Mbói has a girl. Valeria. She works in a restaurant around the corner. He'd never seen her, doesn't know what she looks like."

I wait. A little while. A little longer.

"I can't show my face in there."

"Why not?"

"I'm not welcome. If you see old Sierra, you'll know what I mean."

"So, what am I supposed to do? I'm not a spy."

"I don't know, you're smart. You'll think of something. I left you a bunch of coins over there. Go inside, get something to eat while you're at it."

In front of the store is a wet little bag.

"Isn't it bad luck to take coins out of a fountain?"

"If someone's stupid enough to believe in that, it's already bad luck for their brain."

"I meant for us."

There are leather-bound mate cups in the display case, leather knife cases, saddles.

"What happened to Piñata?"

"He's gone."

"What does that mean?"

"If he's smart, he'll be in Paraguay by now. People don't like being betrayed."

"You didn't give him much choice."

"Everybody picks a side, Ambareté."

"You say that like you have some kind of choice about your family."

I lean over and pick up the bag. I take out the coins, dry them on my shirt, and stick them in my shorts pockets. There must be close to thirty pesos in five-, ten-, and twenty-five-cent coins.

"I always wanted a birthday party with a piñata. And party favor bags."

"We'll do that next year. Now stop trying to distract me and get in there."

"You're the worst when you get *pirevai*."

He laughs.

"Good girl, you're going local."

The barbeque place has a sign so old and rusted, you can barely read the name: Guayacán. There are a couple of empty tables outside and a chalkboard that says "BBQ x 2" but not the price. Next to the door, there's a little girl sitting on one of those coin-operated horses. She's sucking on a strawberry popsicle. Half of it breaks off and melts as soon as it hits the ground.

The dining room is huge, full of wooden tables and chairs. A fan blows cool air in my face as soon as I go in, and I'd like to stay there forever. There are a lot of people. Truckers sitting alone at tables for four, whole families squashed in together.

I sit in an empty spot I find at the bar, next to the window that looks out over the highway. A waitress hands me a laminated menu with stickers pasted over the old prices. She must be fifty, and I don't think she's Mbói's girl. She isn't wearing a name tag. I look at the menu. The alibi comes first, the rest later. I decide on a steak sandwich, but I keep holding the menu to buy time. At the end of the bar, the waitresses go back and forth with plates. They're wearing red aprons. If I could get closer, I'd listen to see if the cooks call their names from the kitchen or if they chat with each other, but all the stools are full. I can't hear anything from here. There's a constant hum from the fans, the scraping of silverware, the noise of plates being stacked up, half of a toast celebrating someone.

There are four waitresses working. Two of them are young, one a little bit older than me. She takes forever to jot down people's orders and moves her tongue as she writes. The other is about twenty-five, blond with full lips. Everything smells like smoke and meat, and I imagine their hair must smell like that, and their skin. They must run straight for the shower as soon as they get off work.

An old couple gets up next to me. They leave a two-peso bill under a cup. The same waitress who left me the menu puts the tip in her pocket.

"Shut up, Rodo, don't be a *yapú*, you call everybody 'honey,'" the waitress says to the guy next to her.

"But you know you're my favorite, Susy."

The woman waves off the guy's line like it was a fly. He stares at her ass as she walks away. I cross her off my mental list. Three left.

Behind the shelves full of J&B, Criadores, Old Smuggler, and Gancia, there's a mirror where I can see little pieces of myself. My fluffy hair. A bit of mouth. I close my eyes. I inhale, then let the air out and settle onto the stool next to the guy.

He's got a beard and sweat stains on his stomach and armpits. He squirts some soda water into his cup of red wine, then sees me and raises his eyebrows.

"I was roasting over there," I say, fanning myself with my hand, before he can think I came over for him. Like that'll work.

"Sure is a hot one," he says, looking at my knees.

Susy comes back and sets down a tin of ice cubes. I order the steak sandwich to go.

"I hope you've got a good mouth," the guy says. He bangs the side of his plate, with bits of meat and raw onion pushed to one side. "They don't serve you beef here, they serve you rubber."

I make that face people make when they don't know what to reply.

"So why do you come here, then?"

"For the people," he says. "And sometimes they screw up and actually give you something tender and tasty."

He still hasn't looked at my face. He turns his body so he's facing me. When I put my hands on the bar, crumbs stick to them. I grab a napkin, clean my hands, and push the crumbs to the side.

"Do you know Valeria?"

He drinks some wine, and the ice cubes fall against his lips. He sets the cup down on the counter.

"She a friend of yours?" he asks.

The guy never asks me about my accent or anything. His brain must not pick up too many stations. That's just fine. I don't answer. Let him keep talking.

"Why are you looking for her?" He pops an ice cube into his mouth and pushes it from one cheek to the other. "Don't tell me your boyfriend cheated on you with Vale."

I flick at a crumb still on the bar in front of me. That's what someone would do if they were trying to hide how mad they were. He opens his mouth and shows me the ice cube.

"He'd have to be an idiot. Vale's pretty, but she's got nothing on you."

That's no help. All the waitresses are pretty in their own way, but this guy would think anything that breathes is pretty. He doesn't even turn his head to look at her. How could he look at her if he won't quit looking at my legs? I wish I hadn't cut these jeans so short, that I'd listened to Dad just a little or asked him for a shirt to tie around my waist like I've done before, but I think, that's fine, he can look there, no one can recognize you by your legs.

He pulls out a cigarette and holds the pack of Camels out to me. I say no.

"Good, girls shouldn't smoke."

He lights up. The fan stops the smoke from reaching the ceiling. Out on the sidewalk, the little girl with the popsicle is still sitting on the horse. She moves her legs, kicking its flanks to make it go, but it's no good. I feel you, sister.

"Looks like you're not the only heartbreaker, Susy," the guy says. "Valeria's giving you a run for your money."

The waitress gathers up the napkins, puts them on the plate, and clears everything up.

"At twenty, everybody's a heartbreaker." She looks for the blond waitress and nods—Valeria. "Especially with those tights she wears. But, hey, anything for a tip, right?"

"I always tip you."

"Ten cents isn't a tip, Rodo."

"Don't complain, sweetie, you'll get wrinkles. And pour me a little more."

At the other end of the bar, an old man talks to Susy. With her hands full of plates, she tosses her head in my direction. The old man comes over and hands me a bag with my sandwich. I pull out the coins and look at him. What I took for wrinkles from a distance are really scars once I've got him up close and personal. A long pink one starts on his forehead and runs across his eyebrow and lip in a straight line. It's a miracle he didn't lose the eye. There are two more scars next to the first, one a little smaller than the other, like a mangled Adidas logo. I slide the coins across the bar to him, adding a good tip. The old guy thanks me and walks away.

"Nice facelift they gave him," the guy says. "And he used to be a boxer."

"Were you there when it happened?"

"No. If I'd been there, nobody would have touched Don Sierra."

Sure thing, big guy.

I turn and look around for her. I hope she comes over so I can describe her to Dad. She's got a bunch of earrings along her ear and a red ribbon tied to her wrist. The kind of thing he'd never pay attention to. The one with the ass, I could say. There's no helping it. We're going to spend the whole afternoon baking inside the Neon waiting for her to finish her shift so I can point her out. Or I can point her out to him now and he can wait on his own.

I wonder if Valeria really knows what Mbói does, if she has even the faintest idea, if she puts up with it thinking she won't have to come here to work anymore. To get hit on by a bunch of guys, to get her ass grabbed, to scrape together more crumbs than tips. Maybe Mbói's job is what she likes about him, or what makes her think twice. Or maybe she just likes him. I don't know.

I feel like an idiot for thinking I could leave Dad behind and take off, come here and deal with all of this. Alone.

The guy sees me staring at Valeria.

"There are better ways to get revenge," he says. "I'm not saying you can't slap her in the face."

He's already filming the whole movie. He's hired the extras and planned all the scenes.

"An eye for an eye is old news. The best revenge is an orgasm for an orgasm."

"Maybe," I say, "but you wouldn't be able to help me with that."

I hop off the stool. The fans, the screaming kids, and the noise of the silverware would cover up whatever he might have said back to me, but he just sits there with his jaw hanging open. Before I leave, I pass Valeria, and she says *enjoy* and smiles at me. Her eyes are blue like her earrings.

The sun scorches me as soon as I walk outside. The little girl with the popsicle says, *yah, horsie, yah* and pets its head like she's smoothing its mane. I pull out two coins and put them in the slot.

"Hold on, cowgirl," I say, pressing the button.

The horse starts to gallop, and she laughs.

DAD'S RIGHT WHERE I left him, chatting with a man who hands him a few bills. He puts them in his shirt pocket, pulling out a baggy of coke as he does. I wait for the guy to walk away before I go over.

"It's not my birthday yet," I say, "but I see you're getting the party favors ready."

"Aren't you the funny one. Did your ego hit a growth spurt or something?"

He takes the bag with the sandwich from me, and before he even finishes opening it, he says:

"Don't tell me you got a steak sandwich. They're the worst."

"It's a barbeque place, what was I supposed to order?"

He hands it back to me, and I set it on the ground.

"Did you find her?" I say yes. "What does she look like?"

The sun hits my eyes, and I shade them with my arm.

"Blonde. Nice ass. Big lips."

Dad shows me his palms, like I'm talking to him in a foreign language.

"Come here. I'll point her out. I don't want to sit here melting in the car all day."

I stand at one corner of the restaurant, where the long window starts. I look around until I see her carrying a leaning tower of Pisa made from plates.

"Loving someone isn't the same as choosing a side," I say.

"So?"

"Don't hurt her. She doesn't have anything to do with it. Promise me."

He crosses his fingers and kisses them.

"That's her."

Dad slides his sunglasses down with one finger, looks at her, and then pushes them back up. He heads back toward the parking lot. A dog is eating the sandwich we left there. He hands me five ten-peso bills.

"Off you go."

A family walks over to the fountain. The parents and three kids. The mom gives each one a coin, and they throw them in and clap their hands. Dad shakes his head.

"Everybody believes in what they can," I say.

"Do you want to make a wish?"

I say yes. We stand next to the fountain. There are Brazilian coins and Paraguayan ones, too. He hands me a bullet from his pocket and hangs onto another one for himself.

"We don't have dreams," he says. "We have plans."

I bite my lips. The sun glints off the bullet in the middle of my palm. It looks alive. I squeeze it, think, and toss it into the fountain. Dad's bullet falls next to mine.

"What did you wish for?" he says.

"If I tell you, it won't come true."

17.

After walking around town for two hours, even my shadow is sweaty.

I wander around, go down one street, turn onto the next, stretch out the walk. There are hardware store signs, a two-star hotel, brightly colored posters advertising a carnival. The coins bouncing around in my pocket make it sound like I'm walking with spurs. I feel like I'm in one of the Westerns Dad watches and always says: *If you do that, they'll blow your head off.* Or, *that's fake*. Or, *John Wayne wouldn't last half an hour in Eldorado, Misiones. The Río Bravo's nothing compared to the Paraná*. And he goes on and on like that, until I say, *Sure, Dad.*

There isn't much to do. I'm tempted to go into the church because of the whiff of damp coolness and the earthy scent I get when I walk by. I turn on a tap outside someone's house and splash it on the back of my neck, being careful not to get my T-shirt wet. I tie my hair back in a ponytail. I don't like how it looks, but I also don't want to die of heat stroke.

Then I stumble across an oasis. An arcade with huge fans, those old ones. I can feel the breeze from the sidewalk. Between the neon tubes that are still there and the black scorch marks where they're missing, I piece together the name: Hechavy. Who knows what it means.

More than once, Dad used arcades like daycare centers. He'd load me up with tokens and say, *I'll be back in a little bit*. They were safe areas. Nobody smoked or drank—except late at night—and the only ones getting knocked around were the machines. That was before I had the Sega. Once he got me that, he could just leave me plugged in, in a hotel room.

It always seems like it's nighttime in arcades. And judging by the machines, it's been the same night for about ten years. Wonder Boy. 1942. Pac-Man. A soccer game. NBA Jam. Space Invaders—the only one Dad plays—and Mortal Kombat II. Mortal Kombat Ultimate, where there's a line of people waiting. There's a Daytona USA in the corner. The wooden stools are painted red, blue, and yellow. In the back is a pool table and a couple of pinball machines. There aren't many people here yet.

There's a kid at the cash register. He's behind a sheet of protective glass covered in stickers. He's trying to grow a mustache, without much success. I pull out the coins and toss them on the counter.

"Did you rob a fountain?"

"At gunpoint."

He hands me a bunch of tokens. When I head toward

the Mortal Kombat II machine, I see it's busy, and I want to play against the computer. No boy likes losing to a girl; he asks for a rematch, again and again, and then a friend shows up to save his honor, and that's how you end up calling attention to yourself.

Dad left me alone so long that I learned all the tricks and cheat codes. My head filled up with all the button combos so I wouldn't have to think about what he might be doing. I learned the Scorpion fatality and repeated it over and over so I wouldn't have to wonder why Dad came back with a cut in his eyebrow. I memorized the trick to make Human Smoke appear so I wouldn't be tempted to open the suitcase Dad brought back. There's a whole part of me full of information I tried to use to block him out.

I spend tokens on the Pac-Man machine for a while. I reach the apple and get bored. The place is filling up. Mostly boys. Now there's a girl at the Mortal Kombat II machine. He hair reaches her denim skirt. She's playing as Mileena, who moves like she's having an epileptic seizure. She tries to do a trick, smashes all the buttons.

"It's high punch, not low," I tell her.

Mileena finally throws her little daggers.

"Thanks."

I walk over to the Daytona USA machine. I don't like cars, but I want to sit down without having to balance on a stool with uneven legs. I do two races, both with manual transmission. When I lose, I stay there.

The girl from the Mortal Kombat machine flops down next to me. She's wearing thick glasses. Her makeup softens her strong features. Red lipstick, a little mascara. Her crop top shows a belly button ring with a pair of dice on it.

"Are you from Buenos Aires?" she asks. I say yes. "Did you come for the carnival?"

I tell her that my dad—my old man, I say—is here looking at some property. He's an adviser for a company. The best way to keep people from asking questions is by saying something really boring. They say, *ah*, and it's like they're closing an MSN chat window.

"What about you? Are you here on your own?"

"I came with a friend, but the guy she likes showed up, and I lost her."

She points them out to me at a pool table. They each have one arm around the other and are holding their cues in the free hands. The guy is shorter, and she doesn't care that the fan is blowing her hair all over. She's wearing a little jacket that won't zip up over her boobs.

"You want to play?" I ask.

"I'm out of tokens."

I toss her one.

"I'm terrible, though."

"Me, too."

We both choose automatic transmission. I get way out ahead of her. She crashes into everything. She should play that game where you get points for running people over. The last time around the track, I hit all the curves wrong. On the final stretch, I take my foot off the gas, and she passes me. She celebrates her win, tapping the steering wheel with her hands.

"It's a good thing you're so bad at this," I say.

After she loses the first race, she introduces herself:

"Martina."

"Alejandra."

Her backpack has writing on it in Liquid Paper and some pins. Blink-182. Green Day. She tells me she's studying because she failed math and chemistry. I tell her I passed. *It must be nice living in Buenos Aires.* Luckily, she's satisfied with me mentioning the Obelisk or Plaza de Mayo. She asks me about the night clubs. *My dad doesn't let me go out much.*

"Did it hurt?" I ask her, nodding at her piercing.

"A ton. But it was worth it."

"It's nice."

"I want to pierce my eyebrow."

"I'm saving up to get a tattoo."

I rub my arm.

"Do you already know what you want?"

"I can't decide. I want to be really sure."

Her friend leaves with the guy. She looks at her over her shoulder, then turns and makes an *I'm sorry* gesture with her hands pressed together.

"I don't know how she does it."

"Do you want me to spell it out for you?"

"No . . . I know."

There are more and more people. Most of them are at the soccer machine. They yell every time someone makes a goal. They jeer at each other and laugh.

"You're good at Mortal Kombat, right?" she says. I shrug one shoulder. "There's a boy I really like, but it's like I'm invisible. He always comes in and plays Mortal Kombat. I think maybe if I beat him, he might realize I exist."

"Have you tried talking to him?"

"Are you crazy?" She laughs, quietly, her shoulders shaking.

"Come on."

I stuff the Mortal Kombat machine full of tokens and teach her everything, right up through Kitana and Mileena's fatalities. She's a little slow. She gets nervous and mixes up the buttons.

"How come you know so many tricks?"

"My dad travels a lot and leaves me at home with the Sega."

She opens her mouth, and I'm sure she's about to ask about my mom, but she switches gears halfway through.

"Your dad sounds cool."

We sit on a long bench next to the pool table, against the wall. People parade by us to get to the bathroom. A few people go in to splash water on their faces and come out drying themselves off with their T-shirts. A couple of guys wave to Martina from the other side of the table, and every once in a while someone comes over and gives her a kiss on the cheek. They bum a token or a cigarette. When they leave, she tells me stuff about each one. *He's always walking around with his skateboard under his arm, but I've never seen him use it. There's hardly any asphalt. That other guy was with a friend of mine. I mean he was* with-*with her*, she says, raising her eyebrows. I don't say much. Talking means I have to remember everything I say so I don't contradict myself. And I don't really feel like lying.

I pull my feet up on the bench, my knees against my chest, and I see a cut on my leg, a thin scab. I have no idea when I got it, but if I had to guess, I'd say it happened last night. Adrenaline blinds your body. I'm running my finger over it, back and forth, when I hear:

"Little sister."

The guy is tall. His hair is buzzed, and he's wearing a black Chicago Bulls jersey. The strong nose and cheekbones look better on him than they do on Martina.

"Big brother," she says. "Alejandra. Marcos. Marcos. Alejandra."

The guy gives me a kiss on the cheek. I lean back as fast as I can so he won't smell my sweat, and I bang my head against the wall. My cheeks burn. Marcos, holding back his laughter, introduces me to a friend who's with him, but the name goes right by me. He has a bike chain looped across his chest. He sticks a token into the pool table. They ask us if we want to play. I say no. Marcos breaks. *Solids*, he says. I listen to the sound of the ball running through the table's guts.

Martina comes over and whispers to me that the other guy is from Buenos Aires, too. That he's the only one in the whole town who uses a bike chain. *As if someone would steal that rusty piece of crap.* I hope she doesn't say I'm from the city, that they won't put me to the test. She keeps talking. Marcos looks at me and smiles. He has little teeth that look like Chiclets. When he hits the ball, the muscles in his arms stand out for a second and then relax.

"So weird, right?" Martina says.

"Totally," I say, but I have no idea whether she's talking

about the guy with the bike chain, her brother, or UFOs in Chile.

For a while, there's just the sound of the balls clacking around the table, laughter. Sideways glances. Marcos only has one solid left, close to a pocket, but the eight ball is in his way.

"Jumpshot," he says. Before taking the shot, he makes sure I'm looking at him. I lift my chin, challenging him. He jumps the white ball off the table. I stop it with my foot and hand it to him.

"I thought this was pool, not baseball."

"Outsiders, *yurú chupita*," he says.

Martina laughs.

"What's wrong, bro? You nervous?"

"These cues suck." He rubs chalk on the tip angrily. He's blushing. "I guess you already went by Roberto's to pick up the part for the blender."

Martina winces like a dog that's about to get hit.

"Mom's going to kill you."

"I totally forgot," she says, jumping up. She slings her backpack over her shoulder.

Marcos sets the cue down, shaking his head.

"Come on. I'll take you on the bike before he closes."

She says goodbye and gives me a kiss on the check. *See you in a little bit.*

"If Mom doesn't kill her first," Marcos adds.

The guy with the bike chain looks at me with a *now that we're alone* look on his face, but by reflex, I get up and stick some tokens into the first machine I see. Tetris. The second-worst game in the world. Out of the corner of my eye, I see the guy start playing Gals Panic. That's the one where you use a pointer to undress a girl. *That's* the worst game in the world. Period. Another guy comes over to see which girl will appear naked. I look at my screen, a bunch of blocks piled up and the GAME OVER sign.

It's dark out. There are mosquitoes around the light outside the arcade. I wonder what time they change shifts at the restaurant, whether Valeria's done or still in there with smoke in her hair. I wonder, when she takes a shower, if she'll have to wash blood off herself, too, her own blood, or Dad's. I want to go home, see if he's there so I can stop worrying. But if he isn't there, I'll go even crazier.

I put a couple tokens into the Cadillacs & Dinosaurs machine. I'm about to choose the girl, but when I see her name is Hanna, I like Jack better. I hit the punks, the hunchbacks, the guys who look like Cormano from Sunset Riders. I get to the next level. And the next. The plastic that covers the controls has cigarette burns in it. There aren't many people left, so I can see him coming. He changed out of his Bulls jersey and into a polo shirt. The collar is folded at the back of his neck. He also took a shower and put on cologne. He must live nearby. Everybody here must live nearby.

"My sister said you're from Buenos Aires."

He leans against the machine. He's a good head taller than it is. I keep playing, punching avatars. They surround me, and I have to do a trick to get them off me.

"She told me you're great at Mortal Kombat."

"Did she tell you, or did you ask her?"

He snorts out a laugh.

"It's hard to find anybody else around here who likes Pantera."

He looks at my T-shirt. I know it's an album cover, but I don't even know what it's called.

"Yeah, I like that song Respect."

It's the only one I can remember. I thought it was cool that the guitarist's beard was dyed pink. But after about a minute, I couldn't stand the music and I'd change the channel.

"Respect? You must mean Walk. That's a real anthem."

"I have a pirated CD. The song names weren't on it."

He walks around behind me and leans on the other side of the machine.

"All the girls I know play Pac-Man or Pinball."

"Pac-Man? Those aren't girls, those are old ladies."

"Have you ever beaten this one?"

"Nope."

He's quiet for a minute, looks at the table, maybe looking for the guy with the bike chain or some other friend.

"I heard the final boss is a T-rex, but I don't think so," I say.

"There's only one way to find out."

He holds up a couple tokens and I make an *okay, let's do it* gesture. He picks the hunchback and breaks all the barrels. We share the food that appears. He leaves the shotgun for me.

"What a gentleman."

"You aren't doing very well just kicking."

I give him a kick in the heel.

"You think?"

He grabs his ankle, making a big show. Then he straightens up, but I can see he's looking more at my legs than at the screen.

"You drop something?"

"No, no."

He talks slowly, with a voice that sounds like *excuse me* and *please*, a voice that's in no hurry, that flows, that could carry you away, but never drag you.

We pass level after level. He gets killed on the last one, and he's out of tokens.

"Avenge me," he says.

I'm getting beaten to hell, and I don't have a moment to let go of the controls. I stick my hip out toward him, showing him my pocket.

"Get some tokens," I say. He hesitates. "Come on, I'm getting killed here."

When he touches me, I freeze. He sticks his hand in until he finds the tokens that seem to hide from his fingers. He pulls them out. On the screen, I see myself get killed and come back to life.

"The cavalry's here," he says.

The final boss is a mutant T-rex. We kill him twice. Then everything explodes.

"Nice work."

"You, too," I say, and we shake hands.

We're still looking at each other when the guy at the

cash register says he has to close. I ask him what time it is. Eleven. Dad's going to kill me. Marcos must be able to see the panic on my face because he says:

"I'll take you."

He has a little Zanella. He gives me his helmet. I hold on tight even though there aren't many potholes. I tell him the way. Two blocks before we get there, I look for a substitute house. *Never tell anyone where you live*. I see one with a big yard, no dogs, that's key, and the typical front light turned on that says, *we're not here, but we're pretending there's someone home.*

"This is it."

He stops next to a trash can. He looks left and right. He must wonder what the hell we're doing in this part of town, but he doesn't say anything. Even his silence is nice. I give him back his helmet, and he hooks it on his elbow.

"You should come to carnival, it's worth it."

I nod and paw at the gate, trying to open it. It takes me a long time to find the latch. I go in and close it behind me. Please God don't let a dog come. I pretend to look for the key, like there are many places I could have put it. I'm sure he's going to wait until I go inside.

"It's me," I yell to no one. "I'll be right in."

I make a *what a pain* face and turn toward the house. I hear him go, wait for a few seconds in the dark waving away mosquitos, and then finally go out.

I want to think up some excuse, but nothing comes to mind. I've got a short circuit. In my stomach and in my head. When I go in, I see he isn't here and hasn't been back. I let out a sigh and feel my shoulders relax away from my ears. Everything is the same, the half-finished coffee on the table, the fruit flies on the banana peel.

I flop down on the bed, tired, as if I'd run all the way here. I bring my hands to my face and smell his cologne. In my reflection in the TV screen, I find my smile the way someone might find money in the pocket of a pair of jeans they haven't worn in a long time.

I'm all sweaty, and my body itches from walking through the grass. I've got red dirt all over me, and the Pantera T-shirt smells horrible. But I bring my fingers to my nose and leave them there.

The shower can wait a little while longer.

18.

It takes me a couple hours to check every corner of the house. There's a false back in every closet. There are chests, and the wood feels like cardboard because of the humidity. Twisted drawers that don't open right and are worse when you close them. I find all kinds of knives with tired old blades that don't shine anymore, guns all throughout the house, crumpled receipts with prices from years ago, papers that fall apart when you touch them, tools for castrating animals, things I don't even know—and don't want to know—the use of. There are also toys of mine, books with the pages stuck together and the covers eaten away by mold, tiny clothes. It's like going back to a version of me that doesn't fit. A bunch of stuff to start a fire. Things I didn't even know I'd lost. But there's no iron, or anything like it. Or a fan. Much less deodorant.

It's so sticky out. I'm wearing just my bra and shorts. I try to open the windows to get some air in, but all the shutters are locked. So no one can get in or out, depending on the situation.

I read somewhere, or someone told me, that steam works to get the wrinkles out of clothes. I turn on the hot water in the shower and hang up the three T-shirts I have on a clothes hanger, the towel hanger, and the curtain rod. All three are wrinklier than an eighty-year-old grandma. The red one shows it the most. The mirror fogs up, and I draw a happy face. I go out and close the door so the steam will build up.

I munch on the fries that came with the hamburger. They're pretty good hot, but cold, it's like chewing on gum made out of oil. It's the cheapest thing I could find nearby. I don't know how long the money has to last. I toy with the idea of buying myself a dress, something airy, but I don't want to run out of money and not be able to sleep because I'm hungry. That's happened before, when I wanted a book, or a pair of jeans, or a Sega game. I count the money, separate the coins from the arcade tokens. I pick one up and flip it. It doesn't matter how it lands. I smile.

I turn on the TV, but the only thing that comes in is the local channel. The afternoon news shows the preparations for carnival. People setting up stands, lighting fires, melting in the sun. I hope it's better live.

I take the batteries out of a flashlight and put them in a stereo that has a tape deck. The cable has been ripped out, probably to tie someone's hands with. I rewind until I get to "Even Flow." I'd like to turn it up as loud as it'll go, but it's better not to call attention to myself. The song makes me want to move around. I jump, dance, sweat, clean up, sweep, put away plates, wash the mugs, dance a little more, get tired all over, my arms, my legs. Everywhere except the smile that's still on my lips.

The Christmas tree is covered in spiderwebs that look like garlands. I try to take it down, but the branches won't fold. I take it outside and leave it in the middle of the backyard. The grass is long, except for one place where it's just dirt, under the tree. I could put in an orchard with this much space. I pick up a couple of bottles and throw them in the trash. I gather up some rotten pieces of wood that are covered in bugs and leave them out front. It's like the sun is following me around with a spotlight and I'm the star of the show. I was outside for ten minutes, and my skin is already darker. I like how it looks.

The steam is coming out from under the bathroom door, and when I walk over to it, I can feel the heat. A hot mist hits my skin when I go in. I check the shirts. They're the same. I leave them there another half hour.

I grab a folding lawn chair and wipe it down with a rag so grimy, I can't tell if it's cleaning it or making it even dirtier. I check to be sure there's no one in the neighboring yards. The hedge is thick, and the long grass tells me nobody lives there. The other times we were here, I always wondered who the hell would have a house around here. Today I feel like I could have a good life here, not just pass through.

I don't want to be passing through anymore.

I take off my shorts and set them aside, along with the

sweaty Pantera T-shirt in case I have to cover up in a hurry, and I start sunbathing.

It takes me five minutes to realize that sunbathing is hard, despite what you might think. It's not just lying there. I don't know how to be still, and my head's even worse at it. It flips through images, memories I can't quite tune into because I don't know if they really happened, or I made them up.

I was here one summer. It wasn't really the whole summer, just two weeks, I found out later, but it felt longer. What happens to you when you're little feels eternal. It probably is. I was always alone. I learned to identify the sound of the neighbor's car. When he left, I'd climb the tree and jump into his yard and go swimming in his in-ground pool. I can remember the wrinkled bark, my palms white and painful when I swung over. I liked when it got dark in the pool. Swimming in the reflection of the moon. I'd go through it again and again. I also liked to cup my hands together and trap it there, trying not to move the water so the reflection wouldn't break up. If the moon fit in my hands, I was grown up, and I couldn't be afraid to be alone anymore.

But there's no in-ground pool next door. Maybe it was above-ground.

I know that I swam at night in a pool the whole moon fit into. Or that I needed to believe that to be strong, so that being little and in the middle of nowhere wouldn't get to me. Maybe fear messed with that memory and distorted it.

Honestly . . . I don't care anymore.

What I care about is that now, everything that happens to me is mine alone. No one's going to tell me how things are, or how they feel, or what I like, or how something smells, or what I'm afraid of or stop being afraid of. I know that Marcos has little teeth, that we killed dinosaurs together, that he has a scent I want to suck in like the smell of rain, that I would have liked to ride without a helmet so I could rest my head against his back, that right now the sun isn't feeling so much like a caress as a pinch, and I'm going all red and I should get inside before I'm the color of strawberry ice cream.

The steam fogged up even the kitchen window. On the table, the shotgun peeking out of the bag looks out of place. I put it away properly so it can't be seen. It's still a couple of hours before nightfall. *The Columbia space shuttle returns tomorrow.* Images of it on TV. Then they show someone taming a horse.

When you're waiting for something nice, time passes slowly.

The steam heated the house up, and I can't take it anymore. The black T-shirt looks the closest to ironed. Or at least it carries off the wrinkles the best. It smells stuffy. Damn. I go outside and hang it from a branch. The TV is a distant sound, and I can't make out what they're saying. I watch the reflection I can make out through the shutters, the way the lights and shadows paint the living room differently when the image changes. With the news on in the background, it's almost like Dad's home.

It's the first time in my life that I've thought so long about a man other than Dad. That I'm not wondering where he is or what he's doing.

I don't feel guilty.

I go inside, turn off the TV, and head back out to the yard. The heat is waning. I put the folding chair under the tree. The moon is out, but I don't need it anymore. There's a breeze so lazy I can feel it on my face, but I can't hear it in the branches or the leaves. The T-shirt barely moves. A dog barks at a car that creeps by at ten miles an hour. The dirt road forces everyone to go slow. The sun spills redness across the sky as it goes down, slowly, like something drifting and unhurried. It grows as fast as a vine. I can't hear the dog anymore. The only speed is in my heart.

19.

Far off, in the middle of that nothingness, of that ground won from the hills at the end of a machete, the fair looks like a fire. The smoke rises from different points, a spotlight scrapes the clouds, and the glow of the red and yellow lights are like flames.

Inside, it's not a fire, but it's just as hot. People push each other and walk as slowly as if it were a procession. On one side are the food stands. *Sopa paraguaya.* Hot dogs, hamburgers. *Choripanes. Mbeyú* pizza. A guy with a cart pours bottles of beer into plastic cups and hands them out, one after the other. That's the longest line.

On the other side are the games, guys inviting you to try your luck in their stands and win some prize from the two-peso store. There's a bingo hall, people in numbered plastic chairs looking at their cards. A haunted house. *Survive the Pombero, the Jasy-Yateré, and the Werewolf.*

I look the crowd over to see if I find any faces I know. I walk past the guy with the bike chain and am tempted to ask him if he's seen Marcos, but I don't want to get stuck with him, so I pretend not to see him and keep on walking, to go watch the show at the stage in the back. *We're the Tanimbus*, says the singer, who's wearing a leather jacket. He must be melting. They're terrible, they miss notes, a garage band that shouldn't ever have left the house, but it helps me hide the fact that I'm alone. I can pretend I'm just another person watching the show, and that I'm out here for a reason. The songs end and begin. I'm afraid it might have permanent effects on my ears. I fend off mosquitoes and shoves from other people.

I should have stayed home.

The singer asks if we want to hear another one. And a bunch of kids yell back, *Yeah, we want to hear another band.* The Tanimbus don't pay any attention to the booing and finish off with a cover of a song that sounds familiar, but they butcher it so badly, I can't quite place it.

It takes me a minute to realize that the *Ale* someone is shouting to is me. Martina is sitting in the stands with a couple of friends and waving at me. She's wearing a plaid skirt and a Cadena Perpetua tank top cut above her belly button. She changed the dice ring for a regular one.

"This is the girl I told you about."

She introduces them to me. One of them is the girl from the arcade. Verónica.

"Oh, the *porteña*," says a girl who's trying to hide a zit on her forehead under her bangs.

None of them moves over to make room for me, so I stay standing. Zit-face whispers something to the other girl, a blonde, who laughs. She takes a drag of her cigarette and coughs out the smoke. She holds it one way, then another. This must be the second time she's smoked.

"So, how's our town treating you? Did you see the sights?"

Oh, you know. I visited a lady who reads lines of coke, also a retired hitman, then I helped my dad kidnap a guy.

"Not really."

A group of guys comes over and says hi. They look us up and down. They're passing around a cup of beer that looks like it's even hotter than they think they are. When they realize they're not going to score here, they move on.

"I'd love a beer," says Zit-face.

"Then let's buy some," I say.

"Fat old Fugaza is being uptight this year. He won't sell to anybody underage."

"He got in trouble with the township."

"It's no problem."

I have an ID for a Victoria Vizcarra that says I'm eighteen. The line moves slowly. Zit-face and Blondie look at me, waiting to see me get caught. Martina stands next to them. I order the beer and stick my hand in my pocket. I get the ID ready like an ace up my sleeve, but the guy hands me the beer looking me dead in the face, and I'm so unnerved that I almost walk away without paying.

"I guess the *porteña* looks old as hell," says Zit-face.

I give her a smile so fake, a blind man would realize it. The beer makes my hand cold. I take a drink and pass it.

They barely wet their lips. They make faces like they're taking cough syrup. They're not used to drinking. They look from side to side. What matters is for people to see you with the cup, not that you actually drink it. There has to be a picture so you can say you got shitfaced that carnival, that that was your third beer, or your fourth, *I was such a mess*, something unforgettable has to happen. At some point, we lost Verónica.

So, where's your brother?

"Where's Vero?"

"Take a wild guess."

Martina takes two long drinks and hands me the cup. She's got more makeup on than yesterday. I want to ask to borrow her mascara. Or just some lipstick.

"Are you looking for the Mortal Kombat guy?"

"No. No."

"You sure look like you've got your eyes peeled."

"There's a guy from another town who might come."

"Well, anyway, everybody's got their eyes peeled."

"Those two are just making sure their dads don't see them. They're supposed to be studying at another girl's house."

Did your brother say anything about me?

I don't like the beer much, but it helps with the heat. I take a sip. And another. I hand it to Zit-face, and like bait it attracts two guys who come over and talk to her and Blondie. One's tall and looks German, like a fake rugby player who wears Kevingston shirts. He leans in to say something in Zit-face's ear, and she touches her hair and laughs.

She offers him my beer. The guy drinks a few swallows and keeps talking in her ear, moving the cup around like he's explaining something to her. I step down and trip—or something—and run into Kevingston, who spills the beer on Zit-face.

"What the fuck!" she says. "What are you doing?"

"Sorry."

"God damn it. My dad is going to kill me."

She and the blonde go get napkins from the *choripán* stand and then head for the bathroom. Kevingston gives me back what's left of the beer.

"You're so bad," says Martina.

"I tripped."

I sit in the space they left on the stands. They're still breaking down the stage, rolling up cables.

Aren't you going to say anything about your brother?

Okay, that's it, enough quiet time, but when I'm about to ask her, I see her face light up, and she waves at a guy. He's older than us, maybe twenty. He has a wispy beard and is wearing a Green Day T-shirt. She looks at me.

"I don't want to leave you on your own . . ."

"It's fine. Have fun."

She runs over to the guy like she's a little girl and he's the Christmas tree at the stroke of midnight. I look at my reflection in the last of the beer. The lights go on and off. Some of them show more of me, my hair hanging down, my eyes down there, sunken; others just show the outline of me, my face a blur.

The mosquitoes are in love with my legs. I kill one. And

another one. I give myself one more dead mosquito until I admit defeat. I want to listen to a sad song, "Nothingman" or "Black" by Pearl Jam. Or "Fell on Black Days" by Soundgarden. Or even a Cartola song. It's like there are parts of me those songs could translate, to understand what didn't make sense until yesterday. Songs that have names and faces now.

And then I hear it, and I think that there are voices that are like songs.

"I thought you weren't going to make it," Marcos says, and the smell of him reaches me a moment after his voice.

He's wearing a black tank top and shorts that go past his knees.

"Were you waiting for me?"

"It would have been too bad for you to miss this party."

"You call this a party?"

"You're so *argel*."

I hold out my hand so he can help me up. He pulls so hard, he has to catch me. Or he does it on purpose so he can hug me. I look small in his arms.

We walk around. We buy a hot dog. The guy puts five pounds of mayo on it, and I eat it with my neck stretched out so I won't stain my shirt. I'm washing it down with a sip of Coke when he makes me laugh and I almost spray it everywhere. It's easy for him to make me laugh. He says random things, like that game is rigged, or his dad saw a werewolf. He talks about the hills like someone who's been there, like the mountains are his childhood and not a place you go to hide.

Marcos stops at a stand where you have to shoot an air

gun at ducks. The attendant puts some bills into a fanny pack that hangs low like a three-month baby bump.

"Go on and impress your girlfriend, Romeo," he says.

He doesn't correct him. I don't, either.

The attendant reaches his arm out to show us the shelf full of stuffed animals wrapped in plastic bags, like they're being suffocated. Coatis, caimans, toucans, bears with hearts that say *Rohayhu*. No jaguars.

"My jaguars went extinct," the attendant answers with a smile. I want to shoot his face full of pellets. "Five shots. If you make three, you get a prize."

Marcos hands him a bill, and the attendant passes him the air gun. He doesn't really know how to position it against his body. I like that he doesn't know about guns. I stand off to one side. He shoots and hits a duck. He doesn't show off. He doesn't look my way or wink at me. He's on a mission. He misses his second and third shots.

"You can do it, Romeo," says the attendant, concentrating on getting a rubber band around a roll of bills.

He knocks another duck over on the fourth shot. He takes a breath and relaxes his shoulders. On his fifth shot, he doesn't hit anything. He scrunches up his eyebrows, and his eyes become two little slits. He hands the air rifle back.

"The sight is crooked."

"Don't be a sore loser. You'll get it next time."

I take out a wrinkled bill and hand it to the attendant. He sets the ducks back up and hands me the rifle. It's light. It doesn't weigh anything compared to a shotgun or a revolver. I'm sure the sight is crooked. I just need to know how crooked. I aim at a piece of cardboard behind the ducks and shoot. One finger-width to the left.

"You've got to hold . . ."

"Shh, shh," I interrupt him. "What was it you said? Outsiders, *yurú chupita*."

I get the gun comfortable, the butt against my shoulder. I hold my breath, and when I let it out, I shoot, and once, twice, three times in a row I hear the tinny sound of a duck falling. I hand the gun to the attendant, who has a cigarette between his lips. A gust of wind knocks off the ash.

"Which prize would the little lady like?"

"Let Romeo pick, it's for him."

Marcos chooses the caiman and frees it from its bag.

"Where'd you learn to shoot?"

"Beginner's luck."

He looks so sweet holding the caiman. He doesn't try to hide it, even though some of the guys he knows laugh at him. When they see he's with me, they shut up. I like being seen with him. When he smiles, his eyes get narrow, and I get goosebumps.

It feels weird. These things shouldn't happen to me, nobody should be able to describe me or remember me, and every time he calls me *Ale*, I snap back to reality. That's not me, this doesn't mean anything, but he looks at me with all the time in the world, he looks into my eyes like I'm a landscape, and I forget about what I'm supposed to do, what I have to do, and I kiss him. Our lips crash into each other, then they understand each other. The taste of beer and melon-flavored gum. I hate melon. I used to hate melon. He gives me a hug that's squashy because of the stuffed animal. He laughs, and I laugh. He pulls back and looks down, shyly.

"You jerk," he says, looking at the caiman. "You're trying to steal my girl."

He hands it to me.

"Give me a minute?" And he heads to the porta-potties.

I sit on the stands. There aren't many of us there. A couple of kids play on the empty stage. Little by little, the carnival shuts down, scatters in the headlights of the cars that are leaving, first a bright flash when they hit you straight on, and then red when they brake before turning onto the highway and shrinking in the distance. Most of the stands have closed. Fat old Fugaza is still there. Except for the bathroom, that's the only place with a line. There's a guy drinking beer alone, looking around. When he lifts the cup to his mouth, I see he has a tattoo in the same place as Mbói. It could be a snake. It could be anything. He sees I'm looking at him and smiles at me. He comes over. I can't see his tattoo. When he sits down to my right, the ink is hidden by the position of his arm. He holds the beer out to me.

"Want some?"

"No, thanks."

"It really cooled off."

I look him in the face. A trimmed beard, neat, no scars.

"I'm waiting for my boyfriend."

"Don't worry. I'm taken, too."

I look at his finger, and there's no wedding band. There are some cuts on his hand, though. A bead of sweat rolls down my back, stretches out, gets so long I could call it Paraná.

He takes another sip of beer.

"Sure you don't want some? I can't drink any more."

"What happened to your hand?"

"Work. I'm kind of clumsy."

"Everything okay?" Marcos says, standing next to me.

"Don't worry, friend. I was watching her for you. Lot of snakes around here."

The guy gets up and leaves the beer behind. The tattoo doesn't look anything like a snake, it's the Iron Maiden monster, but the uncomfortable feeling doesn't go away. It makes me remember we're not on vacation, that Mbói could be anywhere. Marcos gives me a kiss that I barely respond to.

"Did something happen?"

"It's just getting a little late."

"I didn't come on my bike, but if you want to walk home with me to go get it, I'll take you. It's just a couple blocks."

I don't know if he's got other intentions. For a moment, I can't think. He takes my hand and makes me start walking. The cars go by us, our shadows get longer and then shorter, making an M on the red ground. We come to a little house, white and neat, on a corner.

"This is it," Marcos says. "Wait here, I'll be right back."

There are stickers in one of the windows. One of them says Green Day, a few others are bleached by the sun. That must be Martina's room. I wonder what it's like inside. What a girl's room is like when she's lived there long enough for the sun to make her stickers fade. But what I really wonder is what Marcos's room is like.

The lights of a car hit me, blinding me, and it's like coming out of a dream and into reality. When it passes me, I recognize it. It's the Neon. It stops right across from me, on the other side of the road. Dad gets out, and a woman steps out the passenger side. I see her from behind, waiting for him to come around the front of the car. She hugs him. Dad looks my way, and I rush to hide behind a pile of bricks.

"Hey, what's wrong?" Marcos says, pushing the motorcycle by the handlebars.

"Nothing. You startled me."

He stops on the sidewalk and looks where my eyes are pointing. Dad's waiting in front of the house while the woman looks for the key in her purse.

"It looks like you were hiding. Are you sure you're okay?"

I give him an uncertain kiss that ends before he expects it to. I hug him and use him as a shield so I can look at them without them seeing me. The woman smiles when she finally finds the key. She has really long legs, and her short dress makes them look even longer. She adjusts the strap. I think I recognize her. I remember being here, stopping by to drop off money and thinking she must be the wife of some friend of Dad's who ended up in jail.

You idiot, I say to myself.

Marcos lets me go and turns to look at them. I can't remember her name. She and Dad get tangled up in a kiss next to the door. Marcos shakes his head like he can't believe it. I'm worried he might know Dad.

"What?" I say.

"La Gringa," he says, raising his eyebrows. "I never saw her with a guy, and now that I do, he looks like a total jackass."

Gringa, that's it. She opens the door, and Dad smacks her on the ass. Before closing the door behind him, he checks to see no one's following him. You're getting sloppy, Dad.

"The prettier the woman, the bigger the idiot."

"You know what, I never thought I was the prettiest girl around, but I must be, because you're the biggest idiot."

"Hey. Come on. It was a joke."

I turn away, wrap my arms around myself, and take off walking.

"Ale, wait. Alejandra, come on, stop."

I don't know anybody named Alejandra.

I keep walking. He doesn't start running or come after me. I wait to hear the motorcycle starting, catching up to me, but there's nothing. It takes me three blocks to realize I'm going the wrong way. I turn around.

Assholes.

Both of them.

20.

Noise in the kitchen wakes me up. Dad bangs on the filter of the Volturno to knock out the old coffee grounds, scrapes it out over the garbage, refills it, and puts water into the coffee maker. I hear the scratch of the lighter. He must have bought himself a new one.

Looks like Gringa's place doesn't offer breakfast service.

When he comes in to ask if I want him to bring me the coffee with milk in bed or if I'm going to get up, I'll pretend to be asleep. The heat tells me it's closer to noon than dawn. The shoulders of my T-shirt are damp with sweat, and so are the sheets.

The coffee takes a while. As if you need more time if you live here. I hear him walking back and forth, setting things down on the table. I hope he's just here to give me more money. I hope he hasn't found Mbói yet.

I hope he has.

I don't know.

I don't want to leave so soon. I'm tired of resetting my life, my lives, of having to make up stories, of my friends, if you can call them that, only lasting me a month or a semester, of constantly saying goodbye.

I don't want to look for letters anymore, or open gifts that are for someone else. I'm tired of being what other people have left behind.

I cover my head with the pillow so it's easier to pretend I'm asleep. The sounds from the kitchen are muffled. The knife opening a sachet of milk. He pours some. The cabinet doors, a pot, another burst from the lighter, the burner coughing because it's dirty, or because the gas tank is almost empty. There are some sounds I can't make out. But others are unmistakable; he pops the shells out of the shotgun. Dad doesn't use my guns.

The coffee bubbles over, and the smell reaches me. His footsteps on the wood are light, as if a shadow were walking and not a person, and I think it's because of the pillow. I take it off my head, but I can still barely hear them. I put on my shorts and go out into the living room.

The man is sitting next to the table. A sliver of light comes in through the shutter and cuts across his body, as if the light on him were a scar. With one hand, he holds my shotgun in his lap. In the other is a cup of coffee.

"Sorry, I didn't mean to wake you," he says, "but I haven't had breakfast yet. Lot of work, we had trouble at the company, and I couldn't squeeze in a break."

"Who are you?"

Even sitting down, you can tell he's tall. He's wearing all black, a T-shirt, Adidas sweatpants, and I think he's Mbói, but he only has a tattoo on his neck. I don't know what it is.

"I didn't pour you a cup because I wasn't sure how you take it." He stands up with the shotgun and sets it on the table. I try to think where Dad left the guns, but my memory is full of holes, and everything drains out. I also don't think I'm fast enough. "I heated up some milk. I take half coffee, half milk. I'll make yours a little stronger because you look like you haven't really woken up yet. I need you alert."

"Who are you? What do you want?"

"My grandpa always called me Rupave. Do you know what that means in Guaraní?"

"Intruder?"

He lifts the top off the Volturno and a puff of steam rises up. He pours some coffee into a tin pan and puts it on the burner.

"Close. Rupave was the guardian of the only entrance to a land of no evil. Guaraní paradise, basically. *Mitaí, you're our Rupave*, he'd say, really serious. My grandpa was a smuggler, so I was basically a lookout, but he liked to call me that."

"Okay, Rupave, I'm sorry to tell you this isn't the land of no evil, so I don't need a guardian."

"You should have one. Especially with the mess your old man's kicking up trying to find my brother."

He motions for me to sit down. My legs are shaking, and I obey mostly to keep from falling down.

He pours the coffee into a mug, adds some milk, and hands it to me. He's arranged Dad's guns on the table, the bullets on one side, the red and yellow shells all lined up, some of my fake IDs, my underwear, a pair of jeans, some socks. Everything is laid out neatly, like he searched my life and entered everything into evidence.

"Let me know if it's okay or if I should heat it up more."

I bring the mug toward my mouth, and my hand is shaking so badly that it splashes, and I burn my lips. I spill even more on my T-shirt.

"Sorry, I'm used to the microwave."

He sits down across from me, still holding the shotgun, so that he's covering the door.

"Now the question is, who are you?" He touches the IDs, opening them, the first and second pages. "Whoever made these did a good job. They look real and everything. You even look nice in the picture. A pretty little doll. How old were you in this one?" I don't answer. "I'll call you Alejandra because that's the name you've been using around here. Sound okay?"

My mouth is dry. My heart is beating so hard in my ears that I miss some of the words he's saying.

"If you came looking for my old man, you'll have realized by now he isn't here."

"I came to look after my business. Nice sawed-off." He pats the barrel. "They didn't get carried away. It's a good length. Must punch some nice holes. Have you tested it out?"

He picks up a yellow shell, sets it on his palm, weighs it. He empties it onto the table. The grains of salt spread out.

"I haven't seen one of these in forever. When I was little, my grandpa would send me to steal chickens from an old guy who'd shoot at you with this shit. He went off on me, but he never managed to hit me. I always wondered what the hell they did to you."

He flicks one of the shells, and they fall down one after the other like dominos. His cell phone rings. He pulls it out of the pocket, looks at the blue screen, and sets it on the table. He scrapes the salt together into a little pile.

"I've never liked Russian roulette, it doesn't feel very local. How about we play Guaraní roulette?" He grabs a red shell and a yellow one and puts his hands behind his back. "Pick one."

"I want you to leave."

"Pick one, Ale."

"I don't have anything to do with it."

He doesn't take his eyes off me.

"Left."

He raises his eyebrows twice. I can't see which it is because the table blocks my view. He loads one shell, then the other. I hear a car coming, and we both look outside. He stands up and goes over to the corner, aiming at the door. I don't recognize the motor. Please don't let it be Dad. I try to swallow and get ready to scream, to warn him, but I feel like my voice is full of holes, too, like I'm full of holes all over.

The car goes by. Rupave comes back, sits down, sets the shotgun across his lap again.

"Shame it wasn't your old man." He's about to say something else, but his cell phone rings. He looks at the screen and picks up. "Tell me something good, Loza. Nothing?" He drums his fingers on the butt of the shotgun. "Yeah. I'm on it. It'll take me a little longer to finish up here. We're just getting started." He looks at me, stares at my wet T-shirt that's stuck to my skin where I spilled coffee on it. I pull at it. "Half hour. Maybe more. And don't call me unless it's important, this shit is expensive."

He sets the phone aside.

"You're right. You've got nothing to do with this. You just have to listen. To me or to the shotgun. I'm going to talk, and if I don't like your answer, we're going to start in with Guaraní roulette."

It bothers me that my clothes are there, my thong, my panties, like he's opening me up and saying: *this is you, little girl. You can't hide.*

"Where's your old man?"

"I have no idea."

"You want to push your luck right off the bat?"

The guy swings the gun back and forth.

"Looking for Mbói."

"This is the part where you tell me something I don't know."

"He told me he saw a guy named Piñata." He waits. The eye of the shotgun stares me down. If he made it here, he must have followed me from somewhere. "And then a girl Mbói goes out with."

"My brother goes out with a lot of girls. I don't know what the hell they see in him."

"I don't know what her name is. My old man doesn't tell me what he does."

He takes a sip of coffee. The tattoo on his neck is a skull in flames.

"When is he coming back?"

"Sometimes he's gone for weeks at a time."

"How long since you last heard from him?"

"Two days."

"Aren't you worried something might have happened to him?"

I rip a piece of dead skin off my lip. I didn't even realize I was chewing it.

"And you've got no way to reach him? Doesn't he have a cell phone?"

"He doesn't believe in those things. He says they can trace you with them."

Rupave shakes his head. His nails are cut right down to the skin. He cocks the shotgun, and a shiver shakes my body. The sweat runs down my face, a drop falling on my shorts.

"Sometimes you've got to make space for the truth to come out," he says. "It gets stuck in teeth, or on clothes. Or on loyalties. Loyalty is a motherfucker. It must be the leading cause of death, and the people we don't want to betray, they probably deserve to be given up. It's their fault for putting us in that position."

I lower my hands, rest them on my thighs. I drive my nails into my skin like stakes, so my legs won't move, so I can control them. He leans his body over the table to see what I'm doing and pokes at my hands with the shotgun barrel.

"What are you hiding from me, Ale?"

"Nothing, I swear."

The roughly sawed end of the shotgun scratches my legs.

"With legs like yours, it'd be a shame if you couldn't show them off anymore. Or if you lost them."

The shotgun becomes a snout that tries to sniff at me like a dog. I push the barrel away so hard, it almost falls out of his hands. He pokes at me again. His cell phone rings. He looks down, checks the screen, picks up.

"Hey, sweetheart. How are you?" He has a sweet voice that doesn't match the guy resting a shotgun on my legs. "Yeah. I'm still in a meeting. No, you could never bother me. What do you want for dinner? Of course I got you a present. What did you think? I'll finish up here and head over."

He puts the cell phone in the pocket of his sweatpants.

"Do you know what a good gift is for a girl who's turning thirteen?"

With the end of the shotgun, he picks up a black string thong.

"How old were you when you started wearing these?"

"What do you care?"

"Are they for a thirteen-year-old girl?"

He drops the thong on top of my IDs. Then he rests the shotgun on his shoulder, his finger on the trigger.

"I'd love to hang around and wait for your old man, especially with such pretty company, but I'm sure you understand that today is an important day, and I'd like to spend it with my daughter. Family's an expensive bitch, so when you get a free pass, you'd be an idiot not to enjoy it.

"Between you and me, my brother's an asshole. It's his fault we had to leave our town. It was a shithole, but it was ours. He's always running around doing stupid shit, and I'm sick of cleaning up his messes." He looks exhausted for a minute. His shoulders slump, he rubs his forehead, blows air out one side of his mouth. That tiredness looks dangerous on men, and it makes me think of Dad. "If I'm honest with you, I can see where your old man is coming from. But if anybody's going to set my brother straight, it's going to be me. Nobody else. You get me?"

I nod.

"When you see your old man, you're going to tell him you have to get out of here. Tell him to consider that money lost. If he's as tough as they say, he can make more. Convince him. I don't care how. Your family is your problem. Mine is my problem. But if you fuck with my blood . . ." He points the shotgun at me. "There'll be enough of your blood to paint these walls."

He pops out a shell, and it's red.

"You got lucky," he says. "The next time I'm here, it won't be a courtesy visit."

Rupave scrapes the salt together and pushes it to the edge of the table. He throws it over his shoulder.

"Got to scare off the devil and death."

"I didn't know Guaranís believed in that stuff."

"You're wrong. My grandpa's the one who believes all that nonsense. I just have Guaraní blood on my hands."

He stands up and brushes off the salt stuck to the thong. He picks up another one and smells it, sniffs it.

"With how nice your *cachi* smells, it should be a crime for you to wash these."

He puts it in his pocket and sets the shotgun down on the chair he was sitting in. He takes the mug over to the sink, washes it, and sets it on the counter upside-down. He rubs his wet hands over his face and then dries them on his T-shirt.

"If I were you, I'd be careful about deciding which ID you keep on you. You don't want to get buried under the wrong name."

When he closes the door, I punch myself in the leg. I try to feel my body, to feel that some part of me is still mine and doesn't belong to the fear.

21.

The wind chime is still there, hanging between the door and the window. It's different from the regular kind, with the little sticks that keep you up at night when it's windy. This one's made of woven circles that are orange, red, and white.

Ñandutí, that's what that weaving is called. It means spiderweb. That was one of the first words Dad gave me. I wonder if he got it here.

I remember waiting for him in the car while he went in, for a long time that I understand better now, and I'd look at the *ñandutí* and at the sun that filtered through the leaves and made me sleepy. I also have an image of seeing the wind chime through the window, of spending the night on the sofa and waking up with a blanket covering me. No. I wasn't covered up. That was in Tandil. There were mountains, and it was cold. Here it was pouring rain, that's why we didn't get back on the highway. I woke up with a Siamese cat staring at me, curled up on my legs. I think. Maybe there wasn't a cat. My childhood is a tattoo that was never finished because they kept changing the design as they went, or maybe I leave it unfinished because I can't take the pain.

The *ñandutí* is still there. The Neon isn't.

Where the hell are you, Dad?

A few strands of hair blow across my face, and I tuck them behind my ear. I must have been standing here a while because I can feel the sun prickling the backs of my knees. My mouth is open. I have bad breath, no matter how many times I brush my teeth. It's like I can't make any saliva, like I can't put my fear into words. I turn around and look at Marcos's house. There's no one there. The shutters are closed. In the background, the green stretches out like someone just waking up.

At Gringa's, the curtain moves, and a few seconds later, the door opens. She's wearing a black tank top and a long red skirt that goes all the way down to her ankles.

"Ámbar?"

The heat waves make her squint. She looks from side to side, like she's expecting someone else to appear.

"Come inside, you're going to get heat stroke."

I rush in with no hug or kiss hello. The living room is separated from the kitchen by a table with three chairs. In the back is a door that leads to the yard. She walks over to the boiling kettle. A few times she starts to turn and ask me something, but she goes and turns off the burner.

It looks like a house set up to last, a home. The furniture

is sturdy, not the way they make it now. Everything is where it should be, not because that's where it got left but because that's the spot that was picked out for it. Plates hanging on the walls with recipes in Italian painted on them. An old map of Asti, Turin. An embroidered picture of some *cholas* over the couch where I slept. I don't remember if it was there before. A CD tower, a bamboo bookcase, an acoustic guitar. There's no TV, no photos. Some gardening gloves with dirt on them on the table. I wish there were more things to discover so I could take longer before looking at her.

The silence comes down and settles like a layer of dust.

"I'm sorry I came."

"It's fine."

She gestures to the sofa and rests her hands on the back of an armchair. The steam is still rising from the kettle. She looks at me like she doesn't know what I'm doing here. That makes two of us.

"Did something happen to your dad?"

"I was hoping you'd know that."

"Did he ask you to come here? Did he tell you about me?"

"Dad doesn't even tell me about himself."

There's another wave of silence. One of my shoelaces is untied and stained completely red.

"I saw you guys last night."

Her skin is tanned, but even so, I can see her blush.

"You were following him?"

"No. I just was passing by."

"Here? There's nothing around here."

Her face changes, as if something just occurred to her.

"I got lost when I left the fair."

"Did you have fun?"

"It's better than staring at the ceiling."

We exchange a look in the reflection in the glass coffee table between us, like it's more comfortable to meet each other there.

"I was just about to make a cup of tea. Do you want one?"

I say yes. It's a million degrees out, but maybe it'll get rid of my bad breath. I look outside. I can't see the wind chime. Maybe I have to lie down to see it. Maybe I made it all up—or most of it.

Her brown hair looks reddish when the sun hits it. Dad's a few years older than she is. She's barefoot, and her toenails are painted green. She comes back over with a tray, a sugar dish, and two matching cups, each with a tea bag in it, and there's something in that detail, in both cups and spoons being the same, that makes feel calm, something controlled, not made up on the fly. My body relaxes, spreads out across the sofa. She sits down across from me.

"You cut your hair, right?"

"I got sick of having to tie it back." She runs her hand across the back of her neck, shaking out the tips of her hair. "You've got a great memory. You were little."

"You used to have a cat."

"I still do. Mandioca." She calls her. "She must be sleeping on the bed."

She hisses twice. I hear a bump, and the cat comes down

the hall that leads to the bedroom, stretches, and walks over, meowing. She jumps up on her owner's lap, and Gringa pets her.

"Are you sure nothing's wrong?"

The red tea spreads through the cup, slowly.

"I haven't seen him for two days, and I'm worried."

"You say that like disappearing is a new trick for him. You know what he's like. You know him better than anyone. Staying away is his way of taking care of you."

Out the back window, I can see a shed with the door open. There are a few plants and some clothes hanging from a line. Black thongs, no bras, a couple of dresses, including the red one she was wearing last night.

I look at her full lips, her earrings, her birthmark above one eyebrow. I wonder what she sees in Dad.

"You have no idea where he is, right?"

She sets the tea bag down on a plate, then puts some sugar in her cup and stirs it in.

"He's on a job. That's what he says whenever I ask him. And when I say, *what kind of job*, he just says, *a shit job, like there's any other kind*. I don't ask anymore." She takes a sip of tea, the steam blurring her face. "Víctor's not much of a talker. He tells the odd story, but not much. I don't know if it's because he's worried you're going to give him up or that you'll get scared. A couple months ago, he said he was working on something definitive. That's the word he used, definitive. Who knows what he meant."

A couple months ago . . .

I wonder how many quick trips he's made here, how

many times I've waited around in a shitty hotel while he was here with her.

I hear a motorcycle outside. Through the window, I see it's a woman with a little girl or boy sitting behind her. I don't know. The kid's got a helmet on. I don't care.

"Don't worry. No one's going to come looking for you here. Your dad's careful."

You have no idea. Or maybe I'm the one who wasn't careful.

Mandioca comes over, walking across the table, and sniffs me. I remember the coffee and sweat stains on my T-shirt. She looks at them but doesn't say anything. I bet she can even smell them. She doesn't say anything about the fingernail marks on my legs, either. Maybe she's seen them before, maybe she does the same thing.

"You've got Víctor's nose."

"Are you kidding? Dad's nose is all twisted."

"I know, but before it got broken, it was exactly like yours."

"You've known him a long time."

"From back when he didn't use any other names."

I take a drink of tea. The bag has been in it so long that it's strong. It's raspberry flavored, or something like that.

"Do you know how his nose got broken?"

"Trying to remember how he got all his scars is like trying to remember every hot day around here."

"You're the thing in his life that's lasted the longest."

"No. That's you. I . . . I don't know. I'm like a vacation." She looks at the fan, which isn't turned on. "With him, the closest thing to 'forever' is a life sentence. I'm sick of not knowing what dress to wear while I wait for him. One to go out dancing, or to go to a funeral." She notices some dirt on her skirt and brushes it off. "You get sick of waiting."

"It didn't look that way last night."

"I don't wait anymore. If he shows up, fine."

"You're the first girlfriend of his I've ever met."

"Aside from your mom."

"I don't think she was ever Dad's girlfriend."

Mandioca rubs her face against my hands and leaves a shadow of white hairs.

"It's hard to be a woman in Víctor Mondragón's life."

At Marcos's, there's a broken weathervane shaped like a rooster, completely still despite the wind shaking the line of trees behind the house.

"What was he like before?" I ask.

"Before what?"

Before becoming what he is now.

"When he didn't have a broken nose."

She finishes her tea and wipes her lips with her hand.

"I don't know. It's hard not to remember it nicer than it was, after such a long time. We met in his town, when I was about your age. It's funny because most of us wanted to look older, drink beer, smoke, but your dad would walk into a bar and order a glass of water. And he didn't wear name-brand clothes, just the same old plaid shirts, or that green military one. He'd sit there at the bar, and he looked like he didn't fit in at all. Some guys thought he'd be easy pickings, and were they ever wrong. After how he took care of those first few, people started knowing his name. He was always so confident, it was contagious. He could make you believe whatever he wanted. He'd win you over."

She looks around the house. Her mouth moves, like she can't quite tune in to the next sentence.

"I think all that confidence was because he couldn't believe in anything or anybody else, so he just had to believe in himself. I don't know what happened to him before, but I always saw him as a man who learned to live his life looking over his shoulder all the time, who couldn't afford to look at what was right in front of him because when he saw you, when he realized you existed . . ."

She laughs a little. I'd like to know what image of Dad passed through her mind. If there's another version of him that I don't know.

"Sorry, I don't know why I'm telling you all this. Maybe you know something I didn't."

She smiles a little, and two or three wrinkles appear next to her eyes. Most of them must have Dad's name written on them. Or maybe not. Maybe those aren't the nights she sat up waiting for him, maybe they're not the nights she gave up and accepted that when something is drifting on the current, all you can do is watch it float away. Maybe those are the wrinkles you get from living where it's always sunny. Maybe they're just age. Maybe she's a mirror for what I have inside me.

"Sometimes I try to understand him," I say. "Most of the time, I just have to love him. But there are times he makes himself pretty hard to love."

As soon as it's said, I regret it. I hear a tap-tap and realize it's my foot bouncing against the glass tabletop. She looks at me like she wants to hug me, and I'm glad she's too far away, that there's a table separating us.

"Your dad's got a huge heart. The problem is he thinks his brain and his balls are even bigger, and I'd like to think he's starting to realize that. But I'd never doubt his heart."

The house feels small. There's no air. I want to get out.

I wonder if that's how Dad feels.

A motorcycle goes by slowly. It's a kid wearing shorts and a helmet who brakes at the corner and then speeds up, leaving Marcos's house behind. I realize I've seen his motorcycle twice, but I don't even know what it looks like. Still, I could recognize him just by his smile. When I take my eyes off the window, they run into Gringa's gaze.

"He left early this morning," she says. "You've got a pretty close eye on the Cardinals' place. That kid with the shaved head, who listens to heavy metal . . . Marcos?"

"How did you know?"

"I know what it's like to look out a window hoping he'll show up."

She sets the cups on the tray and takes it over to the sink.

"Are you guys going to the party for the end of carnival?"

"I don't know. We had a fight last night. Nothing big. He said something stupid . . ."

I shrug one shoulder. I feel silly for telling her, as if I had anyone else to tell, as if my problem was a boy and not the guy who broke into the house. As if I was a fifteen-year-old girl.

She throws the tea bags in the garbage.

"When they can't open their hearts, guys open their mouths, and it's usually to say something stupid. You do whatever you think is best, but if it was me, I'd go. It's better than staring at the ceiling."

I stand up and brush some of Mandioca's hairs off me. They float in the air and stick to my nose.

"But if Dad decides to come back, I don't want him to not find me there."

"Leave him a note," she says. "You can't hold off living your life while you wait around for Víctor."

We share a smile that feels like sharing a secret.

"Do you have anything to wear?"

"Are you saying I don't look gorgeous like this?" I say, crossing my arms to hide the stains.

She goes into the bedroom. Mandioca follows her. I hear the sound of closet doors and clothes hangers. She comes back with a short black V-neck dress. It's beautiful.

"Just in case," she says. "It's hard to get Mandioca's fur off it. I think this'll fit you." She holds it up against my body to see. It's got a ribbon that ties around the waist. It must have been expensive. "Keep it. I'm too old for this kind of dress now."

"Thanks."

She gives me a bag, and I put the dress in it, folded up. We stand there, avoiding each other, knowing that anything we say from now on will create more doubt than certainty.

"I think . . ." I say.

"Yeah," she interrupts me.

"Don't tell him I was here."

"You, either," she says, laughing. "Don't worry."

She walks me out, and we nod goodbye to each other. She closes the door. Mandioca's meowing fades as she moves deeper into the house. I stop on the corner. Nothing's moving on the whole block, not in her house or at Marcos's, except the *ñandutí* swaying in the window.

I think it makes sense that outside the house Dad goes into, there's not a regular wind chime, but instead, one that doesn't make any noise, one a girl could get tangled up in.

22.

When I see the Neon parked in front of the house, I stop, close my eyes, and blow all the air out of my lungs until I feel like I've shrunk. I inhale, fill up my chest, and my body gets its shape back, like it's rising from its knees and standing up.

Then I remember the dress and swear under my breath.

I could walk in with a shotgun and probably get a proud smile out of him, but a dress—especially one from her—I'll have to sneak in like contraband. I go up to the door without making any noise. I can hear the news, *the destruction unleashed by the fire*, the sound of the tap. I go around the house to the backyard and hang the bag on a branch that faces away from the house.

I go back around and knock with our code.

"I was getting worried," he says.

"I went out to get something to eat."

"In the next town over? I've been here for three hours."

"They had a fan and a TV that got more than one channel."

He's drinking coffee and doesn't have a shirt on. The low light from the TV makes the scars on his chest and stomach stand out, long, deformed. His green military shirt is over the back of the chair Rupave sat in.

Even though I rearranged the living room, moved the TV and table, put all my stuff away, my head can't undo the image, erase the name that was stamped on what used to belong only to me.

"What about yesterday? I called you a few times, and you never picked up."

"I went out for a while. It's boring here. Is that a problem?" I sit down, my back to the wall, my eyes toward the door. I put a piece of mint gum in my mouth. My bad breath still isn't gone. "And if you're worried, how am I supposed to feel?"

He turns down the TV. In the dark, we're just outlines.

"Worried about what?"

"What do you mean, about what?"

"About Mbói? That's just another day at the office. I had bigger problems at school."

"You didn't go to school."

"Up until sixth grade, I did."

The wound on his chest looks a lot better, but he has a bandage around his right hand, covering his knuckles and palm, with little spots of blood on it. I wonder what kind of rage must rise up in him to let him ignore that voice that tells him to sit still, to stop, that he's going to open up his wounds if he keeps that up, but he must silence his body to keep on breaking it a little bit more.

I think about Valeria, but it feels like that was a year ago.

Two of Dad's days can hold another person's whole life.

Or another person's death.

On TV, the fires strip the forest bare, reduce it to bones made of wood and earth.

Unleashed.

It's a word you only hear on TV or read in a book.

Unleashed. Like the destruction was on a leash before.

I can't bear to glance at Dad, all those scars, all that blood coming out of him. That's not destruction. Destruction is *him*. I wish that he would already be unleashed, that I would already know how bad it could get. I wonder if a leashed version of Dad even exists. I wish there were one, and for a second I have the urge to hug him really hard, with everything I have. Maybe, just maybe, that could leash all the destruction waiting to come out. But believing that is just wishful thinking. Because I know that the last time Dad was leashed was seconds before they cut his umbilical cord, that he was born already giving a scar to his mother. What can we expect from life when the first thing all of us do is scar the first person who ever loved us?

Some destruction cannot be put on a leash. Sometimes I think it'll only stop when he's buried.

Once I asked Dad—a man who had been all over Argentina from top to bottom, and parts of Brazil and Paraguay—what the prettiest thing he ever saw in his life was.

His answer was *a horse on fire*. He said it survived—which I doubt—but it was incredible to see it streaking through the night, running out of the stable that was in flames, taking a piece of the fire with it. He said it like he was jealous of the horse.

"You did some cleaning."

"I had to do something to pass the time. I found some of my old stuff. How many times have we been here?"

"Together? I don't know. Two, three times. When I worked for Granny I lived here."

"Has it been a long time since you've been back?"

He doesn't take his eyes off the TV. Even though his mug has a handle, he wraps his fingers around it. Judging by the steam coming off it, it must be boiling hot. He should be burning himself, but I guess he doesn't have any sensation left in his fingers.

"I don't know. A long time. What's with all the questions?"

"I just think it's weird it wasn't that dusty."

"I let some friends use it." He opens and closes the hand with the bandage on it. "And you know you're not supposed to touch my guns. If you're going to, at least put them back where you found them."

It wasn't me.

What I can't unleash is my tongue.

"Why are you here?"

"To see if you're okay."

"Okay, why are you really here?"

I open the door so some air can come in, so I can stop seeing in shadows what isn't here anymore, so I can see that on the table there's a box of Dad's bullets and not my thongs and IDs. Or Rupave scratching at me.

"If you saw I moved your guns, that means you were looking for them."

He opens the .38 and empties the used shells into an ashtray. Little by little, the place fills up with another kind of threat. One I know. One I can almost understand because it has a name. Dad.

"That coffee you made was good," he says. "But don't leave food out anymore, all kinds of animals could come in here." He gives me a kiss on the top of my head.

He sets the mug in the sink and fills another with hot water. He shuffles through his things until he finds his shaving cream and brush, then goes into the bathroom.

I walk across the living room and hear a crunch like bones under my foot. I look down at my Converse and see I'm stepping on the grains of salt Rupave threw.

"Dad."

I'm scared.

"What?"

Mbói's brother was here.

"Did you find him?"

"We're close, Ambareté."

He brushes the shaving cream onto his face, whistling that god damn Cartola song I can't remember the name of. I'd bet my hair there's a Cartola CD in Gringa's tower.

"You're not going to tell me anything else?"

Like that you already killed him. Like that you got your money back.

He runs the razor down his neck. With his hair buzzed and no beard, the shapes of his body are exposed like a tree after a fire. There's nowhere for him to hide.

He swears and stretches his neck up, seeing that he nicked himself. The blood pools in the shaving cream and takes a while to trickle down. He rinses the razor off in the sink and runs it down his neck again. Now that the shaving cream is gone, the blood runs right down, two little lines that get fatter, become one.

I'm sure that if I tell him about Rupave, the most he'll do is leave me locked up alone in a hotel. A hotel where they could find me even more easily. I'm not going to let fear lock me up.

On TV, a reporter is under a bridge, next to a stream. MISSING WOMAN FOUND, it says under the image in big letters. I turn up the volume.

A couple found her right here last night. He points to the edge of the river, eaten away by the passing water, ground that's always muddy. *Valeria Almada, aged twenty-five, had been missing for two days. Her family told police they'd last seen her coming out of the restaurant where she worked.*

"Come here."

"What is it?"

"I said, come here."

Dad stands next to me, holding toilet paper against his neck to stop the bleeding. A woman with cheekbones like mountains comes on the TV. Romina, Valeria's mother. Then an ambulance, police in front of a hospital, a gurney.

"What are you looking at me for?" he says. "If it had been

me, they wouldn't have found her." Then, too late, he adds: "I'd never do that to a woman."

The young woman was carrying no ID. She was finally identified by a scar on her abdomen. Courtesy of her ex-boyfriend, who she'd reported to police and who must have committed the crime, her mother says as best she can with a tongue numbed by sadness.

"She should pick her boyfriends better," Dad says.

There's a quick shot of Valeria being pushed into the hospital on a gurney, her face blurred out because of the bruises and blood. The little red bracelet pushed down onto her hand.

"They shouldn't show her like that."

"Shit, she wouldn't even recognize herself looking like that."

Then they show a guy with a cigarette, the ash bending off the end, forgotten. Ramiro Istillarte, Valeria's boyfriend. *She was a saint*, he says. *She didn't bother anybody. She worked double shifts to bring home more money.*

"What an idiot. Double shifts with Mbói?"

"Will you shut up?"

Dad's about to say something, but he looks at me. I don't know if he'd bother to name the expression on my face, but maybe it would be *shut the hell up or I'll kill you.* Whatever it is he has to say, he keeps it to himself and cracks his jaw.

I bring my hands to my face, then run through my hair to the back of my neck and leave them there. I rest my sweaty forehead on the table and feel all the dirt stick to me.

While the sun was turning my skin red, her blood was

doing the same to hers. While someone's hand was holding mine, someone else's was beating her to death.

"It's our fault."

He puts on a tank top and his military shirt over that.

"The only thing in my life I regret is voting for the president who shall not be named the first time around. Don't let yourself get into that spiral because you'll never get back out."

He takes my face in his hands so I'll look at him. I feel the rough texture of the bandage, the roughness of his eyes. The shaving cream that's stuck to him like scattered rage.

"Having a conscience is a luxury, Ambareté. It's for rich people. They have a clear conscience because they pay other people to get their hands dirty for them, other people who can't afford to have a conscience. If there's one thing I've learned, it's that your stomach growls louder than your conscience. And my hands might be dirty, but up here"—he smacks his hand against his head—"I'm fine. That girl Valeria chose who she got involved with. Not me."

He only lets me go when I nod. I wonder if he even believes the bullshit he says.

"Don't feel guilty." He puts his hands on my shoulders. "If it'll make you feel better, we'll get revenge for her. I promise there'll be a bullet with your name on it."

It doesn't make me feel better. Nothing could make me feel better.

When he finishes shaving, he goes into the bedroom and comes back out with a bag and throws the box of bullets in it. He sets it on the chair. I look at the salt on the floor and go over to it, then I step on all the grains and grind them into dust, easing the name, turning them into just more dirt.

"I'm going out tonight," I say.

"Sounds good. Enjoy your last night here."

"Wouldn't you like to stay?"

"Here? No way. I'd rather be in jail."

He turns away from me and puts his guns in the bag, makes sure everything's in its place, all stuff he'll eventually get rid of. Ready to follow his map of scars, to stretch his path out again with a new one, which I'll have to sew up. If I can.

I bite my lips so hard it hurts. I bite off a piece of skin that's longer than I thought, long like the silence, like everything I can't say, what I can't put into words. As if my mouth were a wound.

Another one. Mine and mine alone.

Fuck you, Dad.

There's a shooting star on TV. Two of them. Three.

Below it a red bar that reads: The Columbia tragedy.

On its return to Earth, the space shuttle Columbia exploded in the air hours before landing. I can see a white line disintegrating into more lines, each with its own separate wake. If you didn't know what it was, it would be pretty. A lot of people must have thought they were shooting stars and made a wish on a bunch of fire and burnt flesh.

I think believing in Dad is something like that.

"Turn off the TV and come look at this," he says, standing in the doorway. "Look at that sky. There's no redder sunset than you see in Misiones. Do you remember the time we pulled off the highway and parked the car on the shoulder, and we sat on the roof and watched the sun sink into the river?"

I remember my legs freezing against the metal, the cold in my face. The only clouds in the sky were the ones coming out of our mouths.

"It was a truck, I think."

"You're right, it was the F100 Méndez gave us."

"It was cold."

"It was freezing. You were wearing that polar fleece jacket and we had to huddle together. That was in Posadas, I think. I remember"—he pauses to snort with laughter—"you were worried because you could see the sun going into the Paraná and you were afraid the water would put it out and we'd have to live in the dark. And I told you not to worry, that nothing could put out that fire." He looks inside, but backlit like he is, I can't see him. "That was one of our first trips. But I can't remember if we stayed long enough to see the sun disappear. You kept saying, *Dad, let's go, how long til we get home*. No. I think we left before it got dark."

He's talking about a sunset but not the fact that we stopped so he could throw a gun into the river. He said he was going to go take a leak, but there was a heavy sound in the water, like he'd thrown in a rock, and if we sat around for a while, if we weren't in a hurry, it was only because he had no idea where we were going to sleep that night.

Maybe he really doesn't remember.

Everyone dulls their memories however they can, so they hurt as little as possible.

He stands there, leaning on his elbow against the doorframe, and watches the sunset. His arm cuts the sky in two. Blue above it, only red below it.

"You were so intense when you were little. All day long, you'd ask me how long until we got home. At least you don't ask that anymore."

There's a wasp's nest in the corner of the doorframe. He looks at it and gives it a little flick. No wasps come out. He reaches up, pulls it off, and squeezes it between his hands. Little pieces come out either side. He comes in, picks up his bag, blows me a kiss, and leaves.

"Because we can never go home now," I say, as the Neon makes its escape.

The only place we can go back to is ourselves.

And that's a pretty shitty place.

23.

Some nights are tattoos.

They mark you, forever.

And others are the blink of an eye.

Dad might live his life looking over his shoulder, but I live mine looking at everything in the rearview mirror, falling away behind me, blurry, indecipherable from the speed, something born to be forgotten. Nights that are bug bites, that bother you for a few days and then disappear like they'd never been there.

Some nights are deep, dark wells.

And some nights are tattoos.

I want to carry this night on my body, forget the shit from this morning, the guilt from the afternoon, leave just the night, tattoo it on myself, be able to come back to it and say, this happened, with all the details, before I'm pulled away from here.

I go into the fair, I walk through it, I leave behind what I see, I'm not interested in this stand or that one, if there's a line to buy beer or get your fortune told. When I come back to this moment, I'm not going to remember that I almost got beer spilled on me, that a guy tried to grab my ass, anything that happens until I find Marcos on the stands and his smile opens slowly like a flower. I know there are more people around, people yelling and dancing, but even now that I'm dodging them, I've only got eyes for those teeth, that mouth I take possession of, pull toward me, take with me, stealing the taste of beer, the echo of mint gum. I occupy it. I make it mine.

Where do you put something to keep it forever?

Where does a kiss last the longest?

In your head?

On your skin?

In your heart?

After a while, we separate, we sit on the stands, and the world gets bigger. A couple arguing over there, she won't look at him, a little girl hugging a stuffed coati toy, people's hands clapping at the end of a song, and later the words come, unnecessary, inevitable.

"I'm sorry about yesterday," I say.

"No, I'm sorry. I'm kind of an idiot sometimes."

"Sometimes?"

"Let's not talk about last night, deal?"

"Deal."

I think that maybe in five years, I'll remember the band on stage, probably not the name, Los Mistoles, maybe I'll give them the name of another kind of tree, maybe that space will be empty, maybe I'll remember that they were all dressed the same, in blue suits, or maybe my brain will say red, getting confused by the color of the dust lifted up by those hundreds of feet that are moving. A red mist. That's what I'll remember, maybe retouched, exaggerated.

But more than anything, I'll remember that Marcos is wearing a new shirt, a black one, and you can still see the creases in it, like it was just taken out of the bag. He must have bought it to wear today. That clumsy neatness is sweet.

The band says goodnight, and the presenter announces the next one. He reads the name from a piece of paper, twice and messing it up, like he can't read the writing or he's drunk, and I think that if he'd said it right, the moment would have gone on by, but now, imperfect, it takes shape while Marcos holds my hands in his, looks at them, and rubs my thumb. I wish my nails were painted. I could decorate the memory and make them green, replay it again and again until I make it true.

"That dress looks nice on you, Ale."

Ale . . . it's like when you're recording your favorite song on the radio, and they jump right into another one before it ends.

Don't make the moment go off-key, Marcos.

I deflate a little, rest my head on his shoulder. The wind blows a few loose locks of my hair that used to be pink. The rest is tied back in a bun that took me half an hour to get right. The music saturates the speakers. I lean in and see a scar where he had his ear pierced. I'm glad he took it out.

"There's something I have to tell you."

He lifts his head like a dog hearing a noise.

"I don't like Pantera."

"I know. You said 'Respect.'" He laughs. "What do you really like?"

"You."

His brown eyes get narrow, just little slits, and I want them to spill onto me like paint, for them to be the ink I use to tattoo this moment on myself.

Where does a memory last the longest?

In your head?

On your skin?

In your heart?

"You're amazing, Ale."

Ale, Ale.

Fuck every single Alejandra in the whole world.

I don't say anything because what I have stuck in my throat can't come out. The band comes out, a tropical vibe, and they pollute the air with a few songs. He pulls me up and we stand in line to get a beer from fat old Fugaza. He says hi to a guy, they talk about a party at Tote's next weekend, *his parents are going away, we've got the house to ourselves. You guys should come.* Marcos's shirt is untucked. I'm not sure if I did that. I don't remember having my hands on his waist. I think about the speed of what you feel, that it's impossible to hold onto it all. When I come back from inside my head, the guy has left and we're almost at the front of the line. *Next weekend.* The silence, our silence, grows. Next weekend. And where silence grows, so does doubt.

"Do you have any idea when you're leaving?"

"I don't know." I don't want to think about that. Or lie to him. "Tomorrow, the next day. You never know with my dad."

We stare at the ground like it's the most interesting thing in the world, like there was something more there than bottle caps. Someone behind us says to move up in line.

"Are you going back home?"

"We have a long way to go before that."

"It must be so cool traveling all over the country."

The mosquitos are chewing on my legs. I brush a couple of them away. Marcos pays for the beer. *Don't let your mom find out*, says Fugaza. We go back to the stands. He takes a sip, then another one.

"If you give me your address, I could go visit you." He says it fast, like he's pushing up against his embarrassment to get it out. "If I save some money, I can go see you. I always wanted to see Buenos Aires."

Me, too.

"If you want to see cement, go into construction."

"Are you telling me it isn't nice?"

I want him to be quiet, but I don't want to ruin a kiss by using it to shut him up. He hands me the beer and I drink it fast so it'll wash away what's in my throat or help me say it, I don't know. I start to give it back to him, but I drink a little more first. He takes a few sips while he stares at the people walking by. The cup sweats. He has a chicken pox scar next to his eye. I want to touch it. He hands the beer back to me, and I finish it and squeeze the cup, but it doesn't crush the way I want it to, and it drips on me. I plan to delete this from the memory.

"Do you know how to dance?" he says.

"It's not my thing."

"I'll teach you."

Mr. Confident. He's even worse than I am. He pulls me, spins me, and brings me close. Our bodies match each other, he puts his hand on the back of my neck, his fingers cold and wet from holding the beer, his mouth wide open, laughing, his mouth, my mouth, one mouth for a while. We clap, out of time, to our own time, the lights paint us blue, red, I don't know what the song is about. It's just background noise.

Everything,

except us,

is background noise.

Us, I think, a word I can barely use when it comes to Dad.

No, don't go, don't let your head go away from here, Ámbar, don't be stupid, because this night belongs to you and Marcos, and I give him a kiss, our teeth collide, he bites my lips, it hurts a little, I like it.

Feeling is the closest thing I've found to not thinking.

A slow song comes on. I rest my head on his shoulder and look at the faces around us out of the corner of my eye. The world returns, all of it, and I'm scared because I'm searching, I'm searching for them among all those faces, and the fear, the echo of the fear, gropes me. I'm crushed by all those stares. I close my eyes and rub his buzzed hair, sweaty, I dig my nails into his scalp, and I can't feel anything, or at least not what I want to feel, which is the same as nothing because I think about all those faces, about those stares crushing me, which of them is following me, looking for Alejandra.

And the night trembles, blurs the tattoo. It becomes a snake, a skull in flames on a neck, a name on an arm.

I don't want to think. I want to feel.

"Let's get out of here."

I don't know what expression was on my face, but the doubt I can see at first on his changes. It becomes a nervous smile he tries to hide, and I want to smack him, laugh it up, kid, the world is lighter when you laugh.

He takes my hand and leads me to the edge of the fair where the hills begin. We go down a little path beaten down by other feet. I can hear people, couples, but we keep going until we reach the river, the shore, the moon reflected on the water. I can still hear the music, but it's just a buzz.

Marcos sits down at the base of a tree. I don't know what kind it is, and I don't care. I settle down next to him. He looks at me, happy and not relieved, not like Dad, not glad I'm still there, complete, more or less intact; no, Marcos looks at me and he's happy, it's so great you're here, he looks at me, and instead of beating, his heart is banging around in a mosh pit, and I want him to touch all of me, right down to my shadow. I undo one of his shirt buttons, I kiss his neck, then his chest.

And I feel safe with him, and safety is the closest thing I know to pleasure.

He touches me, but his hands stay on my back, barely moving down, and it's like, come on, man, I undo another button to kickstart him, let's make a blanket with your shirt and my dress, but he can't get up the nerve to take it off me, and neither can I. I want to feel, but there are too many things running around in my head, and I could do with another beer, or a girl friend. No girls have talked to me about this, nobody gave me advice on how to translate desire into action, on how to move it into your hands, your mouth, on how to let your urges eat up your nerves, eat up the unknown, and he goes stiff, he doesn't touch me, doesn't hold me. I don't understand. Guys always want to touch you, all over, and you have to stop them, and here he is completely still, and it makes me mad, and then I give him a kiss and then another, maybe he needs me to take the lead, to touch him, but I have no idea how, he's still sitting there paralyzed, and I want to scream at him, ask him what the hell is wrong with him, what his problem is, and immediately I feel terrible because I think that if he isn't touching me, there must be something wrong with me, he must not like my body, the way I kiss, I must be clumsy, or naive, or I don't know what.

He looks at me, his lips tight. He tucks my hair behind my ear and strokes my cheek.

"I love you, Ale."

I shake my head.

"I ruined it, didn't I?"

"Not at all."

That's it, enough. When I come back to this moment, I want things to have their real names.

"I love you, too. But don't call me Alejandra." I run my

finger over his chicken pox scar, like I'm wiping dirt from his eye. "My name is Ámbar."

"Come on. Don't joke around about that."

"I'm not joking. My name is really Ámbar. It's a long story."

He laughs.

"I already said I'm sorry," he says. He leans back, and my hand is left hanging in the air like a branch. "And you're still mad about Gringa, come on."

"I don't understand. What does that have to do with Gringa?"

He looks at me, his eyebrows pinched together like he doesn't understand, his eyes scrunched up, not with happiness now but with anger.

"What do you mean what does it have to do with her?" It's a short pause, but I'll remember it lasting a lifetime. "Gringa's real name is Ámbar . . ."

I know he keeps talking, but there's a part of me that unplugs. Now I don't know what I'm going to take away from this night because I realize that you don't get to choose what you remember. Because if there's one thing I don't want to remember, it's what he's saying, and that's the only thing from this moment I won't be able to forget.

There are nights that are like tattoos.

And there are nights that are just scars.

Where does a scar last the longest?

In your head?

On your skin?

In your heart.

III

ÁMBAR

24.

My name is a place where I always felt safe. I thought, I believed—told myself the lie, even—that everything I experienced in those temporary towns, the things I saw or did, was happening to Mariana, to Anyelén, to Victoria, but never to Ámbar.

It was Mariana who, at nine years old, had to hang around a corner until the cop across the street, who stood outside the jewelry store, came over. *Tell them you're lost, you don't know where your daddy is*, said that man I barely knew, who didn't look anything like the pictures I had of him, who was only recognizable because of his tattoo of a name he barely let me use, like it was something that didn't belong to me. *If anyone asks what my name is, say Octavio, okay? Octavio, not Víctor, be sure the cop comes over, cry if you need to, I'll buy you some ice cream after*, and of course I cried because I really didn't know where my daddy was, if he'd left me alone in the corner of a plaza in some place I'd never been and would never come back to.

Anyelén was the one who stood in a supermarket parking lot, who had a hundred eyes pointed in every direction, who kept a lookout while Antonio broke into a car, hotwired it, and took off. It was Anyelén, not me, who changed the plates a hundred kilometers later, who skinned her fingers taking out screws while Antonio complained that he'd only gotten a hundred pesos at a gas station, that everybody paid with cards now, *what a piece of shit world we're leaving you, Freckles.*

Victoria was the thirteen-year-old who sewed up a knife wound in her dad's stomach, closing the cut like silencing a mouth. She didn't want to know where that stab wound came from or who had made it.

She sewed.

She silenced.

She forgot.

To become Ámbar again later.

Where do I go back to now?

To a place that's been demolished, looted.

To someone else's name.

To a name that's only an echo.

To ink in an arm.

Now my name is my favorite scar, too.

No. It's not a scar yet.

There are things that will never become a scar.

And there are things that only disappear in fire.

I think to myself.

And I light one.

I feed it.

The Christmas tree burning in the backyard, my clothes hanging from the branches, the flames moving from one to the next, swallowing, taking on strange shapes, a circle that appears in the center of a T-shirt, grows, bites cloth, spits out black smoke that climbs leadenly and is camouflaged in the night. There is beauty in that fire, there is calm in those flames under the sky, the calm of finally recognizing yourself in the mirror.

Why did you do this, Dad?

Because I also wanted to believe that you weren't Antonio or Germán, that one day you would just be Víctor, and maybe you are, maybe that's the worst of all of it. Because I'll never know if what they say about you is true, but I don't need that anymore, because one truth is more than enough.

Where do I come back to?

I'm not coming back yet.

All roads are longer on the way back.

Ámbar.

I never knew what it meant.

Now I do.

The woman he couldn't have.

Or the one he could never admit he really wanted.

I have another woman's name.

No.

I am the other woman.

What did you do, Dad?

What the hell did you do, you fucking asshole?

One by one, I throw in my fake IDs. They wrinkle up,

disappear. Goodbye to all those girls. I can't feel the heat even though I'm wearing just my bra and underwear. I want to tear the night off me like a dress, like I tore off the one I'm holding in my hand now, reduced to a ball of fabric, the one I wanted to end up on the ground, and that's where it will end up, when it's nothing but ash.

The fire is the only thing that separates me from the darkness. I get up and walk over to it, lay the dress over the flames until it catches, the fire caressing it, grabbing its waist, its neckline, until it bites at my fingertips, and only then, when I can't take it anymore, I let it go. It falls across the branches and looks like a broken body. The fire releases bits of cloth that float up toward the sky, but then they fall, ashes landing in my hair, on my skin, at my feet.

I let the fire grow, trying to shut out the night, to end it, but I'm still here, watching what is no longer mine burn away, be eaten up, leave me alone.

Alone with the fire.

Isn't that what you're good at, Ámbar?

That's all he ever taught you.

To close up other people's wounds, but never your own.

To burn everything that belongs to you.

To disappear.

To be someone else.

But I'm not going to be someone else anymore.

I'm Ámbar.

And that means whatever I want it to.

25.

Like a photocopy of yesterday, I'm standing in front of Gringa's house. If anyone asked me, I couldn't really say how I got here. I feel like I'm coming out of anesthesia. Rage is a lot like anesthesia.

The memories come back as pictures, not video, the last flame from the fire staying there inside me, the shower, the dirt coming off my feet, leaving a reddish trail in the bathtub, my legs going into a pair of shorts, a cup of coffee I don't remember making or finishing, my last T-shirt, full of wrinkles, but what does it matter now, and then, in the end, the lightest bag I've slung over my shoulder in my whole life. A Walkman without batteries. And the shotgun, the only possession I never had to throw away because I couldn't be identified by it, the shells clacking against each other with every step.

The Neon isn't there, or any "new" car parked by the door.

I didn't even look to see if someone was at home at Marcos's. I think about turning around, but why bother. I don't need him. I don't know what I could say to him.

I also don't know what I expect to find at Gringa's, but I knock, once, twice. There's no doorbell. In the tree at the house next door, there's a balloon caught in the highest branches. How the hell did it get up there? I knock again. I want to scream *open the fuck up*. I hear a motorcycle in the distance, a dot two blocks away. He's got a helmet on. I try to make out whether it's him, but I'm too far away. Judging by the long shorts and sneakers, it could be. Him or any other guy who dresses like he's in a heavy metal band. The door opens. The confusion between what I expect to see and what I really see freezes me. Rupave points his gun at me, blood dripping from his hand. He pulls me inside with a jerk, and I'm so limp, I fall right to the floor. I land on my side and grope around for the bag hanging from my shoulder. It's gone. Before I can find it, he picks me up and pushes me against the sofa.

"Sit down."

Flowered board shorts reveal a tattoo down near his heel. I'm too nervous to see what it is. He locks the door and puts the key in his pocket. Whatever he touches is painted red. He talks in the direction of Gringa's room.

"Come in here, fix yourself up, we have company."

Gringa comes out, walking slowly, dragging herself along. She leans against the wall. Her hair is a mess, and she tries not to look at me, but she does. Her face is covered with red spots, blood flowing from her eyebrow right down to her chin in a steady stream. Her blue dress is ripped, one of the straps torn loose.

"Next to her, babe." Rupave walks to the back door to make sure it's locked, whistling. He grabs a half-eaten cookie from the counter. Chews a little, looking at us. As he smiles, I can see pieces of chocolate glued to his teeth. It's a rotten grin. "Víctor Mondragón's two little whores. From what I heard, you're not mother and daughter. Who knows. It's hard to see right now if you look alike. Maybe in a little while."

He puts his hand under the faucet, and the water tears away the blood. He dries off with the kitchen towel, comes back, and leans on the back of the armchair. He looks at his right hand, at how blood appears on his split knuckles and from teeth marks in his palm.

"Glad I have my rabies shot."

Gringa's nose doesn't look broken, but she has cuts all over her face, on her cheekbones, her eyebrow. One eyelid is swelling shut, and her eye is just a slit. She can't stop touching her knees.

"We were just talking about your old man. I was, mostly. I couldn't get her to open her mouth much." He sucks at his hand where the bite marks are. "People think I'm crazy when I say you can see silence. Take a good look. That's what silence looks like," he says, pointing at Gringa, who's pulling up her dress where the strap is broken so it won't fall and show her breasts. "Maybe you're smarter and you'll talk. Where's your old man?"

"I thought he was here."

The answer is as sincere as it is primitive, and it comes out all on its own.

Rupave clicks his tongue, comes around, and sits on the arm of the sofa. The gun is resting on his knee. I think it's a 9mm, as if naming fear could somehow make it manageable.

"I'm afraid he isn't here, but he was."

He points at Dad's green military shirt hanging on the line.

The dress insists on falling down on the side where the strap's broken. She reaches to adjust it because her head can't remember it isn't there anymore, and her bloody fingers brush at her shoulder.

"You should be glad she interrupted us. Do her a favor and talk. Guys talk after they come, and you look like you'd be pretty good for that."

"I already told you, he doesn't talk to me about that stuff."

Rupave scratches the back of his neck. He comes around the table and sits on the armrest on my side.

"You know how they show those pictures in ads to regrow your hair or lose weight? The before and afters? Well, you're the before. She's not the after. She still has a good long ways to go before she's the after."

The image of Valeria appears quickly and is gone, but the mark is stamped into my brain like a handprint on a window.

"Where's your old man?"

"I don't know."

The punch to my gut leaves me on the floor. It knocks the wind out of me. I roll over, squeeze my body between the sofa and the coffee table, breathe, try to open my eyes, and the pain expands, throbs, grows.

"Oh, come on, I barely touched you."

He jerks me up by the arm and sets me back on the couch. He grabs me by the chin and forces me to look at him. The sweat beads on his face like tears. I try to pull away. My hair falls over my eyes, and he blows on it to push it aside. There's an arid smell, like something that's been buried.

"Where the fuck is your old man?"

I shake my head, barely, and he squeezes my face so hard, his fingers sink into my skin.

"I don't have time for this."

The impact explodes in my nose and mouth and throws me to the other side of the couch. The world trembles and then comes back tasting like blood, my mouth is full of it, I spit and cough.

"Still don't know? Let's try another one. Where's my brother? Where can I find him?"

"We don't fucking know," says Gringa.

"You shut your mouth, bitch. Or do you want some more?"

Gringa tries to come over and help me, but I hold up my hand and lean my back against the front of the couch. My jaw, my lips, my teeth, everything is throbbing, begging for attention, dazing me. Blood drips from my nose and mouth, landing on my T-shirt.

"I don't know if you've had any dick yet, princess, but let me tell you, if you don't start talking, it's going to be real hard for you to get any. And you'll miss out on the best thing in the world, right, Gringa?"

He comes over to me, and I hide my face behind my arms.

"I asked you nicely yesterday," he says, but his cell phone rings before he can say any more. He takes it out, looks at the screen, and answers. "Did you find them? Then why the fuck are you calling me, Loza? Yeah. Same here." While he talks, he fiddles with his gold chain with a G pendant instead of a $. He looks at Gringa first, then at me. "No, not yet, but any minute now."

I get back up onto the sofa, and Rupave waves the gun at me. I read on his lips, *don't move.*

"I don't care. An almost is no good to me. Don't call again until you've found one of them."

He puts the phone back in his shorts pocket. He steps back, scratches his forehead with the muzzle of the gun, sees something behind him that catches his eye, and I think it must be my bag. He bends over, and I lose him behind the couch. When I can see him again, he's holding Mandioca, who gives a pitiful meow.

"Finally, somebody who talks," he says.

He pets her. Her white fur turns red and pointy as he does.

"What's his name?"

"Put her down," Gringa says.

"That's a stupid name for a cat."

Her tail twitches, a nervous pendulum.

"Mandioca."

"Good, you know at least one answer."

He strokes the cat's head so hard I can see the shape of her skull.

"I can never remember if they have seven lives or nine.

Mandioca here wants you to say where Mondragón is, because whether it's seven or nine, she's only got one left."

Gringa tries to say something, chokes, reaches out her hand. She doesn't know what to do, like she has too much body and too few words.

That's how I feel, too. "Let her go," I say.

Mandioca keeps flicking her tail, and she scratches at him, then again, and she slips out of his arms and runs into the bedroom.

"It looks like, out of the three of you pussies, she's the only one with any fight in her," he says, looking at the scratch on the back of his hand. He nods his head a couple of times. He rolls his shoulders and takes a deep breath. "Okay, that's enough, I'm done being a gentleman."

I look at my reflection in the glass coffee table. Blood is dripping from my nose, cutting my face in half down to my chin, flowing down my neck to the collar of my T-shirt.

"You might not know this, city girl, but around here, when somebody has a big mouth, we call them bucket *yurú*. *Yurú* is mouth, so you get the picture." He spreads his hands wide, drawing a big circle. "This is the part where one of you makes like a bucket *yurú*, or you're going to have a bucket *cachi*."

He comes over, grabs my hair, and yanks at me until I'm shoved up against the wall.

"I don't know where he is," I say, over and over, but I'm not sure where the words are coming from.

He smashes the butt of the 9mm into my mouth. My body unplugs, falls away like mud from a riverbank, and drops straight down, a heap of bones and skin piled on the floor.

A buzzing sound rises from my jaw up to my eardrums and blurs out whatever he's saying. I roll over until I'm face up, and the blood flows down my neck. I try to open my eyes, bring a little light into the darkness, but everything vibrates, like my vision has an echo. He's standing next to me, long, hungry, talking, spitting, blood dripping from his hands, my blood, falling on the floor next to me.

I manage to tune the house back in. The ceiling is very far away, Rupave's mouth is screaming, at Gringa, I guess, the gun's pointing at her, but the voices still aren't reaching me, it's just noise, and the blood is dripping into my ears. *You're underwater, Ámbar, come up to the surface, stick your head out, even just your eyes.* Spitting out the blood that's filling my mouth is the closest thing to breathing, little gasps, the waves come and go, and I can see the *ñandutí* wind chime outside. There's so much blood that I swallow it. I see coins under the sofa, they're so little, and cat hair, and my bag under the armchair, Rupave's legs, his sneakers touching the shoulder straps, his ankle tattoo right up close, a dagger stabbing a name into his skin: Delfina.

Who the hell is Delfina?

How many people have wondered *who the hell is Ámbar?* while my dad did this exact same thing to them?

He squats down and looks at me, the patience in his eyes an hourglass where the sand's about to run out. I think about lying to him, saying anything at all, but I know it wouldn't work, that the only sand I can give him is my blood, for him to break me so much that he's sure no one could take a beating like that without talking, for him to destroy my mouth so much that it becomes a thing that will be open forever, that can't hide anything or stay silent, but I don't think I can take it. Or that that would be enough for him.

Then he looks at Gringa and says something that sounds like *last chance*, but the blood is going in my ears. Rupave overlooks me, forgets about me, and I feel bad for knowing that for a little while, he'll entertain himself with her, slap her around, that my skin will get a break. I roll across the floor, as fast as I can, but it's slow, like a snail that leaves a trail of blood instead of slime. *That's what you are, Ámbar, slow.* I reach out my hand, touch the straps of the bag, pull it toward me, but he steps on it, and his tattoo comes into the foreground. He pulls the bag away from me, unzips it, and takes out the shotgun.

"You brought toys, huh, you little cunt?" he says and sticks the 9mm in his waistband. "Now we can play Guaraní roulette."

Gringa jumps on him before he can raise the shotgun, wraps her arm around his neck, but he smashes the butt of the shotgun into her stomach and shoves her off of him. She lands on the sofa, which rams into the coffee table and shatters it. The shards of glass fall, so close I can see my face broken up into bits of a reflection, eyes, mouth, lips, in pieces, like they've been torn off of me, loose parts.

And as if I'm trying to gather them up, to bring them back to me, I grab a piece of glass that looks like a knife, deformed, deep. My skin splits open when I grip it, my hand goes red in the blink of an eye, it burns like lighting a fire, but it's just a piece of glass that's cutting me, deep, and before he can aim at me, I stab it into Rupave's thigh. I bury a lot of it, and more is sticking out, and through the glass I see him scream, his face distorted. He drops the shotgun, which falls to the floor far away from me. He hesitates between pulling out the glass and grabbing his gun. He hesitates a long time, too long. I roll to the side, far enough to be behind the sofa. Gringa fires, and the buckshot hits his leg, the shell that pops out is yellow, and where there used to be skin, now there's ground beef. Rupave falls face first, and before he can roll over, Gringa pulls the trigger again, but there are no more shells in it. She jumps on him out of pure instinct, out of fury and desperation, and she goes at his head using the shotgun like a club, once, twice, three times, until he's out. She kicks him to make sure he's unconscious. She ties up the strap of her dress, covering a body spattered in blood that's not only hers now. She breathes through her mouth. She reaches her hand out to me and helps me up.

"Thanks, Ámbar," I say.

I can't see what face she makes behind all that red, behind all those cuts, but it doesn't matter. Not anymore.

"Take that arm," she says, and we drag Rupave.

We take him out back, like he's just a pile of bones.

26.

"I don't think even he knows why he gave you my name," Gringa says.

The first aid kit is on the table, along with bloody cotton balls, a couple of thin little pieces I used to plug my bleeding nose, and a tube of super glue squeezed down to the last drop. Packages of bandages and gauze. The open back door lets in a tired wind that knocks a wrapper off the table and onto the floor every so often. The shotgun, close at hand, is reloaded. The 9mm is off to one side.

Gringa tended to the wounds one by one, tying together each bit of pain so they stopped screaming separately to become a single voice, one pain. First the cut on my nose, then another under my eye. There was nothing she could do about my lips. Now she's using hydrogen peroxide on the cut that goes clean across my hand.

I take the washcloth with ice in it away from my mouth

to talk. My gums are fat, like someone tried to bury my teeth in my flesh.

"You never asked him?"

"An answer from him doesn't mean he knows. Or that it's not another lie."

Her face is closing like a flower that never got any light or water. The flesh takes bites, and I can barely see her right eye. That makes things hard for her, and she does everything slowly, carefully. She has bloodstains on her neck that the water didn't erase. She's wearing a new T-shirt and a couple of improvised bandages. I did the best I could, not like for Dad, because for him, another scar doesn't mean anything.

She holds a kitchen towel full of ice against her nose for a few seconds.

"It's not broken," I say.

"It hurts like it is."

She stands up and gets us a glass of water and some pain killers. She had to throw away the stronger ones because they were past their expiration date. *He found someone else to patch him up*, she said, like she knew that if there's one thing that's never going to change, it's Dad needing someone to patch him up.

I stand up to make sure that Rupave is still in the garage handcuffed—with a pair of pink fuzzy handcuffs I didn't want to ask about—and tied to a grate. Every once in a while, he screams something, but Gringa gagged him with his own T-shirt, so all that comes out is a zombie noise.

"When you came over yesterday, I thought you'd found out."

"Why didn't you tell me?"

"Why would I?"

She pours rubbing alcohol on the cut, and it burns, like the chorus of the whole song of pain. I wonder how many times she's patched Dad up.

"He told me once he'd gotten the tattoo for me," she says, "to show me he'd carry me with him forever. That he was ready to sacrifice the most precious thing he had, being anonymous, that's what he said. Becoming identifiable for me."

Outside, the sky looks like a wet rag, heavy. It's impossible to know what time it is by looking at it.

"Then he told me he was going to stay with your mom, that she was pregnant and he got the tattoo because that was what he was going to name you. That he had to be there. Other times, he told me he just liked the name. It's hard to know why he does things. Did you know exactly what you were doing when you came here?"

In the living room, Mandioca sniffs at my blood, bits of flesh torn from Rupave, the broken glass. She doesn't find anything interesting and lays down to clean herself. The CD tower is on the floor, cases spilled everywhere. I can make out one by Teresa Parodi, one by Caetano, and a little farther away, one by Cartola, the same one that was at Charly's.

"I don't know. Sometimes I don't even know why I do some things, not even while I'm doing them."

"Don't worry, it's always that way."

Even a half smile hurts. Outside, Rupave's legs move, the dirt sticking to the shredded part.

"One time he told me he was on a bus, in Buenos Aires," she says. "They were stopped at a light on Córdoba Avenue. He saw a kid on the sidewalk hit a girl, take something from her, and run across the street, behind the bus. Your dad stood up, calm, and rang the bell like it was his stop. He got off the bus and took off running after the kid."

She cleans the cut on my hand with gauze soaked in something I can't identify, which burns. The cut is wide, but it doesn't look too deep. She opens a package of bandages.

"A block later, the kid took off his white T-shirt to throw it away, and underneath it, he was wearing another white T-shirt. Your dad laughed. *How could he be stupid enough to wear two white shirts when you know you have to change your identikit*. I remember him using that word. Identikit." She gestures to me, and I give her my hand back, palm up. She puts the bandage on. "Hold it with your thumb," she says and starts to roll it up. "He caught up with him two blocks later. He kneed him in the back and had to fight him to force his hand open. And for nothing. He hadn't managed to take anything. *I didn't know what to do*, he said. He rolled him over, and it was just a little kid. He couldn't have been older than thirteen. He was wearing a plastic rosary that was missing the crucifix. Víctor was holding him there and he didn't know what to do. Why did he run, why did he throw away one white T-shirt for another one. The only thing he could think to do was make him go apologize to the girl, but the kid didn't want to, and he started crying. No, no, no. Your dad said the kid got out his wallet and took out a necklace he'd stolen earlier and offered it to him to let him go. He stared at him for about two minutes. *I had no idea what to do. I expected to catch him, beat the shit out of him, get back what he'd stolen, and give it back to the girl, and there I was with a little kid who was more of a dumbass than a thief, and I didn't know what to do. In the end, I let him go.*" The blood comes through the bandage on the first wrap around, a tiny bit on the second, and then the third is clean. It's good and tight. "Sometimes I think he did beat the shit out of him, because he felt helpless and angry, that he only got off that bus to beat him up because someone gave him a chance to get some shit off his chest. Other times, I think he took the necklace and it's one of the ones he gave me. There are times I think that, really, he's the kid in the story. But I never once believed he let him go."

She tries to rip the tape with her teeth, but it hurts her. She gets some scissors and then tapes the ends of the bandage in place. Wrapped up like that, it looks like a boxer's hand.

"When I try to understand your dad, I remember that story, and I stop trying. Things just happen. Except that some things last forever. Especially mistakes." She looks at Mandioca, then at me. "Your name is yours, nobody else's."

"It's a nice name."

I set the washcloth down on the table. The ice makes my face numb. I can't feel my lips or nose, and the throbbing is dying down, like my breathing is coming back to normal. I touch my injuries because I prefer to discover them with my fingers and not my eyes.

"They're going to get a lot worse before they get better."

"Well, isn't that nice."

I get up. The first step is the hardest, but I try not to pay attention to the pain of walking, of staying in motion. We spread Rupave's things out on the kitchen counter. His cell phone. Ten house keys and a motorcycle key. A wallet with no ID in it, but a picture of a blond eight-year-old girl. It's an old picture. This must be the one whose birthday it was. Slips of paper with phone numbers on them. Two condoms. A pack of mint gum.

"What do we do?"

"We wait. We've got lots of practice."

The washcloth gets thinner as the ice melts, and drops of water that are stained red drip off the edge of the table. Dad's green military shirt whips on the line. For him to take it off, it must have been filthy, heavy with blood.

"Where the hell did he go?" I say. "He didn't say anything to you yesterday?"

"Don't worry, I'm sure he's fine."

The cell phone starts to ring, and I jump. It vibrates on the counter, moves forward, passes over the picture. The screen lights up blue. Loza. I show it to Gringa.

"Don't answer."

"What if they found him?"

Her face wrinkles up in pain or hesitation, or both. She closes her eyes and drums her fingers on the counter. The wind blows the gauze wrapper along the floor until it gets caught on the broken glass. The phone stops moving. It hangs on the edge of the sink.

Gringa seems to get smaller, the adrenaline leaving her body after hammering Rupave's head.

Did she know she had that in her?

The cell phone rings again. It falls into the sink between two plates and a cup. I pick it up, along with the shotgun, and head for the garage. Whoever's calling has hung up by the time I reach Rupave. There's a message: *Pick up.*

The blood covers his face. It looks like a ten-pound red candle melted in his hair. I take in the whole picture: the electrical tape holding the T-shirt in his mouth, his scream, his insults, his hands cuffed above his head. His leg is nasty to look at. The skin will take a long time to grow back. It looks worse than a burn.

"I guess you finally know what a salt shell feels like."

More muffled noises. Fury in his eyes.

"I don't speak zombie."

Gringa walks behind me and tears away the electrical tape, uncovering a white strip that contrasts with all the red.

"Your partner won't stop calling you," I say. "You're going to call him back and see what he wants. And I'm going to stay next to you and listen. And if you say something I don't like . . ."

"You think I'm afraid of two little whores like you?"

"You should be," says Gringa, "but men have no idea what fear is."

It hurts to squat down. I move next to him.

"You don't have the balls to kill me. Neither of you."

"No, I don't have any balls," I say, "I've got ovaries. Maybe not enough to kill you, but more than enough to rip your dick off."

I press the barrels of the shotgun in his crotch. I put my

finger on the trigger, and Rupave's expression changes. With my other hand, I hold the phone up between us.

"Finally," Loza says, with an old man's voice. "Were you playing bucket *cachi*, you bastard?"

I press the shotgun harder against him, and he tries to close his legs.

"What do you want, Loza."

I hear laughter, then a rough sound, like he's calling from somewhere outside. I lean in a little closer, being careful not to let this asshole bite me.

"We found him, boss."

"Who?"

"What do you mean, who? That *añamembú* Mondragón. Solano ran into him at the river, he's at the Puerto Kerayvoty place. We left him there snooping around. We're on our way to get the guns. Get over here, we're going to fuck him up good. Leave that *cachi*, I'll pay for another one for you when we're done." When he starts laughing, I hang up.

"Where is that?" I ask.

"It's up in the squatter shacks, about ten miles," says Gringa.

"You're fucked," Rupave says.

I go back into the house, and Gringa follows me. She's having a hard time walking.

"Do you know how to drive a motorcycle?" I say, seeing the key in Rupave's stuff.

She shakes her head. I take a deep breath, which hurts, and let all the air out. There's no way around it, I say to myself. I go and pull down Dad's shirt and put it on over mine to at least cover up the blood on my clothes. Rupave is talking, swearing at me, but I don't pay any attention to him. I put the shotgun in my bag and sling it across my chest. Gringa looks at me. There's no need for me to explain.

"Take care of yourself," she says. "And take care of him."

I KNOCK ON THE door. Let it be him who answers, I pray. No one opens up, but I can hear a TV, far away. I knock louder with my good hand. The volume goes down, and I hear footsteps. The door opens.

"Ale . . . Ámbar, what happened?"

He's shirtless. Flowered boxers peek out over the top of his board shorts.

"A guy beat the shit out of me. He wanted to know where my dad was, and . . . I had to tell him. He wanted to steal the money from a sale. I need to warn him before he does something to him."

He looks at me, trying to decide how much of all that is true.

"Don't lie to me, Ámbar, or whatever your name is."

"I'm not lying to you. Not anymore. But I need you to take me there. I'll explain later."

He closes the door, and I'm left there talking to myself. I imagine Loza's truck. I don't know why, but I imagine them in a truck, all of them piled into the cab, holding guns with the serial numbers filed off and a shotgun or two, the music on full blast and a big smile on Loza's face, his arm out the window, a cigarette between his fingers, and I feel far away from the whole world.

But Marcos comes out, pulling on a T-shirt and carrying the keys in his hand.

"Where are we going?"

27.

I've been fantasizing for two days about being in this position, holding him, up against him, my face buried in his back, my hair flying, far, but this version of now is a crappy remake of that fantasy. Instead of his scent, now there's the smell of the river and blood. Cloth instead of skin. The marks from my injuries are stamped on his T-shirt from holding him so close, without knowing whether it's to keep from falling off, or so the holes in the road won't hurt, or to avoid letting him go.

But the biggest difference is in what's making my heart race.

I look at the signs on every dirt road that starts at the edge of the asphalt. Rust has erased some of the names, and bullet holes make others illegible.

Marcos doesn't say anything. He doesn't take his hands off the handlebars, as if his whole body were part of the motorcycle. He turns down a long road with trees along the sides. The dirt is an intense red. The road stretches out and up, and the stink of the river gets stronger. There's an overturned boat off to one side, the painted letters peeling. A flock of birds move from branch to branch as we go along. On the other side of the hill, where the road splits into three, Marcos stops and takes one foot off the pedal.

"The dock is over there," he says, pointing to a wooden shack two hundred yards away.

The Paraná flows along oblivious to us, to everyone, sounding like interference between us.

This is the easy part, Ámbar: saying goodbye.

"Wait for me," I say and get off the bike. The bag swings, and I hear the sound of the shells rolling back and forth. "I'll warn him, and we'll get out of here."

"Be quick."

He doesn't look at me. He scratches his elbow and unsticks his T-shirt from his skin by pulling at the neck. I bite my lips, forgetting they're split. I don't know what I'm waiting for, but whatever it is, he's not going to give it to me.

I walk slowly, take a few steps, then go a little faster. The adrenaline or the pills shift the pain out of focus, cut the claws off that thing that's trying to stab its way in, hold on to me, tell me to stay still.

"Ámbar."

Maybe I was wrong, maybe this isn't a goodbye, maybe there's a spot on my face that isn't a wound, and he can give me a kiss there, but I turn around, and he's different, his eyes and fingers tight.

"You dropped this."

He throws something to me, and when I catch it, I open my hand to see that it's a yellow shell.

"I'll explain later."

I could open it, show him the salt, tell him it's a souvenir or something, but I don't feel like lying anymore. I put it in my shirt pocket. I don't walk anymore, I run. I hear the motorcycle moving away, and I run even faster so I'm the one who's leaving, so I'm the one doing the abandoning and not being abandoned, again. Lying to other people might be easy, but lying to yourself is a lot harder.

I run. I prefer to hear my body telling me I'm a piece of shit and not my head.

There's a shack to my right, facing away from me. The windows are boarded up. It looks like it's been painted red, but the sunset and the dirt make me wonder if it really is. A little closer to me is an F100 pick-up resting on wooden blocks. On the other side of the road, there are trees, pure hills, pure hideouts. There are canoes piled up, stacked one on top of the other, posts with barbed wire that fence in nothing, that just hang there on their own, disjointed. I remember they have someone looking out and check for them, but they might be anywhere. Or they might not be there at all.

I take out the shotgun. I listen: birds, the river, no cars. I don't see the Neon. I want to scream *Dad*, but I don't want to give myself away. A few yards in front of the shack is a steep bank, and some stairs cut in with a shovel lead down to a wooden dock, where a rope is floating. On the other side of the water is Paraguay.

I don't know if I'm too early or too late. The birds hush and I hear someone whistling, calm as anything. A Cartola song.

O sol nascerá.

That's what that fucking song is called.

I peek around and find Dad sitting on a beer crate in the door of the shack, scraping dirt out from under his nails with a knife. He's wearing a white muscle shirt with spots of dried blood on the chest like an archipelago. He sees me, and in one fast movement, he drops the knife and pulls out his revolver with the same hand.

"Stop right there," he says.

"It's me."

It takes him a moment to recognize me through all the wounds.

"Ámbar . . ." He sticks the .38 in his waistband and comes over to me. "What happened to you?"

"We have to go."

"Are you okay?"

He grabs my face to look me over.

"What motherfucker did this?"

"They're coming for you." Dad lets me go and blinks twice, like he might see me better that way. "Mbói's brother."

He takes one step back, and his gaze is lost in the river. He rubs his arms. First one, then the other. He scratches at his tattoo.

"We have to get out of here, Dad."

"It's fine. Don't worry."

"You don't understand."

Some birds fly out of the branches on the riverbank, flap around, and then disappear deeper into the trees.

"No, I do understand. Wait . . ."

The shot is so close that splinters from the shack bounce off my face. Dad grabs me and pulls me inside with him. The shots punch holes in the wall, make dots where the light comes in and lands on barrels, vegetable crates, things covered by tarps on the front wall, mold, rust. Outside, right next to the door, is my shotgun. I didn't even realize I'd dropped it. He reaches out and grabs it, passes it to me.

"Stay there and aim at the door. Do you hear me?" He snaps his fingers in front of my face. "Hey, do you hear me?"

I nod my head. He gets up, pulls back the tarp, checks his bag, and shoves a pistol into his waistband, along with two clips. Crouched down, he shuffles to the back of the cabin.

"Wait, where are you going?"

"To get those fuckers. Anyone comes in here, you waste him, Ambareté."

He goes out the back door and closes it behind him. He shoots. They shoot. I hear the sound of different guns. Dad's .38. The others mix together. They're loud, a rifle, pistols, a shotgun in there somewhere. Death has so many voices. I try to count how many of them there are by the sound of their guns. Three or four. Against Dad, on his own.

I drop the bag and leave it close by, open. I settle into one corner. They're still shooting, punching holes in the wall that protects me. A shotgun takes a few bites out of the wood near my head and the sunset comes pouring in like a bucketful of light.

When they're all quiet, when their guns are empty, just shells on the ground, I can hear the Paraná flowing, adrift.

Everything is adrift.

I use one of the holes to look outside. I see Dad, hiding behind the F100 they're shooting at. Two of them, on the other side of the road, are sheltered behind the pile of canoes. One's stomach is so big, he'd need the Titanic to protect him. The other one is old. He peeks his head up and fires a small machine gun. Loza, I bet. A third one is next to the river. He takes a few steps, kneels on the ground, and reloads a rifle. He drops the clip. Before he can pick it up, a bullet hits him in the neck and knocks him down. He tries to hold his hand against his throat, but the blood spurts up. He's a man who's become a geyser. Then the pressure drops, his arms fall.

The other two pound away at Dad. The sound of bullets hitting metal is dizzying. I hear desperate swearing in Guaraní and Spanish, and more than swearing, it's prayers.

The fat one tries to run out to one side, but he trips and falls. When he gets up, he has barbed wire embedded in his stomach. The posts shake when he moves. He looks like a clumsy puppet with wire strings that get buried deeper and deeper. Dad doesn't shoot at him, he just laughs. The fat guy runs without really knowing where he's going, and two lines appear where the wires have dug in. His hands yank at them, are cut open. He screams.

I don't want to see any more and I curl up into a ball. I aim at the door, that's it, that's all I have to do, but the shotgun feels so heavy, sweat is pouring down my forehead, and it makes my hair stick to my face and makes my cuts itch. I wipe it away with the bandage on my hand. My ears are throbbing, and so are my hands and my head. There are shots and yells, they mix together and are lost. I hear a thump against the cabin, but I can't tell where. I see something go by the door out of the corner of my eye. Maybe I imagined it. There's noise. Close by. I think. The shots distort everything. The birds fly away, screeching, leaving the branches bare.

The sunset comes in through the holes in the wall and makes little marks on the floor, as if someone lit a bunch of little candles there. And one candle goes out and then lights up again, and then a different one goes out, where a body is moving forward, around the house to get Dad in the back.

I stand up, my knees trembling. I walk carefully so I won't step on anything and make a noise. I open the door with my shoulder, slowly, and I look for the guy, but all I see are trees, shadows, other abandoned cars, rusty as if they grew out of that red dirt. Dad peeks over the hood of the truck, looking the other way. Someone is dying farther off. I don't know if it's the fat one or the old one. There are no more shots. Dad moves forward, slowly, crouching down, one hand on the ground and the other, holding the gun, against the truck. He takes a step, and there's the tinny sound of the butt hitting the metal. I hear some branches creaking. I see the man detach from the darkness, how he stops being a shadow to slowly become an arm, a shoulder, half a body, and the hand holding the gun raising toward Dad. I shoot, but I miss him. The guy spins around and aims at me. I can't see his face. The second burst from the shotgun hits him, just barely, like a push against the shoulder, and he raises his gun again and fires. I pull the trigger, hit him full on, reload, and the shotgun roars once, again, once more, until the shells run out. The man is lying on the ground. Alive. Blasted apart, but alive. There are pieces of his flesh strewn around, like he's a garbage bag that a dog tore into and scattered.

Dad looks at him and kicks his gun farther away. He doesn't know the man doesn't have any fingers left to hold it. He asks me if I'm okay, but I can't answer him with my mouth, so I do it by nodding my head or blinking, I don't know. I don't realize I'm still pointing my shotgun at him until Dad comes over and pushes down the barrel.

"Stay here."

He walks the other way, toward the shouts of the old guy dying over there. He crouches down, and I hear his voice as a murmur. He laughs, and then he shoots. Twice. A few birds fly out like a scar in the sky.

The one I shot gropes at his side, where half of his stomach is gone, and I can smell the shit in his guts. A couple of words try to drag themselves from his mouth, but before he can say them, they're submerged in the blood he spits out, coughs onto his chest. He looks at me, his eyes like wells, like instead of being reflected in them, you just fall down inside. And can never get out again.

Dad shoots him in the face three times so the death will carry his name, and his alone.

He doesn't have eyes to look at me with anymore.

I'm not here anymore.

"He saw our faces," Dad says.

That's the best lie he's ever told me.

I drop the shotgun to one side and sit down on the ground, resting my head on the wood. I close my eyes and listen to the river. It bothers me that it's still oblivious. To everything. Or that it doesn't carry me away. Far away.

Dad crouches down and checks the bodies, their wallets, their necks, looking for a tattoo.

"None of these guys is Mbói's brother."

"No," I say. "He's tied up at Ámbar's."

The words come out on their own. I don't even think them, they just come out. He keeps going like I haven't said anything, drags the old man's body over to the other one. He wipes his hands off on his jeans. He comes over to stand next to me and sees that I'm looking at him. Only then does it click, and he closes his eyes, inflates his chest, and lets the breath out through his mouth.

"How is she?"

"Alive."

He waves away a fly with his bloody hands.

"I'll explain later." He goes to pick up the dead men's guns.

The red shells all around me are like the petals of artificial flowers that someone left on a grave. My grave. I pick one up and throw it far away from me.

Then another.

And another.

All of them.

I'll explain later is what you say when there's nothing to explain.

In the distance, lost among the abandoned cars, I find the Neon. Leaves have settled on the windshield. It's been here a while. I stop and turn around. My shoulder hurts from the recoil of the shotgun. I rub it. In a while, when my blood calms down, it's going to hurt like a bitch.

Leaning against the shack, I watch Dad throw the guns into the water, a drowning noise. The rifle sounds like a kid doing a cannonball into a pool. He bends down and washes the blood off in the river, a red streak carried away by the current. He looks off to one side. There's a buzzing that gets louder, a motor approaching. He stands up and shields his eyes with his hands, his shadow broken up in the current. He jogs up and motions for me to go inside the shack.

"What is it?"

"Nothing," he says. "Get inside."

We go in. He leans down, moves the tarp a little more, tugs at it. I peek out through the hole in the wood. A motorboat with two guys in it comes up alongside the dock. They're wearing board shorts and sunglasses. One of them is wearing a Hawaiian shirt, and the other one has on a soccer jersey. There's a garbage bag between their feet, an oar in the back, and a shotgun in the middle.

"What the hell is going on?" I ask.

He doesn't answer. He goes out with a bag like Santa's sack of toys slung over his shoulder. There's a .45 caliber revolver at his back. The one in the Hawaiian shirt raises his hand. The other one grabs the rope and ties up the boat. I stand up, get my shotgun, and settle back in. Dad reaches the dock and drops the bag like a dead body.

"Mondragón?" says the guy in the Hawaiian shirt. His Brazilian accent deforms the emphasis in the name.

"In the flesh."

I open my bag and take out a shell. It falls through my fingers, and I don't know where it rolls away to.

"What happened to Mbói?" says the other one, in nasal Spanish. The jersey has black and white stripes.

"He had a crisis."

"Oh, yeah? What kind?"

"A crisis of faith. He realized this wasn't his thing."

The men laugh. Jersey looks left and right, then at the cabin.

"It wouldn't have anything to do with all the shots we heard?"

"No idea," Dad says. "Maybe somebody was celebrating the Guaraní New Year."

There are so many flies in here, I can barely make out what they're saying.

"Do you have it?"

Dad points to the bag with his foot. Hawaiian shirt picks it up and sticks his hand in like he's looking for one present in particular. He pulls out a white brick, which he sticks a knife into.

"You'll understand if I don't take your word for it."

"Have at it," Dad says.

He pretends to be pulling up his pants and moves the .45 so it's easy to reach. Hawaiian shirt takes a bump off the blade of his knife and lets out a *sapucai*. Jersey motions for him to hand him the knife and takes his own sniff.

"How come Santa wasn't like this when I was a kid?"

Hawaiian shirt grabs the knife back and takes another bump.

"Is that mine?" Dad says.

Hawaiian shirt throws him the garbage bag. Dad catches it, opens it, takes a look. He pulls out a roll of bills, then puts it back in, drops the bag at his feet, and kicks it a little to the side. He leaves his hand at his waist.

"Are you the Mondragón who worked with Vasco Caneyada?"

Coke is stuck to the sweat between his nose and lips, and he licks at it like a dog.

"That was a long time ago."

"We've heard about you."

"Don't believe everything you hear."

"Shit, if even ten percent of it is true, you're just what we need," says Jersey. "The only thing that worries me is the tattoo. We don't like to work with people who have tattoos."

"That's what people didn't like about Mbói," says Hawaiian shirt.

"I think so, too," Dad says. "But you know, we're always bouncing around from place to place, and we need to take a little piece of home with us."

That shameless prick.

I'm so mad that all I can hear is my own breathing. The flies stop buzzing around and head over to the tarp. Where Dad pulled it aside, I can see two feet.

"Can you get more of this?"

"If you can get more *pirapire*, it's Christmas all year long."

"You've got our number."

I pull the tarp all the way off and uncover a guy in jeans, lying face up, in handcuffs, covered in scars, his face destroyed. I recognize him by the snake tattoo. It wraps around his whole forearm and ends with its fangs on his hand. Fangs and a head that tell me it's a viper. A cloud of flies leaves his face, and it's only half as big as it was. They come toward me, but I wave my arms at them and stumble back until I hit the opposite wall. They fly out through the holes, taking part of the darkness with them, and I can finally see what's left of Mbói.

I'm never going to know the face of the guy who got us into this whole mess.

No, that's not right.

I do know it.

I know it too well.

The motorboat moves away, and the guys yell out another few *sapucais*. The sun bounces off the surface of the Paraná, looking like a bunch of broken glass. Dad crouches down next to the shack, pulls out the rolls of bills, and lines them up on the ground. He counts them, piles them up. It's a ton of money.

Dad yelps out his own off-key *sapucai*.

"Finally," he says. "Finally. Starting from scratch is for suckers. Starting with all this is a whole different thing. What do you say, Freckles?"

I want to tear him a new asshole, but I'm still in what people call "the moment" and my head can't process everything. I don't know what to do with my hands. They're shaking. I put them in my pockets. I find the shell Marcos threw me. I squeeze it so hard I open the cut on my palm. The bandage and the yellow shell are stained red. Everything goes red. I imagine the number of bullets that have cycled through these pockets, the amount of death that's fit into such a small space. How much more is still left. All the death to come.

I can't stop thinking about the fact that Mbói has been dead for a while, that we could have left days ago, that while he was making deals, waiting, whistling Cartola, we almost got killed: her, him, me twice. Dad always takes a roundabout before going home. I think about the next ID, the next *I'll explain later*, the next *you'll understand someday*.

I understand now. My whole body understands. From the scars on his head to the ink that spells my name.

When I stop in front of him, I still have the shotgun in my hands. I load the shell, half yellow, half red.

"Dad."

"What, Ambareté?"

He lifts his head. The buckshot tears off his tattoo, skins it, chews flesh, spits out ink. One hibiscus is left whole, and some bits of black outline, dots. Where Á M B A R used to be, now there's just another scar.

He grabs his arm and screams. A few bills fly like confetti toward the river.

"What the hell did you do? God fucking damn it."

"Me? You did that to yourself."

I walk past him, and his breath against the ground lifts up clouds of red dust. I reach down and stick a few rolls of bills into my bag, along with the shotgun. I take the keys to the Neon from his pocket. He tries to grab at me, but I dodge him. I shake free of his fingers. I throw everything onto the passenger seat and start the engine.

He screams and swears.

Now he only has my name on his tongue.

Now my name is just an insult to him, just like it was to Mom.

When I get to the highway, I undo the bandage, stick my hand out the window, and let the wind pull it all the way off. My skin burns. I look at myself in the rearview and see my injuries for the first time, my deformed lip, my swollen nose, the cuts on my cheekbones. The tears flow down, drag the blood with them, pick up its color.

The sunset paints everything orange and pink ahead of me.

On my face, there's only purple, red, and black.

On my face, it's already nighttime.

28.

The tag in my T-shirt is bugging me and I can't wait to tear it off. Even though the fabric is light, it sticks to me in this heat. Summer hasn't gotten the memo that it's already March, time to pack it in. It keeps hanging around.

I add a third sugar packet to try and cover up the burnt taste of the coffee. There aren't many things worse than gas station coffee, which you only drink if you have to wait. Nobody would risk their stomach for a cup of it if they didn't have to stop, kill some time. On the way there, it's better, but on the way back, it's gasoline. Mine is just burnt. I stir it. A lot. I let the spoon go around and around, get stuck, be pulled around by the current again, and finally run aground. The wind blows at my hair, the branches of a tree, and the shadow we share moves on the ground, little spots of light between the leaves and the locks of my hair. The light on the ground is something that isn't there, a hole.

A gust blows the piece of paper and pen off the table. I lean over and pick them up, then read what I've written. A bunch of words to name what I'm feeling. A way to understand. All of them crossed out.

I can't make any sense of what happened. I thought time would give it another shape, some order, meaning.

Maybe the only shape this has is a scar. The one on my hand goes all the way across my palm. I'm still surprised when I see it. It's thin and barely stands out. You can feel it more when you run your finger over it. From far away, someone might think it's just another line. I have another little one next to my lips that disappears every time I smile.

Maybe smiling is the only answer.

I think about what I'll tell some guy who takes me by the hand, what story I'll make up for the cut that runs across it, if I'll ever love someone enough not to lie to him.

The highway becomes a road that goes through town. On the other side of it, some girls my age are wearing school uniforms. Their backpacks look heavy. Some boys follow them. They laugh together and kick stones on the shoulder. I don't feel like I'm part of anything. I look at my arm, at a couple of black dots from bouncing the pen against it while I search for a word. I turn them into spots, one and then another, make my skin a pelt.

Maybe I could write my story better on my skin than on paper.

I throw the piece of paper into a trash can.

"Ámbar."

I blink, focus my eyes, and see Méndez. He calls me over to avoid walking the twenty yards that separate us. He moves away, limping. The hem of one leg of his jumpsuit is more worn than the other. I never found out how he broke—or they broke—his leg. I grab my bag and sling it across my chest. I still haven't gotten up the nerve to count the money. I catch up with Méndez before he crosses the road. He totters and looks for something to hold onto. I offer him my shoulder.

"Thanks, *gurisa*," he says. "This humidity isn't giving us a break today."

Maybe the only things that are worth anything, that make any sense, are the ones we do without trying, that just come out of us naturally.

"It never gives you break around here. You should move."

He lets out a choked laugh.

"I've got it out back."

Méndez keeps using me as a crutch when we go into the auto body shop. There's a man working in a pit, chains, posters of soccer teams on the walls. Tools hanging from nails, portable lights that are extended like little hunchbacks over greasy parts I can't identify.

"Are you going to get a tattoo, too?" he says, looking at the ink doodles.

"I might."

He clicks his tongue. His saliva makes the same sound as a mate being finished.

"Víctor's not going to like that."

"He can go to hell."

He gestures for us to walk between two pits.

"You don't know where he is?"

"Far away, I guess."

He doesn't stop talking as we cross the shop. He explains the difference between motors, the adjustments he made to the car. He tells me about a cousin of his in Buenos Aires I can visit if I don't have anywhere to stay.

"I put all the papers in the glove compartment. It's all in order. Thanks for the help," he says. He lets go of my shoulder and leans on a table. He digs out the key and hands it to me.

The Neon is out there, shining in the sun. It's got a fresh coat of paint.

"Is that the color red you wanted?" he asks.

"That's exactly it."

I hand him the money, and he tucks it into a pocket in his jumpsuit.

"Have a good trip, Ámbar."

I put my bag in the trunk and get in.

The scar pulls at the skin on the palm of my hand when I grip the wheel. Someday it'll settle in and stop being new. It'll be mine, another part of my body. I look at the pen ink, spread across my arm, unfinished, pure possibilities.

I think that, from now on, I'm going to be the one who chooses the shape of my scars.

I start up the Neon. In the first decent bathroom I

come across, I'm going to cut the tag out of my T-shirt. I turn onto the highway and merge into traffic. I'm part of something. I put my arm out the window. The sun cuddles my skin.

I've got hundreds of miles to choose the shape of my favorite scar.

THANKS:

To Ariel Bermani and his crew.

To my parents, for all the support.

To Lila and Jazz, my cats, for all the company.

To Mallory, for keeping Ámbar safe and not letting her get lost in translation.

To Liliana Escliar, Rodolfo Santullo, Eduardo Antonio Parra, Dolores Reyes and Óscar Alarcón, for jumping in for the ride.

To Miguel Barrero, Xuan Bello, Berna González Harbour, Fermín Goñi and Pilar Sánchez Vicente, for all their work and for making my dream come true.

To Iñigo Amonarriz, for trusting, once again, in my stories.

To *el jefe* Mauricio Bares, *la jefa* Lilia Barajas, Cesar Alcázar and Artur Vecchi for bringing Ámbar to other countries.

To Taz Urnov, for all the love and hard work she put into this book to make it *My Favorite Scar*. On to the next one!

To Juliet Grames, Rachel Kowal and all the Soho Team, for letting me be part of your family.

To my personal Wild Bunch: Ariel Mazzeo and Mariano Sánchez.

To Magui, who makes everything easier every time she smiles.

This book is especially dedicated to the memory of Damián Vives. *Te extraño, hermano.*